The Puffin
of Death

Books by Betty Webb

Gunn Zoo Mystery
The Anteater of Death
The Koala of Death
The Llama of Death
The Puffin of Death

Lena Jones Mysteries
Desert Noir
Desert Wives
Desert Shadows
Desert Run
Desert Cut
Desert Lost
Desert Wind
Desert Rage

The Puffin of Death

A Gunn Zoo Mystery

Betty Webb

Poisoned Pen Press

Copyright © 2015 by Betty Webb

First Edition 2015

10 9 8 7 6 5 4 3 2 1

Library of Congress Catalog Card Number: 2014958048

ISBN: 9781464204142   Hardcover
      9781464204166   Trade Paperback

Poisoned Pen Press
6962 E. First Ave., Ste. 103
Scottsdale, AZ 85251
www.poisonedpenpress.com
info@poisonedpenpress.com

Printed in the United States of America

*This book is dedicated to Barbara Peters and
Robert Rosenwald of Poisoned Pen Press, for their
unfailing courage in giving their authors a voice—
no matter how eccentric that voice may be.*

Acknowledgments

As usual, many people helped in the preparation of this book.

In Iceland, a thousand thanks are due to ever-patient Police Superintendent Árni E. Albertsson, at the National Commission of the Icelandic Police, who aided me in so many ways that cataloguing them all would require a book in itself. I owe you, Árni! My gratitude also goes out to Birgir Saemundsson for giving me details on the Finnish SAKO rifle. Mr. Saemundsson, a 1988 world record-holder marksman and marine engineer, is the founder of BRS Custom Rifles. Thanks and hugs to my kind hosts at Guesthouse Baldursbrá, in Reykjavik, and the lovely people at Hótel Egilsen, in exquisite Stykkishólmur. I also want to thank the everyday people of Iceland who were unfailingly patient and helpful, and who all spoke better English than I do. But my most ardent thanks and kisses go out to valiant Freya, the Icelandic horse who carried me safely across glacial rivers and lava-strewn valleys. Oh, and one more thing: my apologies to the residents of Vik for slightly altering the geography of their beautiful seaside community.

Back in the U.S., thanks again to the loyal Sheridan Street Irregulars, who always let me know when I'm barking up the wrong tree. The same goes for my faithful friends Marge Purcell, Debra McCarthy, and Louise Signorelli. Special thanks go out to Deborah Holt, who—in return for her donations to Friends of Wetumpka Library (FOWL), an Alabama literacy project–continues to let me use her name for a boat-owning character; and to Cathie Kindler, of Moose Hill Llamas, in Alabama, who made a donation to SSLA Youth Scholarship so she could take care of one of Teddy's cats on a houseboat named *S'Moose Sailing*.

Any mistakes in *The Puffin of Death* are due to my own errors, not the intelligent and big-hearted folks who helped me!

Cast of Characters

Icelanders

Bryndis Sigurdsdottir—zookeeper at the Reykjavik Zoo and lead singer in the rock band The Valkyries. Teddy stays with her while in Iceland.

Ragnar Eriksson—Bryndis' ex-boyfriend, an artist and bit player in the film *Berserker!*

Inspector Thorvaald Haraldsson—inspector with the National Commission of the Icelandic Police. He prefers to be called "Thor," and thinks Teddy is cute.

Kristin Olafsdottir—bookstore manager in downtown Reykjavik

Oddi Palsson—very patient tour guide

Ulfur Narfasson—Vik hotelier plagued by a chicken-eating fox

NOTE: A man's last name is taken from his father's FIRST name, with "son" attached, thus Ragnar Eriksson's name means, "Ragnar, Erik's son." A woman's last name is also taken from her father's first name, with "dottir" (daughter) attached, thus Bryndis' name means "Bryndis, Sigurd's daughter." Because so many Icelanders share the same last names, Icelandic phone books have to list people by their first names!

Americans

Theodora "Teddy" Esmeralda Iona Bentley—zookeeper from Gunn Landing, California. While not tending to her animals, she solves crimes.

Simon Parr—founder of the Arizona-based Geronimo County Birding Association (the Geronimos) and winner of the largest Powerball in history. The money has made this birder highly attractive to women despite his Elvis Presley sideburns.

Elizabeth St. John—Simon's broad-minded wife, a birder and world-renowned romantic suspense author. She likes birds just fine, but in reality she lives her life through her books' archaeologist heroine, Jade L'Amour.

Adele Cobb—another birder, and Simon's seemingly heartbroken ex-mistress

Dawn Talley—former model, and another of Simon's ex-mistresses (he had a collection). The only bird she likes is Duck l'Orange.

Benjamin Talley—Dawn's put-upon husband, a birder and ecology-minded traveler. Although from a wealthy restaurateur family, he has a dark past.

Lucinda Greaves—acid-tongued, often-married birder who drinks too much

Judy Malone—Lucinda's timid yoga-instructor daughter, who might be less timid than she acts

Tab Cooper—birder, aspiring actor, deceptively clean-cut

Perry and Enid Walsh—the newly elected president of the birding association, and his birder wife and business partner. Unfailingly kind, patient, and helpful, the couple may be too good to be true.

Icelandic Animals

Magnus—adorable orphaned polar bear cub going to the Gunn Zoo

Freya—Bryndis' Icelandic horse, a sorrel mare

Einnar—Ragnar's Icelandic horse, a black gelding

Loki—Icelandic fox, a male going to the Gunn Zoo

Ilsa—Loki's wife (Icelandic foxes mate for life), going to the Gunn Zoo

Sigurd—male puffin going to the Gunn Zoo

Jodisi—oddly marked female puffin, Sigurd's wife (puffins mate for life, too) going to the Gunn Zoo

Icelandic for Beginners

But first—more helpful tips on the Icelandic language

Because of Iceland's remote location, modern Icelandic is little changed from the Old Norse of the ninth century, and for non-Icelanders, this ancient language—spoken by the legendary hero Leif Eriksson and modern hoteliers alike—is difficult to learn. Fortunately, all Icelanders speak fluent English, and they're all eager to help you. In fact, they'll help you so much the only Icelandic word you'll ever need is *Takk*! which means "Thanks!"

And don't let those long, tongue-twisting Icelandic place names throw you. If the name ends in *vik*, you're near a bay or harbor; if it ends in *foss*, you're by a waterfall; if it ends with *eldfjall*, you're passing a volcano; if it ends in *kirk*, dress up, you're going to church; if it ends in *kull*, you're headed for a glacier, so make sure you're wearing crampons.

Why is the Icelandic language so difficult? Well, Icelanders seem to like consonants more than they do vowels, and this can be especially daunting when you want to ask directions to Skútustathagígar or þingvallakirkja. By the way, that odd letter which looks like a combination of a "b" and a "p" in þingvallakirkja is called a *thorn* and it is pronounced "th." I have used its phonetic spelling throughout this book, especially with Thingvellir (which would correctly be spelled "þingvellir").

Another reason Icelandic is so difficult is that in an attempt to keep the ancient language pure, Icelanders have devised a creative way to refer to modern inventions such as electricity, television, computers, and telephones. In some cases, they simply add several words together in a string to make up one hyper-long word, thus the terrifying: *vaðlaheiðarvegavinnuverkfærageyms luskúraútidyralyklakippuhringur,*

Which (strung together) means hip-wader-moor's-road-work's-tools'-storage-shed's-front-door's-keychain's-ring; in other words, a key ring holding a key to a highway storage facility located on marshy ground. See? In a weird sort of way, stringing all those words together actually does make sense.

Then again, Icelandic doesn't always work that way. Sometimes these descendants of the fierce Vikings use poetic combinations of ancient ideas to create a new word entirely. Thus, the Icelandic word for "meteorology" is *vethurfroethi,* which literally means "weather science"; "telephone" is *simi,* which means "long thread"; the word for "television" is *sjónvarp,* which means "vision-caster"; the word for "electricity" is *rafmagn,* which means "amber power"; and the word for "computer" is *tölva,* which means something like "a woman seer who uses numbers to tell fortunes." Cool, huh?

The only Icelandic besides "Takk!" that you need to know:

snyrting—toilet
karlar—men's room
konur—ladies' room
bilastaeði—parking
heatta—danger
sjúkrahus—hospital

Prologue

Vik, Iceland: August 7

As he snapped yet another photograph of the black, yellow, and white bird, Simon Parr congratulated himself. God only knew why the bird had flown all the way from Egypt to this rough Icelandic clifftop overlooking the North Atlantic, but there it was, pecking its way toward the puffin burrow. Although the morning was chilly, what with that damp wind freezing the tops of his uncovered ears, he had to smile. By sneaking away at four-thirty—the sun was almost up, for God's sake!—and leaving the rest of the group back at the hotel, he would be the first, and perhaps only, person on the tour to snag the hoopoe. So what if he'd forgotten his hat.

Note to self: even in August, mornings in Iceland were frigging cold.

But this trip was working out in more ways than one. First, the conversation back at the airport, where he'd told a certain someone exactly how things were, now the hoopoe. And afterwards…Well, better things were yet to come.

The morning hadn't begun well, what with that stupid hotel clerk blasting away with a rifle at some fox. Simon had been afraid the noise would scare away every bird in the vicinity, but no, after a brief flutter, they all came back. Now all he had to do was wait.

He heard a squawk.

The puffin, another visual weirdo with its oversized red, yellow, and blue-black beak, had stuck its head out of its burrow and was sounding a warning. It wasn't happy with the hoopoe's incursion, but who cared what a puffin thought? Especially that particular one. Instead of the standard, unblemished black crowning its head, this one sported a white streak down the middle of the black. Ugh. Besides, there were millions of the nasty things up here, so if the hoopoe fouled some freak puffin's living room, well, too bad. Parr didn't like puffins, never had. Rats with wings, he'd once called them, bringing down the wrath of the other birders at last month's disastrous meeting of the Geronimo County Birding Association. But had they ever smelled a puffin rookery? It was enough to make a person gag.

The stench was worth it. Same for the damp north wind numbing his fingers. He'd have gone through all kinds of hell to get those shots of the directionally challenged hoopoe.

All things considered, the hoopoe was a gorgeous bird. Not stubby and ungainly, like the poorly marked puffin, but sleek, built for flight and speed. Black-tipped yellow crown. Long, narrow black bill. Dramatic black-and-white-striped wings and tail. Bright yellow body. Given its extraordinary plumage, he could understand why there'd been such excitement when word of its arrival reached them. But in the end, a bird was just a bird. Another notch on his belt, nothing more.

Speaking of belts, another note to self: hire a private trainer and get rid of that incipient pot belly. He had the money now, didn't he? Money to do a lot of things he couldn't do before— dress the way he wanted, smoke what he wanted, wear his hair how he wanted. *Don't like my Cubano Cohiba Esplendido cigar? Hold your breath, wimp. Don't like my sideburns? Babe, if they were good enough for the King, they're good enough for me. Maybe I'll even buy a gold lamé sports coat, a big purple Cadillac, go the Full Elvis.*

Money meant freedom. Money meant no limits.

Simon Parr was so busy gloating over his glorious future that he forgot about the hoopoe. He also didn't hear the footsteps approaching behind him. He didn't even hear the gunshot, because by the time the sound reached his ears, he was already falling toward the puffin's burrow, unaware of sound, sight, or any other sense.

He would never hear another thing.

Or see another hoopoe.

Chapter One

Gunn Landing, California: Four days earlier

When Zorah radioed me that Aster Edwina wanted to see me in the zoo office immediately, I was knee-deep in giraffe droppings. Not that I minded, since that's my job. Most people think being a zookeeper is glamorous work, but the truth is that seventy-five percent of my time is spent shoveling a pile of fecal matter from one place to another. The animals enjoy watching, though.

Being summoned by Aster Edwina Gunn, head of the Gunn Zoo Trust, seldom meant good news, so it was with a certain amount of reluctance that I put my poop-scooping duties aside, climbed the long hill from African Trail, took the long way around Tropics Trail, then cut in front of the new Northern Climes exhibit and joined the crowd by the penguin enclosure. Anything to put off the inevitable. Rory, one of the Emperor penguins, was in the midst of another altercation with Ebenezer, a crested northern rockhopper. The two didn't like each other much, but this was the first time I'd seen them actually go at it. The smaller Ebenezer pecked Rory on the chest. Rory squawked and bopped Ebenezer on the head. Ebenezer bopped back.

I was thinking about breaking it up when my radio hissed at me again. "Keeper Number Four," I answered. "Over."

"Leave those penguins alone and get your butt in here, Teddy," Zora snapped.

"What makes you think I'm watching the penguins?"

"Because that's all you've done since they arrived."

Got me there. It would take a more jaded zookeeper not to be fascinated by the little cuties. They were so people-like. Yet so not.

"Well, Zorah, I'm…"

"Theodora Esmeralda Iona Bentley, do I have to tell you again?"

"Oh, all right," I grumbled. "I'll be there in a minute. But stop calling me by my full name. You know I hate it."

"And I hate being the go-between you and Aster Edwina. She's on a tear today, so make it half a minute. Zoo One, over and out."

While I was clipping the radio back onto my belt, Ebenezer's and Rory's spat morphed into a full-tilt brawl, and the two penguins tumbled butt-over-flipper until they fell off their rocky slope and splashed into the pool. Avian tempers duly doused, they swam to opposite sides of the pool, where they reduced their former physicality to mere glares.

Action over, the crowd left. So did I.

"Well, hi, Aster Edwina," I said, walking into the Administration Building. "What brings you here on this sunny California morning?"

The owner of the Gunn Zoo had to be well into her eighties by now, but age hadn't dimmed her. Hints of her former beauty remained on her face, and her spine was still as straight as a West Point graduate's. Age hadn't tempered her irascibility, either. Glancing at her watch, she said, "It does not take eight minutes to walk from African Trail to Admin."

"It's hot today, so I was reserving my strength. It's August. Happens every year. Plus I'm pulling a double shift, and I…"

"No, you're not."

"That comes as a surprise to me," I said, "especially since you're the one who arranged it."

Keisha, one of the Gunn Zoo's most popular bonobo apes, was about to give birth, and Aster Edwina had ordered that she be observed around the clock. Due to so many keepers on vacation or ill, Zorah, the zoo's director, had pulled a double shift herself the day before yesterday, which meant that today was my turn.

Aster Edwina inclined her regal head. "Zorah has already made arrangements. You're needed elsewhere."

"And that would be?" With Lucy, the giant anteater, who was also about to give birth? Or Wanchu, the koala, whose joey should be emerging from her pouch any day?

Aster Edwina mumbled something I was certain I hadn't heard correctly. "Pardon? Could you repeat that? Where did you say I'm needed?"

"Iceland!" she snapped.

I laughed. "Honestly, I really have to get my hearing checked, because I'd swear you said Iceland."

"You're leaving tomorrow. Zorah's already made the arrangements."

Zorah wouldn't meet my eyes, which meant it was probably true, and she felt guilty about it.

"Iceland? Tomorrow? You can't be serious."

"I am perfectly serious, Theodora. As you know, Jack Spense, our bear man, irresponsibly broke his leg surfing Sunday—compound fracture, I hear—and his doctor won't clear him to fly. You are the only person left on staff whose passport is up-to-date."

At last an out. I began a lie. "But it's not up…

She headed me off at the pass. "Don't bother telling me it's not, Theodora, because I am quite well aware you were in Costa Rica last month, visiting your runaway father. By the way, you should have gotten my permission before you flew off so cavalierly." Here, a harsh stare at Zorah, who had enough sense to keep quiet. "As I was saying before you tried to pull the wool over my eyes, you'll be taking an Alaska Airlines flight out of San Francisco to Seattle at 5:30 p.m. tomorrow, spend the night there, and the next day you'll board the 10 a.m. Icelandic Air flight which lands, weather willing, at Keflavik Airport sometime early Wednesday. We've already arranged for a car to pick you up, and you'll be sharing lodging with one of the Reykjavik Zoo people. The transfer paperwork will take around six days, I hear, because Icelanders move slowly in these matters." She sniffed. "No sense of urgency, those people. Pack for weather."

Icelandic weather. A vision of glaciers and blizzards rose up in front of me. I'm California born and bred, and the thought of spending six days in freezing temps filled me with horror. "Six days? But, Aster…"

"Yes, yes, I know you're worried about that adorable little bonobo, what's her name, yes, Keisha, as well you should, but Zorah and I have already taken care of that staffing problem, and I assure you that everything will be fine."

"But my own pets…"

"I took the liberty of calling your mother, and she agreed to take in your animals, so you see there's no problem, no problem at all." She gave me a beneficent smile, Lady of the Manor to Obedient Serf. "I've even given you several days off with pay so you can see the sights. They say Iceland is a major tourist attraction these days."

"But…But *why* are you sending me to Iceland?" I hated the plaintive tone in my voice, but couldn't seem to stop.

With a look of satisfaction, she said, "To pick up a polar bear, of course."

Grinding my teeth, I drove home to Gunn Landing Harbor to pack. I'm normally an even-tempered person, but the fact that Aster Edwina felt she could disrupt my life any time she wanted enraged me. Still, if I wanted to keep my job, and I did, there was no way around it. The lush green California hills rolled by quickly, and twenty minutes later I arrived at the harbor. Due to severe zoning restrictions imposed by the California Coastal Initiative, the tiny village of Gunn Landing, population five hundred, has no apartment buildings and no rentals other than three already-taken fishermen's cottages. Most of the village's inhabitants, several zookeepers among them, live on boats. Mine is the *Merilee*, a refitted 1979 thirty-four-foot CHB trawler, berthed at Slip No. 34.

I do not live alone. My usual bunkmates are DJ Bonz, a three-legged terrier, and Miss Priss, a one-eyed Persian, both rescued from the same pound. We are sometimes joined by Toby, the unfaithful half-Siamese who adopted me after his previous owner was murdered. Yes, I use the word "unfaithful" advisedly. Neutering hadn't changed Toby's roaming tendencies, and after spending a week or two with me, he always moved on down the dock to whatever boat took his fancy at the time. Right now he was with us again, which presented a problem.

Should I take him to Mother's with the rest of my menagerie?

I realized the problem had already been solved the moment I walked down the dock toward my *Merilee* and saw Cathie Kindler relaxing on the deck of the *S'Moose Sailing*, her refurbished houseboat. In her arms she held Toby, who was licking her ear and pretending he would never love anyone else, the little liar.

"Look who moved in with me," Cathie called, over the noise of a Chris-Craft speeding out of the channel toward the Pacific. She was one of those women who could never say no to a homeless cat. "He spent last week on Deborah Holt's *Flotsam*, but I guess they had a spat because here he is."

"Did you feed him?"

"Just a smidge. Part of a salmon steak."

I had to smile. "You'll regret that, because he'll expect it every day now."

Briefly, because I could hear my other animals crying out for me, I told her my situation and asked her to look after Toby while I was gone.

"Of course. But Iceland! Hope you've got a parka. Don't they have volcanoes? Maybe you should take an umbrella, too, what with all that fire and ash falling from the sky." With that encouragement, Cathie disappeared into *S'Moose's* galley to spoil Toby with more salmon.

I'd forgotten about the Icelandic volcanoes. It would be my rotten luck that one of the things would erupt while I was there, and all the flights would be grounded for a week or two, leaving me to babysit a polar bear on an ice floe where I'd end up as dinner.

Muttering to myself, I opened the hatch and entered the *Merilee*.

Miss Priss wanted food. DJ Bonz wanted walkies, then food. After I gave them both what they wanted, I began to pack.

Chapter Two

Keflavik, Iceland: Three days later

I stood outside Iceland's Keflavik International Airport, bundled in three layers of clothing topped by a Slimfit N-3B parka guaranteed to keep me warm at thirty degrees below zero.

Unfortunately, it was sixty-five degrees *above* zero in Keflavik. The sun was shining and volcanic ash appeared nowhere in evidence. When Bryndis Sigurdsdottir pulled up to the curb in her blue Volvo, I had shed the parka myself and was about to strip to my undies.

"Why's it so hot?" I asked Bryndis, after stowing my luggage in the trunk.

"Well, it is August, Teddy," she replied. The blond Reykjavik zookeeper had to be six feet tall if she was an inch, and was wearing shorts and a tank top. I guess if you're used to sub-zero weather, sixty-five degrees Fahrenheit seems broiling.

"I hear you had an interesting flight," she continued, as she pulled away from the Arrivals zone. "Some sort of ruckus that almost got you diverted to Manitoba." Bryndis' command not only of the English language, even its colloquialisms, didn't surprise me since before leaving California I'd been assured that all Icelanders spoke fluent English.

"Ruckus would be the right word. Some drunk guy sporting Elvis Presley sideburns started a brawl in First Class. He was with a group from Phoenix."

Bryndis nodded knowingly. "Ah, yes. Phoenix, in Arizona. Where the cowboys ride the range. They are wild men, correct? Rugged. Handsome."

"Drunk Elvis wasn't ugly but he was sure no cowboy. From what I heard, he was a birder on his way here with a group of other birders to study vagrants. You know, non-native birds that for one reason or another, show up in countries where they're not usually found. They're…"

I stopped myself in mid-explanation. Bryndis, a zookeeper herself, would know what a "vagrant" was in birder parlance. "Anyway, from what I could hear, the drunk guy started an argument with another birder about hoopoes, those yellow and black Egyptian birds, claiming one had been seen in some place called Vik. When another birder said that was impossible, Drunk Elvis called him a dumb piece of, ah, offal. He got loud enough that the flight steward booted him from First Class to the back of the plane with the rest of us peons."

Bryndis nodded. "But the drunk man was correct. In 2006, a hoopoe showed up at a farm near Vik, probably blown in by a storm. A male, bright yellow plumage. He made our own birders very happy for two days, then disappeared."

"Still, not worth making a scene over."

Bryndis laughed. "You must not know many birders. They can be quite vicious. Especially the Icelandic ones."

For the rest of the drive into Reykjavik, Iceland's largest city, she regaled me with stories about Icelandic birders coming to blows over waxwings and warblers. "But they always make up over drinks afterwards," she finished, as she drove through landscape so weird it looked downright alien. Miles and miles of harsh black rock stretched toward distant, glacier-capped mountains. The rocks were only rarely softened by patches of startlingly green moss; the mountains—volcanoes, actually—looked set to blow at any moment, and they gave me the shivers.

Bryndis noticed me staring out the window. "How do you like the scenery?"

"Nice."

My polite lie elicited a laugh. "Not to worry, this is a centuries-old lava field. After I introduce you to Magnus I will show you downtown Reykjavik, then tomorrow morning we will go riding along the coastline at Vik, a beautiful place that will look more pleasing to you than this. You do ride, yes?"

"Ride? Certainly. And is Magnus, your, um, boyfriend?"

"Yes, and your new one. We Icelanders believe in sharing."

My reaction got another laugh. "Magnus is your new polar bear, Teddy. In Icelandic, 'magnus' means very big. Great, actually. We will swing by my apartment first to unload your luggage, then go over to the zoo first for a quick introduction. You will enjoy a nice walk around there after sitting so long on the plane, will you not?"

Sounded good to me, so I nodded. "Uh, does your car have air-conditioning?" I asked, as another rivulet of perspiration rolled down my face. I was still in three layers of clothing.

She gave me a sympathetic look. "Not needed in Iceland. But tell you what. You can change into cooler clothing when we stop by my apartment."

I liked her already. A good thing, too, since I'd be bunking with her for a week while learning the ins and outs of polar bear care.

Bryndis' apartment, mere blocks from the Reykjavik city center, was quite small. A tiny kitchen, a tiny bathroom, a tiny living room that doubled as an office, and a bedroom with barely enough space for twin beds. Although completely furnished by Ikea, large posters of animals personalized the walls. The rooms were themed, too. The posters in the bedroom displayed mountain gorillas and orangutans. The living room—lions, tigers, leopards, and cheetahs. The kitchen—puffins and whooper swans.

I felt right at home.

The only oddity I found was in the bathroom, where I went to change clothes. Over the toilet hung a big concert poster of a female music group named Valkyrie. Underneath the lead singer, who strongly resembled Bryndis, ran a sentence in Icelandic that said, "*Við syngja af dauðum.*"

Long underwear duly removed and outer clothes back on, I exited the bathroom to find Bryndis waiting for me in the kitchen with a tall glass of iced tea. After gratefully downing it, I asked, "Is that you or a twin in the bathroom poster?"

"It is me, all right. Valkyrie plays all over Reykjavik, sometimes as many as three gigs a week. Is that the right word, gigs?"

"Yep. But how can you handle that kind of schedule? I'm a zookeeper myself and know what a rugged job it is. And from what I hear, being in a rock group is rough stuff, too."

She shrugged. "Icelanders like to be busy, so we all do many things. In fact, there is a joke we like to tell on ourselves. Besides our full-time jobs, two out of four of us are in a band, one is writing a book, and the other works in the movies. Someone is always making a movie here. In fact, two different companies—one of them American—start filming here in a few days. Ragnar, a friend of mine, is going to be an extra in the American one." Considering the bleak scenery I'd seen since leaving the airport, I guessed both movies were horror films. But not wanting to insult her country, I said, "What does that sentence mean, '*Við syngja af dauðum?*' From the expression on your face, I pronounced it wrong."

She laughed. "No problem. Non-Icelanders have a terrible time with Old Norse, which is what we speak. Anyway, the sentence means, 'We sing of the dead.'"

"Cheerful." Yep. Horror movies.

Unaware of my thoughts, she flashed strong white teeth. "Icelandic music can be dark, but you will find that we ourselves are usually of a cheerful disposition. Now I have a question for you. Is it true you live on a boat?"

When I told her about the *Merilee* and Gunn Landing Harbor, her eyes lit up. "As you know, I will be accompanying you and Magnus back to your zoo in California to teach more about polar bears, so perhaps you will show me your *Merilee?*"

"Show you? Heck, if you want, you can even bunk with me.

The *Merilee* sleeps four." And wasn't much smaller than Bryndis' apartment.

Fifteen minutes later, we were back in Bryndis' Volvo, headed toward the Reykjavik City Zoo.

On the way, I found another occasion to be grateful Icelanders spoke fluent English. As Bryndis had explained, their native language—unchanged since the eighth century when Vikings had settled the island—was almost impossible to learn. I couldn't even pronounce the street signs because they were in Old Norse, and as such, had plenty of consonants but comparatively few vowels. For instance, to get to the zoo from Bryndis' apartment, we took Baldursbrá to Snoori, then to Hverfisgata, turned right onto Laugavegur, which eventually turned into Engjateigur, then onto Sudurlandsbraut, made another right on Sigtun, and finally drove into Laugardalur Park. Along the way I'd given the pronunciations the old college try, and my attempts kept Bryndis in stitches until we climbed out of the car at the zoo's parking lot.

The zoo was smaller than I expected, and so was the bear, who was being housed in a small outbuilding, away from the other animals, lest his predator's scent disturb them.

Magnus was a cub, not the ferocious man-eater I'd imagined. White, with adorable black button eyes and nose, and soaked from splashing around the small kiddie pool he'd been supplied with. Although fairly uneducated about bears, especially cubs, I could tell he was underweight. At around six months old, he weighed less than forty pounds. But given the fact that polar bear cubs are usually born during November or December, when their mothers are hibernating, he shouldn't have been alive at all.

Anticipating my questions, Bryndis explained that the winter had been a short one, which had disrupted the polar bears' breeding season.

"The ice sheet is melting, the bears are starving, and many of them have stopped breeding. While others…well, you see the result. A hunter found the poor little thing abandoned on an ice floe up near Raufarhöln, and instead of shooting him, which most hunters would have done because we cannot allow bears to kill our sheep, drove him all the way down here to us." She motioned toward the cub. The roly-poly bundle of fur was sucking from a huge bottle being held by another zookeeper. "As you can see, he is still being milk-fed, which is the only reason we can care for him here. But when he grows up…" Bryndis shrugged.

Because Iceland had only one native mammal—the Icelandic fox—the zoo specialized mainly in domestic animals, not wild ones. Other than one large pool filled with seals, its exhibits were mainly confined to domestic animals, such as pigs, chickens, cows, and Icelandic horses, with a Russian mink and a Lapland reindeer thrown in for good measure. With the sole exception of Magnus, the zoo had no polar bears, and given Iceland's arctic winters, had wisely passed on lions, tigers, and elephants.

"As much as we love Magnus," Bryndis continued, "we must adopt him out. Several zoos wanted him, but when Miss Gunn sent us the specs and photographs of your beautiful new Northern Climes exhibit, the Gunn Zoo became our first choice. So! Shall we head to the office and fill out some papers?"

I could have watched Magnus nurse from that huge baby bottle for the entire day, but business is business, so I dutifully followed Bryndis into the administration building.

Six hours later, and after a quick nap to shake off my jet lag, we were sitting in the Viking Tavern, Reykjavik's most popular watering hole. We'd made the short uphill jaunt by foot, which gave me plenty of time to window shop on the way. Because of the extreme winters and the country's lack of trees, most of Reykjavik's homes and buildings were constructed of brightly colored corrugated iron, which gave the city a cheerful air. Along the way we visited an art gallery, a high-fashion dress shop, three standing-room-only bookstores—apparently Icelanders read a lot—and passed an upscale restaurant whose posted menu announced that they served everything from poached salmon and roasted reindeer to pickled ram's testicles

In a way, the Viking Tavern reminded me of one of the upmarket bars back in Gunn Landing, if you discounted the fierce-looking battle-axes and Viking helmets hanging over the long bar, and the frequent shouts of Old Norse over a background hum of English, Danish, German, and Italian. During a few lulls in the conversation, I could even pick up smatterings of Japanese. It was further proof that tiny Iceland, with a population of little more than three hundred and fifty thousand—almost half of them living in Reykjavik—had become a major tourist destination.

When I asked Bryndis about this, she pointed out the country's spectacular scenery, most of which I'd seen photographs of in the guidebook I bought back in the States.

"But being so small, we do have our problems, especially here in Reykjavik." As if to illustrate, she pulled her iPhone out of her handbag and brought up an app I'd never seen before. "Watch this."

She turned around and tapped the shoulder of a man at the next table. "Hi, Sven. I want to show my new American friend someone, so let us bump phones."

The man, a big handsome guy in a Viking sort of way, grinned. "Anytime, dear Bryndis."

When the two bumped their iPhones together, both phones immediately began to wail.

Several Icelanders sitting nearby began to laugh. "Noh, noh, noh!" they chorused.

Bryndis beamed. "Teddy, let me introduce you to my second cousin, Sven Thómasson."

Sven, who I now saw closely resembled Bryndis, wiggled his fingers at me. "Very pleased to meet you, Teddy. Do not let her get you into trouble, okay?"

When Bryndis turned back to me, she explained, "What Sven and I demonstrated is called the Accidental Incest App. Most Icelanders are descended from only fourteen families that settled here in the ninth century, and so we make certain that the person we have set our sights on at some party is not too closely related. Otherwise we would have babies with two heads!"

More laughter from the bar patrons.

"This is also why we are listed by our first names in the phone book—not enough last names to go around."

Not certain she was having me on, I said, "It sounds like your social life can get complicated."

A big smile. "Teddy, you do not know the half of it."

I was only two sips into my glass of burgundy, but Bryndis was already on her second Brennivin, an alcoholic concoction made from potatoes spiced with caraway seeds. Having had her fun, she left the subject of Icelandic dating behind and began to describe the other animals I would be taking back to California.

"You will like our Icelandic foxes," she said, no slur detectible in her voice. "Sigurd and Freya come from different litters and both are less than a year old. Playful and smart, so be prepared for sneaky business. When winter comes in California, their coats will turn white, like they do here, then dark gray again in the spring. And the two puffins you will be taking with you? Loki has a broken wing which keeps him from flying. He was brought to the zoo a few months ago by the little girl who found him. Ilsa, the female, another rescue, was already here. She, too, has a problem. Part of one wing is missing, not enough that you can see it, but enough that she can no longer fly. She might have been bitten by a fox. But her story ends happily, because when Loki met her it was love at first sight. Puffins mate for life, you understand, so when we told Miss Gunn about their love, she said she would be pleased to take both."

When I expressed surprise, she laughed. "This being Iceland, we can always get more puffins. There's a puffin rookery near Vik, the largest in the world. That is where we're going horseback riding tomorrow so you can see how beautiful our country really is. Iceland is not all lava fields, bookstores, and bars. But we have to go to Vik tomorrow, because within the next few days, two film crews will be setting up there."

"I'm looking forward to…"

The sound of breaking glass cut me off. It was followed by a curse word. An American curse word. Then I heard chairs scraping back, sounds of grappling, more curse words.

"Ah, a fight," Bryndis said, sounding delighted. "Excellent! Fight at night, fair sailing on the morrow."

An old Viking proverb, no doubt. "Maybe we should leave." From my old college days, I knew barroom fights had a nasty habit of spreading.

She gave me a quizzical look. "You do not enjoy a good fight?"

"I go out of my way to avoid them."

She shook her head in disappointment. "Then sit here in peace while I go see who is doing what to whom. That may be Ragnar who is slapping the man with the Elvis sideburns. Ragnar and I used to be, as you Americans say, an item. We still are, when he is not busy with someone else. Or I am."

Elvis sideburns? It couldn't be. But when I stood up and peered over an upturned table, I saw that the man in question was indeed Drunk Elvis, the birder who'd almost gotten my flight diverted to Manitoba.

Drunk Elvis' huge blond adversary had him down on the ground and was slapping the holy hell out of him while a crowd of Icelanders cheered him on. The tourists, alarmed by the physicality, huddled against the far wall.

"Hi, Ragnar," Bryndis said, leaning toward the big blond slapper. "Are you going to Arni's opening tonight?"

Ragnar nodded. Without missing a slap, he said with a slight accent, "I have been looking forward to it all week. He will be exhibiting twelve oils and four sculptures. The Njalsdottir Trio is performing, I hear. And the buffet includes hakari. Will you be there?" Still slapping.

"Too much paperwork to do. By the way, I believe you have punished that man enough."

"You think? Well, here is what he said to her." Ragnar growled something in Icelandic.

I couldn't understand a word, but Ragnar's words appeared to horrify Bryndis.

"He actually *said* that? To a woman?" she replied in English.

Ragnar switched back to English, too. "And much worse. But perhaps you are right. He has learned his lesson. See? He cries now, the big baby."

The blond giant stood up, hauling Drunk Elvis with him. With a consideration that seemed odd under the circumstances, Ragnar swept pieces of broken glass off his victim, bloodying his hand in the process. He didn't notice. "There, sir. All good now. But it would be best if you return to your hotel and never visit the Viking Tavern again. I am not the only Icelander in here who heard you say such things to that poor woman. Consider yourself a lucky man. If you had said such things to an Icelandic woman, you would be dead now, killed by her own hand."

We watched as Drunk Elvis, still sniveling, staggered out of the bar with a middle-aged woman trailing behind him. Her hair, obviously dyed, was almost the color of my burgundy wine. It wasn't flattering.

After giving Ragnar a kiss on the cheek, Bryndis steered me back to our table. "That was fun. Say, Ragnar has a brother who is even more handsome than he is. Would you like me to arrange a date? He could show you a good time for the rest of your days in Iceland." She winked. "A very good time."

I sputtered for a moment, then managed, "I'm engaged."

"That is a problem?"

"In the way you mean, yes. At least it is in the U.S."

She shrugged. "That is all right then, I guess, as long as your fiancé shows you a good time, too."

There were no more fights at the Viking Tavern, but Bryndis wanted to get us to the stables in Vik first thing in the morning so we left at eleven. Given the time difference between Iceland and California, it was somewhere around three the previous afternoon there, the perfect time to call my fiancé. After clearing a space for my laptop on the minuscule desk in the living room, Bryndis toddled off to bed, and due to the miracles of modern electronics, my call went straight through to the San Sebastian County Sheriff's Office.

"How cold is it?" Joe asked, as soon as he picked up.

"It's August, even in Iceland, and it hit seventy today. Since I was wearing ski gear more appropriate for Switzerland in December, I almost had a heat stroke at the airport. But now that the sun's down the temperature's dropping, and it would sure be nice to have you here to cuddle with." I made kissy-kissy noises.

"Sending you an imaginary cuddle." He returned my kissy-kissy noises.

This was one of the things I loved about Joe. To meet Joe Reyes, he looked like your basic rough, tough county sheriff, albeit handsomer than most, but when you got to know him you realized he was sloppily romantic. At least once a week he had delivered a single red rose to the *Merilee*. And then there were those biceps, that chest...

"Is the bear as cute as you expected, or haven't you met him yet?"

I put away my X-rated fantasies and replied, "Met him already, and he's even cuter. They've named him Magnus. How're things on the criminal front in San Sebastian County?"

"No more bank robberies since you left or Circle K holdups, only a couple of domestic disturbances, none of them violent, and a few speeders. You know, the usual. Speaking of Switzerland, have you decided where you want to go on our honeymoon?"

"Hawaii. Rome. Paris. Mexico City. Whatever's fine with you." More kissy noises. "You're so easy."

"That's what all my fiancés say."

Joe also had a good sense of humor, so he got a laugh out of that one. But then, with regret in his voice, he said, "Listen, it's wonderful talking to you, and even though you've only been gone a couple of days, I already miss you like crazy. But I promised to drop by and see Rogers at the hospital. If I don't get out of here now, I never will. The paperwork's about to hit the fan on the First National."

Just before I'd left, Sam Rogers, the newest and youngest deputy on the San Sebastian force, had broken his pelvis when his squad car experienced a blowout and rolled during the high-speed chase of two Nevada men who hours earlier had robbed the San Sebastian First National Bank. Like most good sheriffs, Joe was supportive of his deputies, especially when they were injured on the job.

"Go, go. Spread the solace and put off the red tape as long as possible."

Another laugh, another rash of phone kisses, and we hung up.

Despite my daytime nap, I slept well that night, awakening only once when, during an X-rated dream of Joe, I opened my eyes and discovered that he'd morphed into Drunk Elvis.

"Are we having fun yet?" he leered.

Chapter Three

At four in the morning, a few minutes before Iceland's summer sunrise, Bryndis and I left Reykjavik for Hótel Brattholt—Icelandic for "steep hill," my fellow zookeeper informed me. Brattholt was a combined hotel and farm near Vik, a tiny seaside community southeast of Reykjavik where she and Ragnar boarded their horses. When not slapping Drunk Elvis around, Ragnar was the soul of generosity, and had graciously offered to lend me his gelding so that I could enjoy a day in the saddle.

"Pretty isn't it?" Bryndis said, pulling her Volvo to the right to avoid hitting a sheep walking down the center line of the highway.

"The sheep?"

She laughed. "No, Teddy, the scenery."

Unlike the barren lava fields I'd seen during yesterday's drive from the airport to Reykjavik, the scenery along this part of Iceland's Ring Road, which looped around the entire country, was gorgeous. As the sun rose, I saw glacier-topped mountains to our left, and lush, emerald-green pastures to our right. Herds of shaggy Icelandic horses grazed peacefully in those pastures, careful to make wide berths around the steaming hot springs the country was famous for. Every now and then a shooting geyser erupted from one of the hot springs, splattering the area around it with scalding water. It didn't faze the horses, which were known for their steady temperament.

At one point during our drive, Bryndis parked on the side for a few minutes and drew my attention to a seemingly peaceful-looking mountain capped by a glacier.

"That's Eyjafjallajökull," she said. "Remember back in 2010 when one of our volcanoes erupted and disrupted air travel all across Europe? There is the villain."

"You mean there's a volcano underneath all that snow?"

"That is true of most of our volcanoes—we have more than a hundred—which is why Iceland is called 'the land of fire and ice.' But only around thirty keep erupting, which does cause some inconvenience from time to time. When Eyjafjallajökull blew, a few hundred people had to be evacuated."

I tried pronouncing the unpronounceable. "Eya...Eyafah-alla...what?" My American tongue made it sound like a Middle Eastern culinary dish.

"AY-uh-fyat-luh-YOE-kuutl-uh," she said slowly. "*Eyja* means 'island' and *fjall* means 'mountain.' When you put them all together and add *jökull*, *Eyjafjallajökull* literally means 'the glacier on top of the mountains you can see the islands from.' Not so hard when you break it down, eh?"

"If you say so."

She laughed. "As bad as Eyjafjallajökull was to us, do you see that big hump several miles to the south?"

From here, that "big hump" was a snow-covered slope that looked perfect for skiing.

"That is not snow, Teddy," Bryndis said, as if reading my mind. "It is another glacier, and underneath all the ice lies Katla, an even bigger volcano than Eyjafjallajökull. Much, much bigger! In legend, Katla was a cruel witch who was chased out of a village because of her evil ways, and every now and then, she takes her revenge. Our scientists say she is long overdue for an eruption and that when she blows, we may have to take to the boats. I will bet you hope you are back safe in California when that happens, eh?"

I'd once been in Hawaii when Kilauea erupted, wiping out several homes, so I wasn't eager to see anything like that again. Compared to Eyjafjallajökull or even Kilauea, Katla appeared as gentle as the lambs grazing on the side of the Ring Road. In the early morning light, soft clouds hovered above its peaceful slopes.

Bryndis read my mind again. "No worries! We always get earthquakes before an eruption, and other than a couple of bumps in the past few days, nothing has happened."

"Bumps?"

"You did not notice the one last night? Iceland averages several quakes a week, all perfectly safe. But you being from California, you must be used to them, right?" Without waiting for an answer, she continued, "Now take a look at the pretty green hill in front of Eyjafjallajökull. That is part of a lava flow created by the volcano more than a thousand years ago. See the buildings caved into the rock? Those are ancient dwellings our ancestors used to live in. Now they are used for storage, and during especially bad weather, as shelter for farm animals."

"You're telling me Vikings used to live in caves?"

She grinned. "The heat came in handy during the winter, I hear."

We reached the Hótel Brattholt three hours after leaving Reykjavik, having made a couple of stops along the way. The hotel, with its nearby stables, was popular with all sorts of outdoors-loving tourists. It sat atop a steep hill, a mile back from the famous black sand beach of Vik.

A no-frills structure, the hotel's steeply pitched metal roof must have come in handy during the area's rugged winters. So would its corrugated iron siding, erected to withstand any insult the weather threw at it. The sides of the hotel were painted a creamy yellow with bright green trim, and looked welcoming. The interior was even cozier than the exterior. The combined lobby/dining hall was filled with comfy sofas, booths, and chairs arranged in an arc around the huge stone fireplace. Despite the early hour, several visitors had already staked out the seats closest to its warmth.

As I waited, Bryndis went in to speak to the hotelier, a muscular man of about forty, whose name tag said ULFUR. Like everyone I'd met so far, he spoke fluent English, and was kind enough to caution us about the weather.

"A light rain is forecast for later today, so rain slickers might be a good idea. If you do not have any, you can borrow some from us." He motioned to a collection of jackets and slickers hanging from a pegged shelf on the wall behind the counter.

"We are fine, but thanks," Bryndis told him. To me, she said, "The food is good here, so let us have lunch after our ride."

"My treat," I insisted. Aster Edwina, my usually-stingy boss, had loaned me the zoo's platinum Visa, and I planned to take advantage of it.

Weather in Iceland is changeable. When we went back outside, a front of dark clouds had already sped inland from the North Atlantic, lending accuracy to Ulfur's warning. But having folded a slicker into my fanny pack before we left her apartment, I was prepared for whatever the weather threw at me.

To my surprise, the horses weren't stabled. They ran loose in a large pasture behind the hotel, but catching them proved no problem. As friendly as dogs, they ran toward us at the sound of Bryndis' whistle, so within minutes of our arrival, we were saddled up, Bryndis on her sorrel mare Freya, me on Ragnar's black gelding, Einnar. The horses appeared eager to get some exercise, and we were glad to oblige.

The riding trail led down a steep incline from the hotel toward the Ring Road. Freya's hooves flew as she sped along, trusting my Einnar to catch up. I'd ridden most of my life, but was unused to the Icelandic horses' unusual gaits—especially the fast *tolt*, a rapid gait bearing no resemblance to an American horse's gallop. As Einnar raced in pursuit of Freya I clutched amateurishly at the pommel of my saddle. My horse, speedy despite his gentleness, caught up with Freya as we reached the highway.

No cars were coming, so we crossed safely to where the riding trail continued on the other side.

Bryndis grinned as I reined up alongside her. "How do you like our Icelandic horses?"

"Mag" puff "ifi" puff "cent," I puffed, hoping she understood me, what with all those puffs.

"Our horses, they are different than those you are used to?"

"Night" puff "and" puff "day."

As if trying to figure out what the heck I was talking about, Einnar turned his great head to look at me, snorted, then bobbed his head at Freya. When she nickered back, I was convinced the two were sharing a joke at my expense.

"Caught your breath yet?" Bryndis asked, pityingly.

"I'm good for a few more miles." Puff, puff.

From the highway, it was only a quarter-mile further to the black sand beach, which I found terrifying in its beauty. To the east, a steep volcanic cliff almost two hundred feet high fronted the beach, hiding it from the highway. With that reminder of civilization out of sight, the seaside landscape looked almost alien, which, Bryndis explained, was why it remained such a popular film location, from historical epics like *Noah* and *Beowulf* to sci-fi flicks like *Prometheus*. On the cliff walls, giant columns of gray basalt, thrust up by volcanic eruptions, framed a series of caverns formed by lava flumes. Several yards off shore, three sea stacks rose as sentinels in the turbulent North Atlantic.

"That looks like rough surf," I yelled to Bryndis as we *tolted* along the beach. I was becoming used to my horse's gait, and could speak without turning blue.

"Angry trolls keep the water riled up."

I wasn't certain I heard her right. "Trolls, did you say?"

"Legend says that those big columns in the water are the remains of three fishing vessels the trolls tried to pull out to sea. They could not quite manage it, so to spite other fishermen, they made the water so rough no one has been able to boat near here. Or swim. So whatever you do, do not fall in the water!"

"I'll try to remember that."

While we rode along, flocks of seagulls, grebes, and fat-bodied puffins cawed and shrieked against the rising wind. Our horses weren't bothered by the racket. They were unflappable, and *tolted* across the black sand as if the sea and the sky had remained motionless.

Casting a look at the darkening day, Bryndis shouted back at me, "If we want to see the puffin rookery, we must hurry. Once the rain begins, the trail up will be too slippery for safety." She pointed to the top of the cliff, from which the parrot-beaked birds peered down at us.

Surely she didn't mean for our horses to scale the cliff! I would have shared my concern, but she had already urged her horse forward, and we sped along the black sand at such speed it was startling. A few minutes later we rounded the jutting southern end of the cliff and entered a low, lava-and-grass-speckled marsh at the harbor's mouth. In the distance I saw the picturesque village of Vik, its green, yellow, and red corrugated iron homes bright against the darkening sky. Unlike the sheer rock wall ahead of us, they looked welcoming.

As we grew closer to the base of the cliff, I could see a narrow trail leading up to the top, but it appeared dangerously steep, eased only by a series of switchbacks. One misstep and we would wind up in the churning North Atlantic, food for hungry trolls.

I urged my horse forward until he caught up with Bryndis. Trying to disguise my concern, I said, "You said that the rookery is a popular spot for birders, but most birders I've known aren't mountain-climbers, so how…?"

She reined Freya to a halt and pointed inland, where I saw that the cliff wall was actually the abrupt end of a land bridge that began in the inland hills to the north. Sitting atop the highest was the Hótel Brattholt. We had ridden in a long semi-circle and come out on the other side.

"From the hotel, it is an easy hike along the footpath to the rookery, but nowhere near as scenic as the way we've ridden. If you look hard, you can see the footpath and the pedestrian footbridge that crosses over the road."

Squinting, I saw a serpentine scar winding from the inn to the cliff's plateau. I was about to suggest that we return to the hotel and pick our way along the footpath, a much easier journey, but Bryndis and Freya had already started up the steep incline on the side of the cliff. Without asking my opinion, Einnar followed suit.

The ride proved as unsettling as I'd feared, and a couple of times I had to shut my eyes against the steep drop to the beach, trusting Einnar to make his way along the narrow track without my guidance. Braver and more surefooted than I, he did, and after a climb that felt like hours but by my watch was only minutes, we arrived at the summit, a windswept expanse of flat land interrupted here and there by eerie lava formations. Some of them were vaguely human-shaped, which Bryndis told me might have given rise to the still-prevalent Icelandic belief in gnome-like creatures called the "hidden people."

"Be careful or one might grab you," Bryndis teased, dismounting on the same spot where the footpath from the hotel came to an end. "The hidden people love redheads."

Only half-convinced she was kidding—I'd read somewhere that as many as two-thirds of Icelanders still believed in gnomes and trolls—I watched my step.

By now the wind was blowing in earnest, and the first drops of rain had begun to fall. The North Atlantic roared far below us, the surf's noise eclipsed by the squawking and cawing of innumerable nesting puffins. White-and-black heads adorned with vivid red, yellow, and blue-black beaks stuck their heads out of their underground burrows, shrieking their displeasure at our trespass. Sympathetic to their distress, I dismounted and led my horse toward what appeared to be solid ground, but before I'd traveled more than a few yards, a nesting puffin poked its head out of a nearby burrow and squawked a warning.

"Sorry," I muttered, seeing a downy chick hunkered beside it.

Mama Puffin was in no mood to accept my apology. Believing I meant harm to her baby, she squawked again, then hopped out of the burrow to deliver a swift series of pecks to my boot. Her garish beak must have been stronger than it looked, because I could feel her assault through the thick leather. I stepped further away, continuing my apologies. Not that Mama Puffin cared.

"Avoid the nesting females," Bryndis advised. "They are protective of their young. The males, too, come to think of it. Uh oh. Here comes Papa Puffin now."

A larger puffin swept by me, several small, silver-colored fish dangling from its bill. Once the bird landed at the mouth of the burrow, it ignored me until it had finished stuffing breakfast into its chick's craw, but as soon as that had been accomplished, it fixed me with an evil eye and growled. Yes, *growled.*

My horse and I beat a hasty retreat.

"Come here!" Bryndis shouted over the wind. "Twins!"

I'd read enough about puffins to know that surviving twins weren't common among the species, so I led Einnar to where Bryndis and Freya had halted. The zookeeper took out her iPhone and aimed it at the ground, while her horse stood stoically, ignoring the caws and growls of nearby puffins. From the bottom of the burrow, two small nestlings looked up at us, their dark eyes glittering. Unlike the adult birds nearby, they appeared fearless—at least until their parents returned. Then, goaded by the larger birds' growls and squawks, the nestlings screeched an alarm, further distressing the parents.

"We'd better move away," I said, hoping to spare my boots from another attack.

"Just one more picture."

Leaving her to it, I set off on the footpath, snapping pictures as I moved inland up the slope with the faithful Einnar heeling me like a well-trained dog. All went well for a few minutes, until I zeroed in on a particularly human-like lava formation thirty yards away. Around five feet high and as thin as a fashion model, the moss covering it could have been a haute couture dress. At its feet, half-hidden in the shadow of the morning sun, was another lava formation, this one stretched horizontally across the ground. In the dark shadow, its color appeared more blue than green. For some reason, Einnar decided he didn't like it, and with an alarmed snort, pulled up short, almost yanking the reins from my hand.

"Don't ruin your breed's reputation," I murmured, focusing my iPhone's lens on the lava. The interplay of colors—black, green, blue, pink, and red—would make for a nice print. The shutter clicked at the same time I asked myself...

Pink? Red?

Frowning, I tugged at Einnar's reins and led him closer to the formations.

No.

Only one lava formation.

The horizontal shape was a man lying face-down across a puffin burrow.

Dropping Einnar's reins, I ran forward, scattering puffins in every direction. "Bryndis!" I shouted. "Someone's been hurt!"

When I touched the back of the man's neck, his skin felt cool. But so did the wind and rain whipping across the top of the cliff. Hoping it wasn't too late to render aid, I turned him over...

And saw that nothing could help him now.

The man must have been dead before he fell across the puffin burrow, because he hadn't closed his eyes against the bird's vicious beak. His nose had been pecked to a pulp by the burrow's inhabitant—a female puffin protecting her chick. But the injuries she'd inflicted didn't bother me as much as did the small, neat hole in his forehead.

Although I'd seen plenty of grisly things in my life, I had to sit down on a nearby rock.

The female puffin popped her head out of the burrow and growled. Blood smeared her beak and stained the unusual white stripe that ran lengthwise down her head. Blood had trickled onto her fat chick, too, but the birds were in better shape than the dead man.

"Is he...?" Whatever else Bryndis had been about to say was silenced by a gasp.

"Better call the police," I said, not bothering to turn around. "He's dead. And I think I know who he is. Uh, was."

The man's lush sideburns identified him as Drunk Elvis, the American birder who'd caused a disturbance on my flight, and then proceeded to repeat his churlish performance at the Viking Tavern.

Bryndis had to see for herself. Once she saw him, she made a sound similar to a hiccup, then punched in a series of numbers on her cell. A spate of Icelandic soon followed.

While she spoke to the authorities, I felt his carotid in hopes of even a tiny pulse. Nothing. Not even a flutter. As I leaned over him, a series of panicked thoughts staggered through my head. What was the emergency number in Iceland? My tourist guide to Iceland the number listed the number as 1-1-2 for cops, ambulances, whatever, maybe even for driving directions, since Icelandic road signs were all in unreadable Icelandic. Come to think of it, why didn't these people change their road signs to English so that tourists would stop getting lost, like maybe Drunk Elvis? Yes, that was it. Drunk Elvis became lost and somebody killed him, yes, they did, and then he'd fallen on his face, and, yeah, Mama Puffin pecked away at him....

Wait a minute. Puffins don't shoot people. Besides the hole in Drunk Elvis' forehead, he had a matching hole in the back. And, oh, my God, look at that camera strapped around his neck, an upmarket Nikon D4 with a lens a yard long, and his binoculars must have cost a small fortune, and why'd he look so familiar? Even in my shock, I remembered thinking the same thing on the plane.

Realizing that I needed to get myself back under control, I stood up and brushed the moss off my pant. I took a deep breath to ensure that my voice wouldn't tremble, then said, "Bryndis, we need to back away a few yards. Unless I'm wrong, and I don't think I am, this is a crime scene."

"What are you talking about, Teddy? That man…he…he must have fallen and hit his head. Then the puffin got him." She paused, then began to back up with her horse. "Although I have never seen a puffin do that. Kill someone. How could a little puffin kill a person? They are such small birds and they never hurt anyone other than give them a peck or two. I was pecked once when I…" She hiccupped again. "Oh, this is a terrible, terrible thing."

For some reason, the fact that Bryndis sounded panicked herself helped calm me, and I shook my head. "The puffin didn't kill him, Bryndis. He was shot."

She stared at me in disbelief. "Shot? We don't shoot people in Iceland!"

"Somebody didn't get the memo."

The first policeman to arrive was a black-uniformed constable from Hvolsvöllur, a small village a few miles down the road from

Vik. Given his peach-fuzz beard and reedy build, Constable Galdur Frimannsson looked little older than a high school senior, but after taking one look at the dead man's wounds, he made a quick call on his radio. He spoke in Icelandic, but there was no mistaking his serious tone. He, too, recognized a crime scene when he saw one.

Even if people didn't shoot people in Iceland.

While waiting for reinforcements, I found myself chilled to the bone. A hard rain now blew sideways across the moss-covered plateau. The yellow slicker I'd packed kept off the worst of the damp, but did little to protect me from the plummeting temperature. Turning my back to the wind meant that I had to face Dead Elvis, which made me even more wretched. I wanted to hop onto Einnar's back and return to the Hótel Brattholt, but Constable Frimannsson refused to let us leave the scene. At least he was polite about it.

"You must both be interviewed by Inspector Thorvaald Haraldsson, who will be arriving from Reykjavik with a foren-sics team," he'd explained, looking apologetic. "This death is an unusual occurrence, and given the weather, I'm sorry, but the dispatcher told me to keep you here so that the inspector himself can question you. Since you, Miss Bentley, are unused to Icelandic weather, he might send someone up to the inn to get you some coffee. Or hot chocolate."

Bryndis rolled her eyes. Truth be told, my fellow zookeeper looked as miserable as I, but true to her Viking heritage, she'd begun putting a stern face on her discomfort. Ignoring the dead man, she faced the raging North Atlantic. "Ah, a freshening wind," she said, stretching her arms as if to embrace the rain. "Good for one's blood."

Not dead Dead Elvis'. Constable Frimannsson had covered the body with a tarp harvested from the trunk of his police cruiser, but most of the man's blood had washed away in the rain. Not happy about the continued deterioration of the crime scene, Frimannsson's frown deepened when he spied people walking toward us down the slope from the hotel. As they crossed the narrow pedestrian bridge across the Ring Road, I could see cameras strapped around their necks. Their relaxed body language suggested they were unaware of the drama below. Birders, probably, like Dead Elvis. Then I remembered. At the Viking Tavern, he had been with an unhappy-looking woman. His wife? A girlfriend? She might be part of the approaching group.

Hoping to prevent the constable from having to deal with a hysterical widow, I filled him in on last night's bar brawl. He flicked a quick look up the land bridge—yes, several women were among the pack—then down at the tarp. There was no mistaking the human-sized form underneath it.

"So now we have another problem," he said, his voice so low I could hardly hear him over the screaming wind. "Tourists." He sighed. "Miss Bentley, since those people may all be countrymen of yours, perhaps you would be kind enough to inform them there's been an accident and tell them to return to the Hótel Brattholt, that there will be no birding today. At least not here. Whatever you do, don't mention the deceased person. When Inspector Haraldsson arrives, he will send someone to the hotel to tell them what has happened to their friend." He paused, then added grimly, "And to question them."

Young, perhaps, but no fool.

With a feeling of foreboding because my "countrymen" tended to be less amiable than Icelanders, I started toward them. Before I was halfway there, I heard the whup-whup-whup of a helicopter.

The cavalry had arrived.

Chapter Four

Chief Inspector Haraldsson, head of the Violent Crimes Squad, displayed little Icelandic *politesse* as he and another officer ordered the birders back to the hotel. Above the wind, I could hear snatches of anger.

"Listen, buster, you can't tell me…"

"Do you have any idea how much this trip cost…?"

"The American Embassy will hear about…"

They didn't go quietly, but in the end, they went.

Unlike the other police officers who'd arrived at the crime scene, Inspector Haraldsson wore civilian clothes, a dark raincoat loosely draped over a severe gray suit. A man with sandy hair flecked with gray, he was tall, even for an Icelander, and his sharply angled face was clenched into a don't-mess-with-me expression.

Despite the inspector's forbidding appearance, I noticed that Constable Frimannsson addressed him as Thor, the diminutive for Thorvaald, his first name. As they talked quietly, one of the inspector's uniformed minions began taping off the area, while several officers in forensic overalls got busy erecting a tent over the body to protect the crime scene from the worsening weather. During the commotion, the puffin and her wobbly chick decamped to another burrow, squawking bird-curses the entire way.

Bryndis and I watched as Haraldsson, who'd slipped on a pair of latex gloves, went through the dead man's pockets. He came back to us holding a black wallet. After inspecting it, he said to me, "He's American. A Mr. Simon Parr, with an Arizona address on his driver's license," he said, in unaccented English. "Do you know him?"

Parr. Simon Parr. The name sounded familiar, but I couldn't pinpoint it. I shook my head and repeated the story I'd told the young constable about the scene on the plane, followed by the slap-down at the Viking Tavern, adding that Bryndis had also witnessed the scene. Once he was through with me, he proceeded to interview her in Icelandic. I surmised that she told him pretty much the same thing, with one notable exception: although she mentioned the Gunn Zoo several times, I never heard her say Ragnar's name.

Expressionless, Haraldsson returned his attention to me. "So. Welcome to Iceland, Miss Theodora Bentley, of the Gunn Zoo, in Gunn Landing, California. Bryndis tells me you've traveled all the way here for a polar bear cub."

"True, along with two Icelandic foxes, and a couple of puffins. Our zoo has a new exhibit called Northern Climes. We've already brought in penguins, a couple of species, actually."

"Northern Climes?" A faint smile softened the hard lines of his face. "I was unaware that penguins could be found in the northern hemisphere."

"Of course not, they're…"

"My little jest. What are your thoughts about the fight in the Viking Tavern? Was there blood?"

"Nothing but slaps."

"Was Mr. Parr drunk?"

"As the proverbial lord."

A hint of his former smile came back. "I am certain we will find out more when we interview members of his group. Describe the woman he was with. Young? Old? Did he call her by name?"

"She had dyed red hair darker than mine, kind of a burgundy wine color, and she was around forty, forty-five, maybe even fifty. And no, I didn't hear him call her by name, he was too busy getting beat up at the time. Oh, and I just remembered. On the plane, I was certain I'd seen his face before, but I still can't make the connection."

He raised his eyebrows. "Could you have seen him at your zoo?"

"I doubt it. His group, those birders, they're all from Arizona, I think, and the Gunn Zoo is in California, so I don't see why...."

"I was under the impression the two states touch."

"They're big states."

This smile was fractionally cooler than the other. "Then that will be all, Miss Theodora Bentley of the Gunn Zoo. For now."

I didn't like that last part.

As it turned out, I'd been right to feel apprehensive. Less than an hour after the inspector allowed Bryndis and me to sit out the rainstorm at the Hótel Brattholt, he appeared at our table while I was in mid-bite of an excellent piece of Icelandic cod. Although I'd felt guilty about sitting down for a meal after such a tragedy, the matter-of-fact Bryndis pointed out that starving ourselves wouldn't bring Simon Parr back from the dead. For her part, she was enjoying a heaping plate of fish and chips.

"His widow has been informed," Inspector Haraldsson told us, sitting down. "Her name is Elizabeth St. John. For professional reasons, she does not use her husband's name."

"St. John?! *That* Elizabeth St. John? The writer?"

He nodded. "She is also, with her husband, a big lottery winner. So now you see why the man looked familiar. In June Mr. Parr and his wife appeared on many TV programs throughout the world. Why, I even saw them myself, on the television in my own living room. Lucky devils. Well, her, anyway. Him, not so lucky, considering that he is now deceased."

As the old saying goes, them that has, gets. A few years back, while awaiting my annual checkup at my dentist's office, I'd thumbed through a two-year-old copy of *Entertainment Weekly*, where I happened across an article about St. John. She'd made millions from her chart-topping romantic suspense novels, and her appearances at bookstores in the U.S. and Europe had drawn blocks-long crowds. In London, Prague, and Brussels, riot police had to be called to keep things orderly. Thinking about her probable annual income had made me jealous.

As if that wasn't enough, more money poured in earlier this summer when her husband stopped at a convenience store and bought a loaf of bread, a bag of Fritos, a quart of milk, and one lone Powerball ticket. The ticket won the highest payout in Powerball history—more than a half-billion.

"On the news, Mr. Parr looked cheerful, holding up that big check for six hundred million U.S. dollars," Haraldsson continued, looking wistful. "When I saw all those zeroes, I put myself in his place and thought of red Ferraris and warm vacations in Bermuda. And women, of course, many beautiful women, all eager to share in my good fortune. But what does Simon Parr do? He takes a bird-watching trip to Iceland."

Haraldsson's fantasy life didn't interest me, but Elizabeth St. John's writing did. I had never read any of her novels, but the dentist's office copy of *Entertainment Weekly* had described Jade L'Amour, St. John's protagonist. Jade was an Indiana Jones-type archaeologist who travelled the world uncovering international spies, unmasking murderers, and rescuing orphans, all while wearing designer clothes. The photograph accompanying the article highlighted St. John's startling good looks: long, glossy black hair that hinted at an American Indian ancestor, navy blue eyes, and an aristocratic profile to die for. Sitting next to her was her husband, Simon Parr, who hadn't yet grown his Elvis sideburns.

A few weeks after reading the article, I'd been channel-surfing on my tiny television and happened across St. John being interviewed by Barbara Walters. She was telling a doubtful Walters that today's young women needed more believable role models than those found in Marvel Comics, and she wrote her books to fill that need.

But the woman in the Viking Tavern was not Elizabeth St. John. She was a dyed redhead with nowhere near the author's mature beauty. Which reminded me of something that had come up in the Walters interview before I changed the channel. St.

John said she and her husband had what they called a "European" marriage, which she defined as a marriage that gave them the freedom to occasionally "date" others. It kept their marriage fresh and exciting, she claimed. When Walters asked the writer her if she wasn't afraid that such an admission might hurt her book sales, St. John answered, "I always tell the truth. Besides, Barbara, you of all people should know there's no such thing as bad publicity."

I remembered something else, too. After the Walters interview, St. John's book moved from No. 9 on the *New York Times* best-seller list to No. 1.

"How did Mrs. St. John take the news about her husband's death?" I asked Haraldsson, who was still yammering about warm beaches and beautiful women.

The inspector's face revealed nothing. "When I told her about Mr. Parr's demise, she shed tears, which is only what one would expect. They had been married for twenty-six years, you understand. But that brings me to you, Miss Theodora Bentley." Some of the geniality had left his voice. After a few seconds pawing his big hand through his wet raincoat, he pulled out an iPhone, poked it a couple of times, then turned the screen toward me. It revealed an article in *The Gunn Landing Reporter*, with the headline, LOCAL ZOOKEEPER SOLVES MURDER. My photograph wasn't flattering.

"As you can see, I've checked up on you," Haraldsson continued, "and I think it might be wise to let you know, before things go any further, that the Icelandic National Police do not need your help. We are perfectly competent to investigate a suspicious death, even though—and being from a much more dangerous country than ours you may have trouble believing this—Mr. Parr's is our first murder this year. We only had two last year, one committed by a Lithuanian, the other by a Dane. Both recent immigrants, both stabbings, one over a woman, the other over a card game. We Icelanders might slap obnoxious drunks from time to time, but we do not sneak around and shoot them in the back of the head. The use of guns as murder weapons is almost unheard of here."

"Then where'd the firearm come from?" I asked, stung by his portrait of me as an interfering busybody. "Judging from the wound and the fact that there were no powder burns around it, I'd say he shot from at least several feet away by a small caliber handgun. Or a rifle."

Bryndis gaped at me but Haraldsson's polite expression never wavered. "I applaud your knowledge of ballistics, and, yes, the weapon is most likely the Finnish Sako that Ulfur, the hotelier here, reported missing this morning. I only mention this because he has been complaining to everyone, so it is no secret. Poor Ulfur. He needed that Sako to take revenge on the chicken-stealing fox that has plagued his farm for the past two weeks. But you see? Already you are sticking your pretty nose in. While I sympathize with your concern over the fate of a fellow American, please be aware that any interference on your part can create difficulties for all of us, so I would appreciate it if you concentrated on your little polar bear and your foxes and your puffins."

Oblivious to my ire, he put his phone back into his pocket and stood up. "Good day, Miss Theodora Bentley. Enjoy your stay in Iceland."

Chapter Five

"He likes you," Bryndis said, watching Inspector Haraldsson's retreating back.

I looked at her in amazement. "You're kidding, right?"

"He called your nose 'pretty.'"

"Which means exactly nothing."

"It does in Iceland."

While Inspector Haraldsson had been giving me my marching orders, the hotel's crowded dining room had fallen strangely silent. I suspected a case of mass eavesdropping but recognized that in their place, I'd do the same. A member of their tour group had been murdered in the very spot they planned to visit.

But as Inspector Haraldsson had pointed out, it was none of my business. I hadn't known the victim and I certainly didn't want to know the killer.

Best laid plans, and all that. Later, as I was washing my hands in the ladies' room, a woman approached me at the sink. I'd noticed her earlier in the dining room. A tall, slender, brunette with startlingly green eyes, she was attractive enough to be a fashion model. In her youth, anyway. A closer inspection revealed fine lines parenthesizing her mouth. The man she shared her table with was as handsome as she was beautiful, too, but his chin and nose looked almost too perfect to be real.

"Um, I couldn't help but hear you talk to that, um, cop," she said, her voice high and hesitant as a child's, yet she had to be at least in her late thirties.

"The whole dining room heard us. Inspector Haraldsson wasn't exactly quiet."

"I looked you up on my iPhone…"

Technology has its drawbacks. With a few taps on a screen, total strangers could find out everything about you. I forced a smile. "Don't believe everything you see on the Internet."

As if I hadn't spoken, she continued. "…and thought maybe you can help us."

Us. I looked at her left hand. Yep, a wedding ring. Mr. Handsome was her husband.

"I'm only here to chaperone a few zoo animals back to the States," I said, trying to sound apologetic about it.

"That inspector, Haraldsson, he was asking Ben too many questions."

"Inspectors do that sort of thing."

"But considering everything, I'm afraid they'll pin the murder on Ben." She looked down at her hands. They were trembling. "Given his past and all."

I studied her reflection in the mirror. Either she was sweating, or there were tears on her cheek. "What do you mean, 'given his past and all'?" A little voice told me to follow Haraldsson's orders and keep my nose out of police business. I ignored it. I grabbed some paper towels and began drying my hands. "Sorry, I'm afraid I don't understand."

"Ben's had problems in the past, you see, and there was a big argument between him and Simon before we boarded the plane. He's never liked Simon, so…" She bit her lip.

"If you're that worried, maybe you should find an attorney." I made for the door, but she moved quickly, blocking my path.

"An *Icelandic* attorney? You must be kidding. They'd love nothing better than to blame this on some tourist."

Leave, Teddy. Shove this woman out of the way and leave right now. Go back to your table, tell Bryndis we have to go, and hustle your butt out of this hotel before you agree to do something you'll regret later.

"Look, I have to…"

"Ben's protective of me because of all the weird stuff that's been going on with Simon lately. He bought a Glock and…"

Deflect. That's what you learn to do when you work in a zoo. When a four-year-old asks you where baby chimpanzees come from, you ask them which they think is the smartest—chimps or orangutans. "Your husband didn't bring a handgun on the plane with him, did he?"

An affronted look. "Ben's not stupid."

"Did your husband pack his suitcase or did you?"

"What difference does it make?"

She was beautiful, yes, but no Mensa candidate. "Think about it."

After a moment, she said, "I'd have noticed if he packed his Glock."

Which meant her husband did his own packing. "You need an attorney, Mrs…. Er, what did you say your name was?"

"I'm known as just Dawn."

What an odd thing to say.

My befuddlement must have shown on my face, because she explained, "That was my modeling name, 'Dawn.' No last name, just 'Dawn.' Ben's a Talley. You know, Talley, like the restaurant chain. It's the family business."

Talley's specialized in New American Cuisine, which is to say, gussied-up hamburgers and ten-ingredient omelets named after movie stars. For a while there'd been a Talley's in Gunn Landing, but it eventually closed for lack of business. The one in San Sebastian was still open.

I tried to sidle my way past her to get to the door. She sidled with me. Exasperated, I said, "Look, Dawn, if you overheard my conversation with Inspector Haraldsson, you know he told me to mind my own business. I'm sorry, but I really can't help you. Besides, even if Haraldsson decides your husband is a suspect in the killing, which I doubt he will, Ben can afford to hire a top-notch attorney. He'll be cleared in no time, and then you can continue on your tour." A stretch of the truth there, perhaps. Especially if Ben had packed that Glock.

"I'm not hiring some crooked foreign attorney who'll charge and arm and a leg and do nothing."

Before I could point out that here in Iceland we were the foreigners, she rushed on.

"Ben has no alibi, you see. When I woke up this morning, it was around five and already light, and he wasn't in the bed next to me or in the shower, either. When I was dressing he came back from wherever he'd been and he was wearing his heavy jacket. His hands were freezing, like he'd been outside."

"You spent the night here? At Hótel Brattholt?"

"It wasn't on our original schedule but then Simon, you know he treated us all to this trip, don't you, all of a sudden he asked Oddi, our tour guide, to drive us down here late last night so we could get over to that cliff early."

"Wait a minute. Did you say Simon Parr paid for your trip?"

She gave me an incredulous look. "You think the other birders could afford this trip on their own? As soon as Simon won that big Powerball, he started planning it. First class all the way, air fare, hotels, food, private tour guide, whatever, he took care of the whole thing. Maybe he looked like an idiot with those ridiculous sideburns he'd started wearing, but he wasn't stingy. Anyway, as I was saying, earlier in the evening he was all excited, saying he'd heard there'd been some kind of Egyptian bird spotted down here, a hookah or something."

If she didn't know a bird's proper name it meant her husband was the birder. "I think you're talking about a hoopoe, but those birds are…"

She didn't let me finish. "This morning, when I asked Ben where he'd been, he told me he'd been out enjoying the fresh air. But I'm really worried! What if he did kill Simon?"

Belatedly, I snuck a quick look at the bathroom stalls. They appeared empty, but appearances can be deceiving. Lowering my voice, I said, "Dawn, you shouldn't go around saying things like that to anyone, including me. The wrong person might overhear you."

She ignored my warning. "You can help us, I know you can! I'd ask Elizabeth what to do because she knows all kinds of stuff, but she's upset, and she's gone back to the hotel in Reykjavik anyway, and these awful Icelanders, they want to jail everyone who doesn't look like them!!" The waterworks started again.

Not my problem, not my problem, not my problem…

Oh, who was I kidding? I couldn't stand to see anyone cry, not even a woman with an advanced case of xenophobia. Sighing in defeat, I asked, "All right. Why, exactly, do you think the police might arrest your husband for killing Simon Parr?"

"Because of the fight."

"Fight? Before, you described it as an argument. Now you're saying it was a physical fight?"

"There was some shoving. But there was another one, too, at last month's birder meeting, when the Geronimos…"

"Geronimos?"

"The Geronimo County Birding Association, of course. They were having their yearly elections and Perry Walsh won, he's his friend, but then he claimed he'd cheated because he knew he had enough votes to win and he was really mad about being accused of…"

The flurry of pronouns was confusing, so I stepped in to clarify. "This Perry person, he was Ben's friend or Simon's?"

"Ben's friend, of course. Simon never liked him, said he was a crook."

"Simon believed Perry Walsh cheated to win the election?"

She rolled her beautiful eyes. "Simon believed my husband cheated by stuffing the ballot box for Perry. Isn't that what I said?"

Not really, but I let it pass. "Dawn, if Simon won a big Powerball, why would he care who won the presidency of a birding club?"

"He said it was some kind of honor thing."

Only the misery on her face kept me from laughing. "An *honor* thing? Like, we'll settle this at sunrise, and choose your weapons?"

She gave me a baffled look. "I don't understand wha—'

My salvation arrived when at that precise moment, Bryndis opened the ladies' room door. "Hey, Teddy, I was beginning to think you had drowned."

Chapter Six

"What was that scene in the ladies' room about?" Bryndis asked, on the drive back to Reykjavik.

"Just some woman upset about the murder."

Bryndis took her eyes off the winding Ring Road to glance at me in surprise. "Her husband was the victim? I heard she went back to Reykjavik."

"This one wasn't the widow. Uh, there's a sheep standing in the middle of the highway. It looks lost."

She expertly swerved around the sheep and continued on. "Then why was she crying?"

"Worried, I guess."

"You Americans worry a lot. We Icelanders, even though our volcanoes chase us down to the sea every few years, do we worry about it? No. We simply keep our bags packed. Speaking of volcanoes, there's Katla again, over on your right. So beautiful, the way the sun makes rainbows on the ice. Maybe the old witch will erupt while you're still here. Would not that be fun?"

"No."

She laughed. "Volcano parties are the best parties. Everyone drinks and sings. Say, I have an idea. Tomorrow you are going with me to learn how to take care of Magnus and the foxes, so we will be busy all day. But Saturday, would you like to drive out to see Hekla, another volcano that's even bigger than Eyjafjallajökull and Katla? In the Middle Ages people believed

Hekla was the gate to Hell itself, that condemned souls traveled through it on their way to eternal damnation in a lake of lava. It's a nice hike. Not the hike to Hell, of course, but through the valley surrounding Hekla."

I marveled at her equanimity. "It won't be so beautiful if the thing erupts."

"The last time Hekla erupted was in 2000, and she is not due again until maybe 2032, so you're safe. It is Katla, the witch, who is overdue."

"All the same…"

She steered the Volvo around another sheep. "See, there you are, being American, worrying about some far off problem, while we Icelanders believe everything will work out in the end. Even if it does not work out, worries will change nothing."

Bryndis was right, of course. Worry alone never solved anything unless you took the necessary steps to solve whatever problem you were worrying about in the first place. For instance, look at Dawn Talley, nee 'just Dawn.' Worried sick that her husband might have killed Simon Parr, when all the while, the scenario was unlikely for two reasons. One, the chances of anyone smuggling firearms onto a flight these days was practically nil, even if Dawn's husband had stowed it in his luggage, not his carry-on. Two, regardless of the feud between Simon Parr and Dawn's husband, the idea that Ben Talley, owner of a big restaurant chain, would commit murder over Dawn or a disputed vote at some birding club was beyond ludicrous. We worry-wart Americans weren't that crazy.

As the Ring Road swept past green pastures, another element of our conversation began to bug me. If Dawn was really all that worried about her husband's possible involvement in the murder, wouldn't it make more sense to keep her mouth shut? Why seek out a total stranger—in a hotel ladies' room, no less—and blurt out possible motives, however far-fetched? Was she truly that unintelligent? Or maybe she wasn't dumb at all, and for her own reasons, had decided to throw suspicion toward her husband. If so, I guessed she'd soon be sharing her "concerns" with Inspector Haraldsson. Whatever was going on with the woman, I felt well out of it.

By the time we reached the barren lava fields outside Keflavik and the Ring Road turned north toward Reykjavik, lost sheep sightings had dwindled to nothing, and the only holdup was traffic congestion. But Icelanders being the polite drivers they were, we encountered few problems, and were soon back in Bryndis' cozy apartment on Baldursbrá Street.

"So. What would you like to do now?" she asked, after changing out of her riding clothes. Apparently no longer concerned by the events at Vic, she was looking forward to the rest of the day. "Shop on Laugavegur? Hit some museums and galleries? See Hallgrimskirkja, the church built to look like the basalt columns at Vik? Or maybe we could take a nice walk down to the harbor and I can show you Harpa, our new concert hall? Harpa's built right over the bay and has become quite the tourist attraction. Coming back we could see the Solfar Viking boat sculpture. And get hot dogs."

"Hot dogs?"

Bryndis now wore gray linen slacks and a blue silk blouse. With her hair unpinned, the combination of chic sportswear and shoulder-length blond tresses made her look more like a fashion model than Dawn. But to be honest, Bryndis was at least ten years younger, and Dawn, stressed about her husband's possible involvement in Parr's murder, wasn't having a good day. Stress can play hell with a woman's looks.

"You will love Bæjarin's Beztu Pylsur. They serve the best, most famous, *pylsurs*—hot dogs—in the entire world," Bryndis continued, unaware of my flashback to the morning's sad events. "So famous that Bill Clinton and Madonna and that bad boy Charlie Sheen and James Hetfield from Metallica have all eaten there. Even Mikhail Gorbachev, when he was having the Glasnost meeting with Ronald Reagan, they say he ate there, too. I will treat you to a big *eina með öllu*, which means 'one with everything.' If a *pylsur* could help end the Cold War, it will help us recover from what happened at Vik. I keep seeing that dead man's face. Ugh!"

So much for Bryndis' Icelandic stoicism.

"Murder aside, I did enjoy the horses," I said. "And yes, a walk down to the harbor sounds wonderful, as well as the whatsis, the hot dogs. But you don't have to treat me, because the Gunn Zoo's picking up the tab for everything." Within reason, of course. The tab for hot dogs wouldn't break Aster Edwina Gunn's bank.

"Then we will have two *beztu pylsurs*! Each! And Cokes!"

On this balmy August afternoon, the temperature hovered around seventy degrees Fahrenheit in downtown Reykjavik, keeping sidewalk musicians and other performance artists busy on Laugavegur Street. Across from an upscale women's wear shop, two "Vikings" dressed in traditional garb play-acted a swordfight for tourist dollars, while a few doors down, a musician—her Chihuahua sitting patiently at her side—played a rousing rendition of Flatt & Scruggs' "Foggy Mountain Breakdown" on her banjo. Cheered by this touch of home in such an unlikely setting, I threw a five-dollar bill into her banjo case.

"*Takk fyrir*," she said, repeating in English, "Thank you."

Although our stroll down Reykjavik's colorful streets was pleasant, the image of Simon Parr's mutilated face kept intruding in my mind. True, both times I'd seen Simon in action, he'd been behaving badly, but try as I might, I couldn't keep the memory of his ecstatic face on television as he held up that check for 610.3 million dollars. Yet his generosity with his friends proved that he wasn't a complete churl.

Unlike animals, people are complicated. A bear acts like a bear all the time, and a tiger acts like a tiger. Even a lizard always acts like a lizard. But people constantly surprise you. Self-centered men risk their lives rescuing kittens from burning buildings. Beautiful women who act as if they don't have a brain in their heads can be hiding a level of intelligence that would impress an astrophysicist.

Besides Dawn's husband, who else wanted Simon Parr dead? That wasn't the only question nagging at me. I was also plagued by the suspicion that I had missed something at the murder scene, something important, but as much as I racked my brain, I couldn't remember.

By the time Bryndis and I reached the Ingolfsstraeti turning toward the harbor, I'd tried to distract myself by contributing to so many buskers that I'd run out of American dollars and had to switch to Icelandic króna. I would have bankrupted myself if not for Bryndis, who put a warning hand on my money arm. "Better save some for later," she said. "While I was dressing, I received a call from Ragnar. He has invited us to a party tonight at his apartment. It is on Skólavörðustígur, in the middle of the arts district, so on the way, you will have plenty of opportunities to make our street performers happy."

Just before reaching the harbor, we paused in front of a small store named Ingolfsstraeti Bókabúð. Despite its difficult name, it was obviously a bookstore. But what caught our attentnion was the big sign in the window, printed in both Icelandic and English.

MEET AUTHOR ELIZABETH ST. JOHN
6 P.M. SUNDAY
HEAR THE FAMOUS AUTHOR TALK
ABOUT HER NEW BOOK
* * * TAHITI PASSION * * *
AND THE PROFOUND NEW LOVE
HER HEROINE JADE L'AMOUR
DISCOVERS WHILE CONDUCTING AN
ARCHAEOLOGICAL DIG
IN AN EXOTIC TROPICAL PARADISE.
FREE REFRESHMENTS

Bryndis looked at me. "Uh oh."

"'Uh oh' is right. Think we should we go in and tell them what happened at Vik this morning?"

"We had better. I know the manager, and would hate to see her spend her kronur on refreshments for a talk that will not happen."

The bookstore wasn't as large as the three I'd visited yesterday. Having no room for a café, nothing but books lined the four walls. Banks of free-standing floor shelves provided more space for books, leaving only narrow aisles for customers, of which there were many. At first I couldn't see how such a small store could host signings for even unknown authors, let alone a superstar like Elizabeth St. John, but as Bryndis led me toward the back, I saw a small alcove near the restrooms. In the alcove stood a table topped by the author's photograph and a small stack of books. Unless there were more in the back room, they would surely run out.

"Follow me," Bryndis said, weaving her way through the racks. "Kristin is usually in her office."

From the entrance, the door to the office had been invisible because some clever artist had painted it to look like a filled bookshelf, but when Bryndis pushed against a book titled *Landnámabók*, it swung open. Inside a room the size of an American closet sat a young woman staring into a computer screen with a cross expression on her face. Small, fine-featured, with harlequin glasses perched on a tiny nose, with her light brown hair shorn in a pixie cut, she looked like a cranky elf. Upon seeing us, the elf pushed her chair away from her child-sized desk and greeted Bryndis with a broad smile and a rush of Icelandic.

When Bryndis introduced me, Krista immediately switched to English. "An American zookeeper! I got my MFA at Georgetown University, and while there, I visited the National Zoo to see the pandas. Does the Gunn Zoo have pandas?"

We talked animals for a few minutes—sorry, the Gunn Zoo had no pandas—before Bryndis got around to delivering the bad news about Elizabeth St. John.

Krista's reaction was unexpected. "It is kind of you to warn me like this, but I have already heard about the unfortunate occurrence at Vik. No problem. Not for us, anyway. Elizabeth called this afternoon to assure me that her signing was still on."

"Still on?!" I squeaked.

"A strong woman, that one." Krista's voice was filled with admiration. "Just like her heroine Jade L'Amour. Yes, she is sad, of course, and yes, she cried a little as we spoke, but she said that—how did she put it?—oh, that the show must go on, that she had made her promise to us and her readers, and despite her personal misfortune, she will honor it."

Honor. Where had I heard that word earlier? Then I remembered. In the restroom at Vik, Dawn Talley had described the argument between her husband and the dead man over their birding organization's vote as being a matter of "honor." Briefly, I wondered if I should inform Inspector Haraldsson, then decided not to. Let the grump solve his own crimes.

Krista was still talking. "It is a terrible thing to say, but all the publicity will help the signing. I have been worried about it, but now everyone will come to see the woman whose husband has been murdered."

"But will they buy books?" Bryndis asked.

Krista's grin didn't diminish. "I will make them feel like murderers themselves if they don't."

Krista's expertise as a saleswoman became apparent when she insisted on showing me around the shop. Without sounding the least bit pushy, she managed to talk me into buying five books: four coffee table books featuring the scenic wonders of Iceland, and the fifth, an anthology of Icelandic sagas.

"You will especially love *Njál's Saga*, which has so many killings in it that even our historians sometimes lose count," she said, swiping the Gunn Zoo's Visa through the card reader.

Books are heavy. Especially coffee table books and anthologies. Fortunately, my going-away present from my mother had been a Coach Studio Legacy handbag that doubled as a backpack, so I slung my haul over my shoulder and set off with Bryndis again, slumping only slightly. Fortunately, the rest of the walk to the harbor was downhill.

"Sorry about that," Bryndis said, as we trudged along. She, too, had been cajoled into buying several books, but unlike me, she'd purchased lightweight paperbacks. "I should have warned you about Krista," she said, with a rueful smile.

Ten minutes later we arrived at Reykjavik's famed concert hall. A modern glass and steel building jutting out over the water of Reykjavik Bay, Harpa's irregular colored panels, each a different shape and size, mimicked the translucent effect of stained glass windows. At night, Bryndis explained, the building provided an extraordinary light show as the colors flashed on and off, twinkling like a million stars going nova in a synergetic ballet. By day, you could stand inside the great hall and watch cod fishing boats steam into the harbor.

As much as I enjoyed the tour through Harpa—in addition to hosting concerts and operas, the concert hall also provided a forum for post-modern painting and avant garde sculpture—it was nice to get back outside into the pollution-free Reykjavik air. And to tell the truth, I was starving, and looked forward to the trip across the street to Bæjarin's Beztu Pylsur, which I now realized simply meant "the best hot dogs in town."

The joint wasn't fancy. It wasn't even indoors. A red and white shack fronting the harbor, it attracted enough customers that we had to stand in line for ten minutes before giving our order. Since the one picnic table was already occupied by a group of Japanese tourists taking snapshots of each other as they ate (what did that remind me of?) we milled around the sidewalk with other tourists and native Icelanders until we heard our number called.

We ate while strolling down the harbor road. Gulls, gannets, and kittiwakes sailed over our heads, shrieking their sharp cries. Ahead of us, but miles distant, loomed Mount Esja, heralding the gateway to the Snaefellsnes Peninsula. Because the peninsula was reputed to be as mythic as it was picturesque, I felt a brief pang that I wouldn't be traveling there. However, in less than two weeks, there was a limit to what I could see and do. As we rounded a curve in the harbor, the sight of Sólfar—Sun Voyager—a sculpture that resembled an old Viking longboat, took me out of my gloom. It had been positioned to face the setting summer sun, and golden late afternoon light gleamed along its steel surface.

Very photogenic, as proved by the gaggle of tourists around it, all snapping pictures.

I started to take out my own camera, then froze. Something had nudged my memory back at the hot dog stand, and now here. But what? Surely that was impossible, since I'd never been in Iceland before.

Still…

"Teddy, why do you frown?" Bryndis' voice startled me.

"I don't know," I confessed. "There seems to be something familiar about this."

"An attack of déjà vu? Ah, reincarnation! Perhaps one of your ancestors was a Viking and his genes are urging you to hop on Sólfar and sail away to loot and pillage."

Although the image of a red-headed Icelandic ancestor made me laugh, it wasn't impossible. The early Vikings had taken thousands of villagers as slaves during raids on the Irish coast, so who knew?

But I didn't think so. There was something about the scene before me that…

"Excuse me, miss, but do you mind getting out of the way so I can take a picture of that thing?" An expensively dressed American, from his accent, a New Yorker, sub genus Brooklyn.

"No problem." As soon as I moved, the man stepped forward, hefted a Nikon D4, and began to shoot.

That's when I remembered.

Vik.

Dead man.

Nikon D4 lying on the moss.

Could Simon Parr have taken a photograph of his killer?

Chapter Seven

The next morning I returned to the Reykjavik City Zoo to help Bryndis with the animals we were readying for transport and learn the finer points of their daily routines. The temperature had climbed to sixty-five degrees, and a gentle breeze blew in from the North Atlantic, making the animals frisky. Cows lowed, chickens clucked, pigs squealed. Only occasional yelps from the seal pool reminded me this was no mere barnyard.

After tossing a few fish to the seals, Bryndis led me to the Icelandic foxes' temporary enclosure.

The six-pound foxes were little different in habit and diet than the Gunn Zoo's coyotes and wolves. Shy, as most wild animals are, they kept to the back of their enclosure while we worked around them. We checked on their automatic watering system, making certain it wasn't clogged, and at eleven-thirty on the dot—zoo animals are keenly aware of time—filled their bowls with a commercial dog food mixture. The only difference was that we added bits of chopped poultry, eggs, and a couple of frozen mice, which more accurately copied their diet in the wild.

Ten-month-olds Loki and Ilsa would accompany me back to the Gunn Zoo. Already separated from the rest of the zoo's foxes for standard quarantine protocol, they were housed in a large pen near Regina, the reindeer. Ilsa, the steel-gray female, sat near a rock and watched curiously as I helped Bryndis clean the area, but Loki, the slightly paler male, ran back and forth along the fence line as if panicked by our intrusion.

"He is more angry than scared," Bryndis explained. "Monday, they received their shots for travel, and Ilsa didn't seem to mind. I distracted her with a piece of chicken. But Loki hates the vet and any disruption in his routine, no matter how minor, so when we get to California, I will instruct your canidae keeper to be careful around him. Loki may be small, but his teeth are sharp."

Looking at the two foxes, it was hard to believe they would turn white in the winter, which in the northern wild, served as protective coloration against the deep snow. Although the commercial freezing units Aster Edwina had spent a fortune on would keep the temperature in our Northern Climes exhibit low, I wondered if they would fool Mother Nature. We'd find out in October, when the foxes were due to start morphing.

Once the foxes were taken care of, we moved into the small quarantine shack where the two-year-old puffins were housed. At first I couldn't see the injuries that Sigurd and Jodisi had received that insured an early death in the wild, but as Jodisi hopped toward me, hoping for a fishy treat, I saw that her injured wing drooped lower than the other.

"She can hardly flap it, let alone fly," Bryndis said. "Same with Sigurd. They are lucky that the parents of the little girl who found them at Vik brought them to us or they would have wound up as dinner."

The most dangerous time in a puffin's life, Bryndis explained, came during their maiden flight to sea, which took place at night, when the former nestling, called a *lundepisur,* was around six weeks old. "They can get confused, and turn back toward their burrows. Sometimes they injure themselves trying to land, and that's when birds of prey, or even foxes, get them. That's what happened to Sigurd and Jodisi. The injuries, I mean. But like I said, they were rescued before they became meals. They've acclimated well to captivity, and have already raised one chick. Since we already had enough puffins, I drove it down to Vik and released it in the middle of the night, as the other *lundepisur* were flying away. And off she flew, a big, strong girl!"

Neither puffin showed any fear as Bryndis leaned over and dropped several small fish into their enclosure. As Jodisi nudged Sigurd aside to get at the fish, I noticed something about her that startled me. Her head had the same white stripe as the puffin at Vik. I pointed it out to Bryndis.

"Genetic mutation breeding true, would be my guess," she said. "Her daughter, the one I released at Vik, had the same unusual marking. A rare coloration, because except for their white chests and cheeks, the top of a puffin's body is usually solid black. I would appreciate it if over the years you let us know if the trait reappears on their other chicks so we can compare our records to yours."

As birds go, puffins are relatively long-lived, sometimes more than twenty years, so as I watched Jodisi gobble up the lion's share of fish, I wondered if she was the daughter of the puffin who had pecked Simon Parr's face as he lay across her burrow. Aggression, as well as unusual markings, can be a genetic trait, and that puffin was no wuss.

I shook away the memory of Parr's ruined face. He might have acted badly at times, but no one deserved to die like that.

"And now for Magnus!" Bryndis announced, unaware of my sudden misery.

There's nothing easy about polar bear care. From food issues to safety issues, if care isn't correct down to the smallest detail, someone's going to die; you or the bear.

When first discovered abandoned on an ice floe in northern Iceland, the cub had been sickly, almost certain to die, and only the pleas of the hunter's young daughter had kept him from putting the little thing out of its misery. When Magnus arrived at the zoo, his age was estimated at four months, but he'd been severely underweight.

It had been touch and go for months, Bryndis said, requiring round-the-clock bottle feeding of a thirty percent fat-enriched formula. "He was too sick then to even think about sending him to another zoo. He would never have survived the trip."

"Did you care for him all by yourself?" I asked, watching Magnus' body language as he stared at us across the kiddy pool he'd been given to splash around in. Small as he was, and surrounded by a child's toys, he was still a formidable presence. With time, he would become even more so.

"Yes, and you should have seen the bags under my eyes. I used to share my apartment with Ragnar, but he became jealous and said I loved Magnus more than I loved him." A flashing grin. "He was right. Magnus was my baby. But Ragnar? He is a big boy and can take care of himself."

Bryndis' personal sacrifice had proven fruitful, because her bouncing baby had achieved a now-healthy weight, and was eating a varied diet of eggs, rodents, fish, poultry, and seal and whale blubber. Since most polar bear cubs aren't weaned until they're over two years old, Magnus' heaping plate of solids were always washed down with big helpings of his high-fat formula.

"I suggest you continue the same diet for another year," she added. "He is thriving, but with the big move to America, he will be set back for a while, so the less change in diet, the better. I will be there to help watch over him for a few days. Oh, and I have been meaning to ask, when we get to California, will you teach me to surf? Not all our coastline is as fierce as Vik's."

The abrupt change of topic startled me for a moment. "I can try, but I'm not much of a surfer. In fact, I almost never do."

"A California woman who does not surf?" She stared at me as if I'd grown two heads.

"Not all Californians are the same, Bryndis, but don't worry, I'll borrow a couple of boards and teach you the basics."

She gave me a blinding smile. "Excellent! Now back to our baby bear. It is time for me to take some blood samples and make sure he is ready for his big trip to America."

As soon as Magnus spotted Bryndis, he jumped out of his kiddie pool and made a beeline for the habitat's back gate.

"One of the good things about getting a bear this young is that you can start their training without being mauled to death in the process," Bryndis said, showing me how she'd taught

Magnus to press his side against the gate. "You see how easy it will be for his new keeper to take blood samples or administer medications? He is so focused on the big fish that will be his reward, he barely feels the needle."

Once the blood sample was accomplished, she threw the cub a large fish. "Now watch while I get him to stand up so I can look for anything out of the way—lumps, wounds, whatever."

Holding another fish high, she stood up. Magnus mimicked her action, raising his paws in a likewise manner, and caught his reward before it sailed over his head. Polar bears being the intelligent species they were, he would always remember these commands, thus keeping his caregivers, as well as himself, safe and healthy. But a polar bear's intelligence had its downside. They got bored quickly, and a bored polar bear is a dangerous polar bear.

"You will have to change his toys several times a day. Throw him new Boomer Balls on an irregular basis. Big and small ones, different colors. He likes to bat them around. Cardboard boxes, he loves those. Also, plastic garbage can lids, traffic cones, PVC pipes, beer kegs, burlap bags, old phone books, anything he can tear up and drag around. Yes, it will make a mess, and, yes, his new keeper will be busy cleaning up after him, but it is necessary. Another thing about keeping him occupied; it cuts down on stereotypic behavior, the pacing and head-wagging we see with so many poorly kept animals in bad zoos. I know his new enclosure is quite large, because Miss Aster Edwina was kind enough to email us pictures, and that it has hills for him to stand on and look around when he's out of his pool. But you might want to think about putting a picnic table in there on one of the flat spots so he can climb around. A child's jungle gym is nice, too. Variety, variety, variety. That is the recipe for a happy bear."

As soon as Mangus had wolfed down his reward, Bryndis threw him a big red Boomer Ball, and he happily chased it around the pool. The expression on her face was that of a fond mother, pleased with her child. It surprised me until I remembered that she had hand-fed him from a bottle while he was still a cub.

"You'll miss him, won't you?" I said.

The besotted expression disappeared. "Zookeepers know better than to become attached to their charges. And we Icelanders are not emotional, anyway."

I hid my smile, knowing from my own experience that she was lying. For a brief moment I allowed myself to remember the many animals I loved. Lucy the giant anteater. Wanchu the koala. Alejandro the llama. Carlos, the gift-giving jay. And my own pets, of course. But thinking about them made me homesick, so I turned my mind back to Magnus' antics.

I wasn't allowed to enjoy them for long. As Magnus executed a half-roll over his Boomer Ball, an unexpected zoo visitor approached us. Inspector Haraldsson, carrying a thick file folder.

He pasted a genial smile on his dour face. "How fortunate! Here are the two lovely ladies I was looking for."

I'd trust a full-grown polar bear more than I trusted him, so I stepped back and allowed Bryndis to take the lead.

"Thor!" she enthused. "How nice to see you!" Icelanders were a lot less wary about police visits than were Americans. Maybe it was because Icelandic police didn't carry guns. "Any news on whoever killed that poor man?"

"We are getting close," he said, the phony smile never leaving his face. "Just a few loose ends left to tie up, which is why I am here. I have photos our Mr. Simon Parr took before he met his untimely demise." He opened the manila file and removed several color prints, which he thrust toward me. "Today our lab downloaded the pictures he took with his excellent camera, and I was hoping our American friend here might be able to identify certain people and places. And birds."

"Oh, I can't…"

He waved away my demurral. "Some places I recognized, so I did not bring those along. But I know nothing about birds."

"I'm not a true birder."

His smile didn't go away, neither did the printouts. "You spend your days with many birds at the Gunn Zoo. I checked. You are said to be particularly fond of one named Carlos. A jay of some sort, I was told. Now, this strange bird, Miss Bentley. What in the world is it?"

Yellow bird, big black-tipped yellow crest, black-and-white bars on wings, white-barred black tail, long curved bill. Standing near the cliff edge at Vik. "Hoopoe. Native to Egypt."

The phony smile widened. "See how much help you are? I have never seen a bird like that in my life!"

"They're rare hereabouts," I muttered. "Blew in on a storm or hitched a ride on a freighter."

He shoved another printout at me. "And what is this?"

Red bird, black mask around its beak, sitting next to a plain brown bird on a prickly pear cactus. "A cardinal and a cactus wren. He took that picture somewhere else, back in Arizona's my guess, which means you're showing the pictures out of order."

His smile turned smug, rendering it even more alarming. "How astute. Despite your denials, you know your birds." He handed me another printout.

Brownish-gray and black bird, black bars on its head, white edging on wings, gray-tipped tail, long straight bill. "Eurasian woodcock. Inspector, is this really necessary?"

"Call me Thor. And, oh, yes, it is. Now this one?"

Soft grayish-brown bird fading to a pinkish brown around crested head, black mask, brown wings with yellow-tipped black tail. "Bohemian waxwing."

"This?"

Large gray and brown falcon, rounder wingtips and longer tail than a peregrine's. "Gyrefalcon."

"This?"

Plump red bird, but no cardinal, black wings with two white bars, short beak, late juvenile. "Crossbill."

"And this?"

Naked woman, not a natural redhead, plump, forty-ish. "Uh...uh..."

"Ever see her before?" No smile now.

I took a deep breath. "She, ah, she's the woman we saw drinking with Simon Parr at the Viking Tavern."

Bryndis grabbed the printout from my hands, gave it a brief look. "Yes. I remember her purple nail polish. I was going to ask her what brand it was, because I have a blouse that color and it would be fun to match it. But then the man she was with started insulting her and she looked like she was about to cry. I was going to go over and tell him to shut up, but Ragnar got there first. After Ragnar got through with him, Mr. Potty Mouth with the Elvis sideburns was the one who cried, not her."

The inspector ignored her and directed his next question to me. "I understand Mr. Parr's wife is a famous writer. Is Mrs. Parr the woman in the picture?"

I corrected him. "His wife goes by the name of Elizabeth St. John. And, no, that's not her. She's a brunette."

As if deeply disappointed, Haraldsson heaved a great sigh, but it sounded a bit theatrical to me. "A rejected mistress could be our killer, then. Or maybe, given the circumstances, a jealous wife. What a disappointingly easy case this may turn out to be. And here I had such high hopes…" Another sigh, this one even more theatrical than the first. "Well, thank you, Miss Bentley. You have been of immense help."

He took his printouts and left.

Chapter Eight

That evening, after our shift was over and we returned to Bryndis' apartment, I finally had a chance to sit down at the kitchen table and read the newspaper.

U.S. LOTTERY WINNER MURDERED AT VIK! screamed *The Reykjavik News* headline. One of several English-language newspapers in Iceland, it went on to describe the crime scene and the ill-fated tour of the Geronimo County Birding Association. It featured several quotes from Inspector Thorvaald Haraldsson, who had the temerity to compare the U.S. murder rate to Iceland's.

Not that there was much of a comparison.

"We are a nation of gun-owners, but the only thing my countrymen shoot is dinner," Haraldsson said in the article.

Yes, he went on to explain, there had been two murders the year before, but neither of them committed by native Icelanders. In a sudden fit of political correctness, he added that Icelanders did occasionally kill each other. Three years earlier, there had been a stabbing over a woman in one of the western fishing villages. One man died, the other survived, and he was still getting intensive psychiatric care to help him deal with his guilt. The year before that, a drunken hired hand beat a farmer to death on a sheep farm somewhere in the country's interior, then hanged himself in the barn during a fit of remorse.

But murder by firearm?

Nada. Zip. Zero.

I looked at the article again. The name of the birding group struck a chord, which seemed rather unlikely since I'd only been in Arizona once in my life.

The Geronimo County Birding Association.

Geronimo County.

Then I remembered. Irene Spencer, more commonly known as "Cowgirl Spencer." She had been a good friend of mine during my teen years at Miss Pridewell's Academy in Virginia. Her parents owned a horse ranch in Geronimo County, and for years afterwards, she nagged me to visit. Time got away from me, as it so frequently does, and the visit never happened. Still, I wondered if she by any chance knew…

No, I refused to have anything to do with the case.

I was about to turn to another page when Bryndis emerged from the bedroom. She looked stunning in a black dress and black stiletto pumps, her blond hair flowing around her shoulders like a sunlit river. She even wore makeup. "Hey, Teddy. Better get ready for the party."

I rattled the newspaper at her. "Inspector Haraldsson says here that the police are following up leads."

"Of course they are. It is their job."

A buttery ray of afternoon sunlight streamed through the kitchen window. Although low and gold on the horizon, the sun wouldn't fully set until almost ten. Ragnar's party had started at nine, but we took time to eat a quick meal before heading out, in case there was no food.

"I didn't know you were into the nightlife," I told her, after wolfing down some spaghetti in a marinara sauce, "so I only packed jeans and tee-shirts. This is the best I've got." Actually, I was rather proud of my HONEY BADGER DON'T CARE tee and the hand-embroidered panda on the rear pocket of my jeans, courtesy of one of my fellow zookeepers.

Bryndis frowned. "You look like you are ready to clean out an enclosure."

"I'd never do that in clothes this elegant."

Despite her obvious disapproval, she grinned. "I have an idea." She disappeared into the bedroom, and emerged a few minutes later with a mint green silk blouse that must have cost her a week's salary. "Try this on."

After slipping into the blouse, I realized that given Bryndis' great height, it reached almost to my knees.

"Not bad." She unbuttoned the top two buttons, which brought the neckline down to such a daring degree you could almost see my minuscule breasts.

"Are you sure…?"

"Oh, live a little, Teddy. There will be many handsome men at the party, and no, you do not have to run off into the hinterlands with them, but flirting is fun and we Icelanders are good at it. Besides, I am not done with you yet." She took another trip into the bedroom, this time bringing back a large, multicolored scarf that picked up the shirt's pale green, and wrapped it across my hips, tying it in a sash at the side. For a finishing touch, she fastened a sparkling crystal necklace around my neck. "Now for some makeup."

Not giving me a chance to protest, she went to work on my face, and a few minutes later, said, "There! Go look in the mirror."

I did, and the transformation astounded me. Despite my resemblance to a giant-sized pistachio ice cream cone, green looked good on me. But there remained one problem—the Timberland boots on my feet. I'd packed a pair of Nikes, but they wouldn't work, either.

"What size do you wear?" Bryndis asked, staring at them.

"An American eight."

"My shoes would flap around on your feet regardless of the style. Maybe…" She paused for a moment, then said, "I have an idea." She headed for the door, calling over her shoulder, "I will be right back!"

A few minutes she returned, bearing a pair of strappy silver sandals. "On loan from Esja, next door. Like you, she is tiny. She said to kiss the boys for her!'"

Once I slipped them on, I was ready. At least that's what I thought.

"One more thing, Teddy."

Before I could protest, she whipped out a flagon of cologne and gave me a spritz. It smelled like roses on fire.

"Nice," I said. "What's it called?"

"*Heitt.* That is Old Norse for 'hot.'"

Bryndis had told me that Ragnar sometimes worked as a film extra, but hadn't mentioned what he actually did for a living. The minute I walked into Ragnar's crowded apartment, his profession became apparent. Ethereal music by Sigur Rós blasted forth from a series of well-placed loudspeakers, providing counterpoint to the vivid paintings of birds covering the walls. No matter how monochromatic the living birds' plumages had been, Ragnar had transformed their coloration into kaleidoscopean hues. In the living room, a depiction of a six-foot by six-foot red, green, and blue puffin with a white stripe on top of its head hung next to a painting of a purple, orange, and yellow eider duck. Across from them, a seven-foot painting of a red and chartreuse eagle reached out with lavender claws, making the five-foot-high blue and orange chaffinch nearby appear tepid by comparison.

"Wow," was all I could say, awed by all that color.

"Last year Ragnar had a one-man show at Harpa," Bryndis said proudly, "and now he has been invited to present at the ARKEN Museum of Modern Art, in Copenhagen. His work is well-respected."

"An artist who's into birds, what are the chances of that?" Now I could identify the faint odor that had puzzled me upon entering to the apartment: the scent of fresh varnish.

"You did not know? Ragnar is not only a birder, but a member of Fuglavernd, BirdLive Iceland, the conservation group. When we were on the phone he told me that is why he was at the Viking Tavern the other night. He was there with the president of BirdLive when…Oh." Her eyes grew round. "That is when he had that run-in with Simon what's-his-name."

"Simon Parr." I tried and failed to keep the frown off my face. Bryndis noticed. "Do not worry, Teddy. Ragnar did not know the dead man, other than to take exception to the way he was treating that woman."

"But Ragnar got physical with him."

She shrugged. "Someone had to."

"Maybe."

"You don't think Inspector Haraldsson would…would…?"

"Nah."

Not my business. Not my business.

Refusing to think any more about the case, I wandered over to the drinks table, around which numerous partygoers had gathered. Above the ambient strains of Sigur Rós, I heard snatches of Icelandic, English, Italian, and Russian. Ragnar sure got around. After availing myself of a beer labeled Ölvisholt Lava, I toured the rest of the apartment.

It was larger than Bryndis', with two bedrooms, one of them acting as an artist's studio, where more paintings of birds crowded the walls. Propped on an easel in the studio was an unfinished oil of a hoopoe, only instead of being yellow, black, and white, the Egyptian bird was well on its way to resembling a red, green, and amber traffic light. Instead of becoming outraged at Ragnar's liberties with nature, the painting made me smile. I had plenty of company, mostly male, while I checked out the other paintings in the studio. Apparently my green "dress" was working, and several Viking types hit on me, albeit politely. In each case I flashed my engagement ring and told my admirer how much I missed my fiancé. To my chagrin, no hearts were broken. My admirers simply moved on to the next unattached female.

The paintings in the back hallway weren't quite as large as those in the studio, but there were twice as many. I sipped at my Ölvisholt Lava while studying another unlikely-colored puffin, this one lavender, scarlet, and pink.

Back in the living room, someone switched the music of Sigur Rós to that of singer/songwriter Brostinn Strengur, and although she sang in Icelandic, the sadness in her voice made me suspect she sang about loneliness. It made me miss Joe. Then I had an inspiration. Why shouldn't we come to Iceland on our honeymoon instead of Italy? I was already in love with the country, and I knew enough about Joe to bet that he'd love its wildness, too. During the day we could ride horses through glacial valleys, and at night we could…

"Here, try some *hákarl*," Bryndis asked, handing me a dish of something evil-smelling. Her sudden appearance, blended with that awful stench, pulled me right out of my X-rated fantasy.

"*Hákarl?* What's that?"

"Rotten shark. Traditional dish. Very expensive, almost as much as the finest caviar. Ragnar bought two pounds!"

"Purple puffins must sell well, then. But, no thanks, I'll pass on the shark."

"You sure?" She looked disappointed. "I do not want to hog it all."

"Knock your socks off."

She appeared puzzled.

"That's American slang for 'be my guest.'"

A big smile. "Your loss." With that, she took a big bite of dead and long-buried shark. "Yum!"

"I don't see how…"

From the living room, a male's voice rose above the usual party noise. Ragnar. Shouting in Icelandic. He sounded furious.

Wondering if someone had been foolish enough to insult a woman in his presence, I turned a questioning face to Bryndis. "Who's Ragnar mad at now?"

The impish look on her face disappeared, replaced by one of alarm. Without answering, she rushed toward the living room. Curious, I followed.

At first I couldn't make sense of what I saw and heard. Bryndis' ex-boyfriend was surrounded by a group of serious-looking men wearing black. Even more oddly, he was holding his arms behind him. But when I spotted Inspector Thorvaald Haraldsson standing among the black-clad men, I realized they were police officers, and the reason Ragnar's arms were behind him was because he'd been handcuffed.

Whatever he'd done to bring the ire of the police down on him, Ragnar wasn't going quietly. As he struggled against the cuffs, he aimed what sounded like Old Norse curses at the inspector. That made everyone else begin to shout in their native tongue, creating a cacophony of babble.

One clear voice rose against them all.

After reeling off a formal-sounding declaration in Icelandic, Inspector Haraldsson added in English, "Ragnar Eriksson, I am arresting you for the murder of Mr. Simon Parr, a citizen of the United States of America. I am also arresting you for the theft of Ulfur Johansson's Finnish Sako, the rifle with which you shot Mr. Parr to death."

So much for Nordic stoicism.

Bryndis' steely reserve crumbled the minute we exited Ragnar's apartment. She didn't quite burst into tears, but her lower lip trembled enough I could tell she was on the verge.

Trying to be helpful, I said, "Maybe I should drive."

She turned her head away for a moment. When she faced me again, her lip had stopped trembling. "Do not be ridiculous."

"Just trying to help."

Sniff. "Not needed." Sniff.

It being after eleven, the summer sun had finally set, and we drove in silence through the dark streets of Reykjavik. Bryndis didn't speak again until she unlocked the door to her apartment.

"I do not love him anymore."

"Of course not."

"I never did."

"Emotions can be confusing, can't they?"

Sniff. "We Icelanders are not like you Americans."

"Oh?"

"We are not run by our emotions." Sniff.

"Commendable, I'm sure."

Once inside the apartment, Bryndis flicked on the kitchen light. "How about some coffee?"

"Sounds good."

As I sat down at the table, she busied herself at the Mr. Coffee, imported, like almost everything else in Iceland, from the U.S., Denmark, or China.

"Strong or weak?" she asked.

"Weak. I don't want to lie awake all night. We have a full day at the zoo tomorrow."

"I have a full day at the zoo," she said. "Not you."

Mr. Coffee gurgled and a thin brew trickled out.

"What do you mean, not me? I thought I was going to the zoo with you, and working some more with Magnus."

She handed me a half-filled cup of coffee. "Sugar? Cream?"

"Neither. You didn't answer my question. Am I or am I not going with you to the zoo tomorrow?"

"You are not." She poured herself a cup then joined me at the table, her formerly vulnerable face set in hard lines. "You go wherever you need to go, but call me every now and then and tell me of your progress."

I frowned in puzzlement. "I don't understand."

Her jaw clenched and her eyes narrowed, making her look like one of her ruthless Viking ancestors ready to lay waste to some sleepy English village. Even her tone scared me.

"Here is how this will work, Teddy. Tomorrow morning you will drop me off at the zoo, then you will take my Volvo. Oh, and be sure and take your laptop along, too. I can catch a ride home from one of the other keepers. A couple of them live nearby."

"You want me to take your car? Where? And why?"

"Because you are going to find out who really killed Simon Parr, that is why!"

Chapter Nine

You can't argue with an Icelander.

Bryndis refused to listen to my refusals and little by little she wore me down. Against my earlier resolve, I agreed to look into the case. Mission accomplished, she tottered off to bed, leaving me alone in the kitchen, drinking more coffee than was good for me.

I knew I was unequipped for the task, being in a foreign country and having already been warned by Inspector Haraldsson to mind my own business, but as the silence of the apartment closed in, I began to wonder. What had led the inspector to arrest Ragnar in the first place? Despite my ignorance of the parties involved, I could already see three possible explanations.

One: Ragnar's slap-fest with Simon Parr at the Viking Tavern proved he had a temper and wasn't loath to act on it. Two: judging from his paintings, he had more than a passing interest in birds, and the unfinished oil of a hoopoe made me suspect he might have traveled to Vik on the day of the murder in hopes of seeing one of the birds in the flesh. Three: most damning of all—Simon Parr might conceivably have photographed Ragnar on the cliff top.

This led me back to Inspector Haraldsson's odd visit to the Reykjavik City Zoo, where he'd shown me the printouts of Parr's pictures of birds and one naked woman. Yet he'd shown me no photograph of Ragnar at Vik. Because no such photograph existed? Or had he withheld the photo because Bryndis was standing next to me? But then why show me any pictures at all, especially given the fact that he'd already warned me not to get involved in the case? Could he have been checking out Bryndis' reaction, and not mine? Surely he didn't suspect the zookeeper of also being involved in Parr's death!

The more I thought about it, the more troubled I felt. To give the devil his due, Haraldsson probably had good reason to arrest Ragnar, but to me, it didn't feel right. Given Icelanders' lack of enthusiasm for murder-by-firearm, touring members of the Geronimo County Birding Association could more rightly top the suspect list, not him. The snag was that other than the tearful Dawn, I didn't know them.

A glance at the kitchen clock showed that it was nearing one, but I wasn't at all sleepy, so instead of turning in, I went into the small living room and sat down at the desk. Upon firing up my laptop, I Googled the Geronimo County Birding Association. It took me a while to land on the right website because I spent the first few minutes stumbling through several Native American sites devoted to the old Apache warrior. I finally landed on the Geronimo County Birding Association website, illustrated by dozens of pictures of birds. When you clicked one, you could even hear its call. After listening to a few tweets and warbles, I moved onto the MEMBERS link, where I found a list of the organization's twenty-seven members. By themselves, the names would have meant nothing to me, but fortunately, the site also featured a MEDIA link. I clicked on that, and found several articles from various Arizona newspapers about the club. The article that interested me most appeared on July 10 in the *Geronimo County Ledger-Dispatch.*

POWERBALL WINNER TREATS BIRDERS TO ICELAND
by Max Avery

> Bird-watcher Simon Parr's motto must be "My luck is your luck" because the winner of the largest Powerball payout in history—$610.3 million—is treating eight

of his bird-watching friends to an all-expense-paid trip to Iceland.

"The coastal towns in Iceland see large groupings of varietals every August," said Parr, in an interview at his Apache Crossing home. "There are the native birds, of course, like the whooping swan, razorbills, and puffins, but because the summer weather is so balmy and the winds so warm, birds from all over Europe and even the Middle East have been known to drop by."

When asked how he chose the lucky people who would be traveling to Iceland with him to see the varietals, Parr answered, "That was easy! I've been a member of the Geronimo County Birding Association for twenty-two years, and these are the members I've traveled with before to various birding sites—Cape May, New Jersey, the Florida Everglades, and once even to Patagonia, which is all the way down at the farthest tip of South America. Everyone paid their own way then, of course, but now that I have the money, why not treat my friends?"

Those lucky people are Geronimo County residents Adele Cobb, Perry and Enid Walsh (Perry Walsh is the newly elected president of the Geronimos, as they are known), Benjamin and Dawn Talley, Lucinda Greaves, Judy Malone, and actor Tab Cooper. All, with the exception of Mrs. Talley, who only recently began accompanying the group on their bird-watching adventures, are longtime members of the Geronimos.

Also accompanying the group to Iceland is Parr's wife, the famed romantic suspense novelist, Elizabeth St. John. She and Parr have been married for 26 years, but because of her career demands, she hasn't always been able to join her husband on his birding adventures.

Both Parrs have already displayed a strong bent toward charity. In addition to treating his friends to the trip of a lifetime, Parr has donated $500,000 to the Apache Crossing Girls & Boys Club and a battered

women's shelter. Ms. St. John, whose books feature an
archaeologist likened to "a female Indiana Jones," long
ago set up an archaeology scholarship at Arizona State
University, but with her 50% share of the Powerball
payout, is she has begun funding a sanctuary for abused
circus animals.

Included with the article was a group shot of the club. Although their faces were too small to be of much use for identification purposes, they all wore bright red windbreakers and matching baseball caps emblazoned with the initials "GCBA." That wasn't all. A sidebar listed the group's touring itinerary—if indeed they decided to continue on their adventure. In light of the tragedy, they might return to Arizona, but given the fact that this was a paid-for trip of a lifetime, I didn't see that happening, murder or no murder.

In reading the birders' itinerary, I saw nothing but Old Norse town names. They were unpronounceable—mainly consonants with only few vowels—but a quick scan of the map in my tour book gave me their locations. The Geronimos were based at Hótel Keldur, in downtown Reykjavik, but for the most part, stayed within the southwestern side of the country, along what was known as the Golden Circle. None were in the Icelandic interior, an impenetrable wilderness of glaciers and volcanoes. Tomorrow the birders would visit something called the Snaefellsnes Peninsula, where they would spend the night in a small fishing village named—Heaven help my poor twisting tongue—Stykkishólmur. I checked the map in the tour book again and discovered that the unpronounceable village was less than two hours away from Reykjavik, all on what appeared to be decent roads. Maybe after I dropped Bryndis off at the zoo, I'd take a little drive.

The next day I arrived in Stykkishólmur—pronounced STICH-ish-HOL-meh, Bryndis had explained—shortly before nine. With a population of less than fifteen hundred, it should have been easy to find eight people wearing red blazers and matching baseball caps, but that wasn't the case. The village was made up of one main street leading to a picturesque harbor, and a few side streets winding to the top of a bluff that overlooked the North Atlantic. The bluff appeared to be perfect bird-watching territory, so I headed straight there, only to be disappointed. Ten minutes later, having driven every one of its narrow lanes, I gave up. After checking my guidebook, I learned that birding was also popular on the rocky island further out in the bay.

Rather than waste more time driving around aimlessly, I pulled into the parking lot of Hótel Egilsen, where they would spend the night. That's when I spotted a large blue van with ODDI'S ICELANDIC TOURS emblazoned on its side.

The hotel, painted bright red with sparkling white shutters, was as charming inside as out. Its small lobby was furnished with comfortable seating, desks, and bookshelves loaded with magazines and books in both English and Icelandic.

The counterman, another tall, blond Viking type who'd been reading a book, looked up with a smile. His name tag said, LEIFUR.

"*Hvad segerōú?*" Leifur asked.

Noticing the panic on my face, he switched to English. "That is Icelandic for 'How are you?'"

"Fine, thanks." I don't like lying, but sometimes it's necessary. "I'm looking for some friends from the Geronimo County…" I trailed off, not knowing under which name the reservations may have been made. "Ah, the friends of Mr. Simon Parr."

Leifur's smile broadened. "The birding group from Arizona! I plan to go there someday to see the cowboys and ride the broncs. Yes, your friends, such nice people, arrived a couple of hours ago, but after leaving luggage in their rooms, they left with their binoculars and cameras."

"Oh."

I was either transparent or Leifur was good at face-reading, because he added, "Do not feel sad. They may have gone to Helgafell, which is popular with birding groups because many birds nest in the ruins of the old church. Or they might be up by the lighthouse on Súgandisey, that little island across the bay. I am no birder myself, but I hear you can see many puffins, guillemots, and eagles near the lighthouse. So perhaps you should try that first, since it's closest. You can climb to the top in a few minutes."

I could see the island's sheer cliff wall from the hotel's lobby window. It looked like a climb fit only for a mountaineer or nerveless Icelandic horse.

"There is a nice, safe staircase up the side of the mountain," he said, reading me again. "You will be fine."

"*Takk fyrir*," I said, using my only two words of Icelandic. Thank you.

With that, I headed out the door.

Leifur was right. A wide causeway led across the scenic harbor to the bottom of the looming cliff. The staircase was steep but, except for sneak attacks by a flock of shrieking Arctic terns determined to knock me off the stairs, I felt safe. Upon reaching the top, I followed the path toward the reddish-orange lighthouse. There I found the Geronimo County Birding Association. Those who weren't taking pictures were listening to a talk being given by a tall, burly man whom I took to be Oddi, their tour guide. Most of the birders dressed in the club's bright red windbreakers, which provided some defense from the brisk wind that blew in from the North Atlantic. It may have been July, but up here it felt more like November.

Several yards away, I recognized the woman Simon Parr verbally abused at the Viking Tavern, and who in what had to be happier times, posed naked for his camera. She was snapping pictures of a guillemot perched on a large outcropping while the other birders concentrated on an eagle preening its feathers on a metal rail crowning the lighthouse. A member of the auk family, the guillemot was fairly large, at least sixteen inches, with striking black and white coloration. But rare? The island was covered with the things, whereas I only saw the one eagle. Why was the woman so intrigued by a more common bird?

Grasping my own camera, I approached her slowly, not wanting to startle the guillemot. For form's sake, I snapped some pictures. In between frames I snuck a glance at Simon's nude model. Her face was pale, and her eyes were swollen. It could have been in reaction to the wind, but I didn't think so. She'd separated herself from the others so she could mourn alone.

A couple of minutes later, the guillemot headed back out to sea. The woman watched until it was a mere dot on the horizon.

"Don't you love watching them?" I said, hoping to start a conversation.

"They're lovely birds," she answered, a polite smile on her face. More prepared for the weather than I, a thick purple turtleneck sweater peeked out of her red windbreaker. Both clashed with her burgundy-colored hair.

"Say, you sound American! I'm Teddy. Theodora, actually, but all my friends call me Teddy. I'm from Gunn Landing, California, in the Monterey Bay area. And you?"

"Adele Cobb, Apache Crossing, Arizona." Her eyes drifted toward the other birders, still enraptured by the eagle.

All except one. Dawn Talley, wearing an Icelandic-patterned wool sweater instead of the official club gear, had drifted away from the lighthouse to the cliff edge, and was staring across the harbor toward Stykkishólmur. A slight frown marred her beautiful face, but other than that, she appeared to have recovered from her concern for her husband. I wondered how genuine that concern had actually been. Maybe she was merely one of those people who enjoyed drama and wasn't averse to creating her own whenever the opportunity arose.

Adele's voice interrupted my uncharitable suspicions. "…and when a friend ponies up for an all-expense paid trip to Iceland, you can hardly say no, can you?"

I returned my attention to her. "No, you can't. But gosh, what a wonderful gift!"

"Yes, it was. Except…" She trailed off, then looked me hard in the face. "Wait a minute. I've seen you before. You were at Vik, weren't you?"

No point in lying. "Yes, I was down there horseback riding with a friend." After a slight pause, I cut to the chase. "We were up on the cliff where, you know…" I let the sentence trail off.

"Oh." The polite smile vanished and her pale face grew even paler. "Are you the woman who discovered his body?"

"I'm afraid so."

"Was he…was he still alive? Did he…did say anything, anything at all?"

"He was dead, Adele, and had been for a while."

"Oh." She took a deep breath. "Then did he…did he…?"

Her words were snatched away by the rising wind, but it didn't take a mind reader to guess what she wanted to know. I crossed my fingers behind my back and told a whopper. "He didn't suffer. In fact, he looked quite peaceful." Other than the hole in his head. And his chewed-up nose.

She closed her eyes for a moment, and when she opened them again, whispered, "Thank you."

Adele had loved him. Remembering the ugly scene in the Viking Tavern and Parr's ill-treatment of her, I marveled at the myriad forms love can take. Maybe that had been the first time in their relationship he'd behaved abusively toward her, but I doubted it. I was about to ask her how long she'd known him when a familiar voice rose above the wind.

"Why, it's Teddy! How lovely to see you here!" Dawn Talley. The stiff breeze had brought roses to her cheeks and a sparkle to those dazzling eyes.

I arranged a smile on my face. "Nice seeing you, too, Dawn."

She hooked an arm around mine and drew me away from Adele. Together we walked over to a guillemot-free area, leaving Adele alone with her grief.

"Thank God you've decided to help us," Dawn said, in a voice so hushed I could barely hear it above the wind. "That awful policeman, Inspector Svensson or Olafsson or whatever, those Icelandic names are so confusing, he's been asking Ben some really scary questions, like, where was he earlier the morning of the murder and why didn't he eat breakfast with the rest of us.

Worst of all, he actually asked Ben if he knew the hotelier's rifle was missing! And between us, Teddy, I don't like the way Ben's been behaving."

After making a mental note of that missing rifle, I asked, "Haven't you read the morning newspaper?"

She threw me a look of disbelief. "You're kidding, right? I can't read Icelandic."

"There's an English language edition, and it announced an arrest in the case."

"Really?" Maybe it was my imagination, but I thought her surprise was tinged with disappointment.

"Whatever's going on with your husband, he didn't murder Simon Parr, and the police know it."

"Then why was Inspector what's-his-name at our hotel this morning, asking questions?"

Now it was my turn to look surprised. "Haraldsson was here? In Stykkishólmur?"

Her frown accentuated the lines at the corner of her eyes and mouth. In the harsh sunlight, she almost looked Adele's age, without any of Adele's voluptuousness. "I'm telling you, Teddy, he took us all, one by one, into a room and asked us where we were at what time and how well did we get along with Simon, which in my husband's case, wasn't very well. Those two never liked each other, not after…" She paused, then clutched at my arm in a gesture of panic too flagrant to be sincere. "That rude man even questioned me!"

Not knowing anything about Icelandic law, I wondered why Inspector Haraldsson had felt it necessary to drive all the way up to Stykkishólmur when he already had a suspect in custody. At the same time, I wondered about Dawn's supposed concern. There was something about it that didn't ring true.

She wasn't finished. "The worst thing was when that cop demanded I tell him where I was between four and five in the morning the day of…uh, the day it happened."

"What did you tell him?"

Her glare erased all remnants of beauty from her face. "I told him I was in bed, of course. Not that it was any of his business."

"Then there should be no problem."

"You don't get it, do you, Teddy? Since Ben wasn't in bed beside me, I don't have an alibi."

Confused, I asked, "Why in the world would you need one?"

She gave a quick glance toward the other birders, then leaned toward me. "Well, I don't exactly want to broadcast it, but Simon and me, we'd been having a thing."

"A *thing*? You mean, like an affair?"

She bit her lip and looked down. I followed her glance and saw two different kinds of lava, some red, some black. The entire island was the result of a massive volcanic eruption. Fascinating, yes, but not half as fascinating as what Dawn said next.

"Yeah, Simon and me, we had an affair, a short one, you understand, but then the creep dumped me."

"Simon Parr dumped *you*?" A man dumping a beauty doesn't happen every day.

Dawn flushed so deeply I knew she was telling the truth. "Oh, yeah, he told me it'd been swell and all but adios, and don't let the door hit my ass on the way out."

That made no sense. A beauty kicked to the curb by a birder? From the pictures the newspaper had run of Simon Parr, the murder victim hadn't been a handsome man, even if his Elvis sideburns lent him a certain rakish appeal. But then I remembered that Powerball win. Six hundred million could be a strong aphrodisiac. "When did this happen?"

"Just before we left for Iceland."

"Did your husband suspect? About the affair, I mean."

"Well, duh."

"I don't understand."

"What do you mean, you don't understand?"

There is nothing more exasperating than talking to a person who thinks you're a mind reader. "Did you husband know about the affair?"

An exasperated sigh. "Of course he did."

"Well, then what did he do?"

"Nothing, of course."

"Look, Dawn, I'm not getting any of this. Help me out here."

She briefly resumed her perusal of the island's volcanic history, then took a big breath, and in the petulant voice of a bratty three-year-old, spit out, "Well, okay, since you can't seem to figure it out for yourself, Miss Mensa, Ben didn't do anything, 'cause the affair was his idea in the first place. So there!"

Somehow I kept my jaw from dropping. "Why in the world would your husband want you to have an affair?"

She said something else I couldn't quite hear over the wind.

"Louder, please. That is, if you want me to help you."

"He wanted me to do it because we were broke."

"But isn't your husband one of the Talleys, of the nationwide Talley Restaurant chain?"

Her petulance vanished and she looked distinctly uncomfortable. "The restaurants have been having financial problems for years, closing locations all over the place. Ben said that if I, um, started sleeping with Simon I might be able to hit him up for a loan, enough to keep the company afloat until the economy turned around."

Suddenly everything made sense, especially Dawn's odd behavior at Vik, a performance which had seemed more designed to draw attention to her husband's guilt than away from it. She resented Ben, and I didn't blame her. There's a word for men who provide women to other men for sexual purposes, and it isn't a nice one.

Still, she could have refused. The fact that she went along with her husband's scheme said a lot about her character, or lack thereof. Out of curiosity, I asked, "Why'd you agree to do it?"

Her pretty mouth twisted into an unpretty shape. "Why not? We were going to get a divorce anyway, and according to the terms of our pre-nup, the more money Ben had when the papers were filed, the better, because…" She didn't finish, but it wasn't hard to see where she'd been headed. *Because divorcing a rich husband was more profitable than divorcing a poor one.*

Judge not lest ye be judged, and all that. "I take it your husband's plans were scuttled when Simon dumped you. May I ask why?"

"Why Simon dumped me?

"If you don't mind."

At first I thought she wouldn't answer, then she muttered, "He said my breasts were starting to sag."

I winced. Given the insecurity most women felt about their bodies, it was a cruel thing to say. Added to Simon's performance at the Viking Tavern, it suggested that, despite Simon's generous treat of the Iceland birding adventure, he had harbored a mean streak.

"Did Ben know Simon broke off the relationship?"

"He walked in on me the day before we left for Iceland, so I had to explain why. He was furious! He blamed me for not knowing how to please a man, and said that, yeah, my breasts were sagging, along with my ass." The look Dawn turned on me now was devoid of all spite and artifice. "Please help me, Teddy!"

I almost turned her down, but at the last second realized that Dawn could provide me with the perfect reason to stay close to the Geronimos. Maybe Dawn needed my help, but Bryndis and Ragnar needed it more.

Aware that I would regret it later, I made a snap decision. "Okay, but you need to do something for me."

"Anything."

"Tell the other birders we're old friends, say, from school, and that we met here by coincidence. Say you've invited me along on some of your outings because I enjoy birds so they won't be shocked when they keep running into me."

She was so desperate she agreed. Tears of gratitude filled her eyes. They might even have been genuine.

Eager to begin building a fake history, I asked, "Where did you go to college, Dawn?"

"I didn't. I had a modeling career, remember? And why does it matter?"

"Because I'm trying to find a believable explanation for us being old chums." Silly me, asking that question about college.

These days models started out in high school, sometimes even earlier, another reason they seldom became rocket scientists at retirement, which in many cases, came in their late twenties. No wonder Dawn was so panicked. She possessed no career skills, just a husband who no longer loved her and a rapidly dwindling beauty.

"Scratch the college question. Have you ever been to California, say, around the Monterey Bay area? Or San Francisco?"

I'd lived in San Francisco when I'd been married to Michael. Before he left me for another woman.

Dawn stared at me. "*Everybody's* been to San Francisco. I even *lived* there."

"And left their hearts there, I know. But when did you live there and for how long?"

She wrinkled her brow. That's when I noticed a tiny scar above the bridge of her nose. "Hmm. My dad was transferred there from Cleveland when I was in middle school, so, let's see, we lived in San Fran for about three years. That's where the model scout saw me at the beach and recommended me to the Ford Agency. Soon after that, we moved down to L.A. where my career really took off, and we moved to New York, where I wound up on the covers of *Elle* and *Cosmopolitan*."

Fat lot of good those covers did her: only marriage to a man who pawned her off to another man for financial reasons. "Here's the way we'll play it, then. When you rejoin the group, tell everyone you've run into an old classmate, that we used to hang out together after school, like at Fisherman's Wharf, Gump's, whatever. It's important you make everyone believe that our running into each other up here is only a coincidence."

"You mean you want me to lie?"

Working with animals has taught me patience, so instead of pulling out my hair, I said, "Yes, Dawn, I want you to lie. What was the name of the school we went to? And what neighborhood did we two BFFs live in?"

"James Lick Middle School. It's in Noe Valley. You know the area?"

I nodded. Since I was familiar with Noe Valley, faking our middle-school friendship shouldn't be too hard. "Okay, so I'll leave it up to you to let the others know about our old connection. In the meantime, what else did Inspector Haraldsson ask when he interviewed you?"

"Not much. I kept telling him that I didn't kill Simon and neither did Ben, and I made up a few whoppers, saying that Ben wouldn't hurt a fly, which is a laugh riot, considering the fact that he's gotten physical with me a few times. But what the hell, all men are like that, aren't they?"

My fiancé wasn't like that at all. He carried a gun, sure, but so did every peace officer in the U.S. And Joe's gentle hands… Shocked by where my mind was headed, I shook myself back into the present, where the behavior of Benjamin Talley of the failing Talley Restaurant chain was sounding considerably less handsome than his looks. "Speaking of getting physical, Dawn, did you tell the inspector that your husband got into a shoving match with Simon Parr at the airport?"

"There was a shoving match?"

"You mentioned it when you were talking to me at the ladies' room in Vik, remember?"

She shrugged. "Sorry, I wasn't thinking well that morning because of the murder and stuff. But, yeah, come to think of it, there might have been a shoving match. Or maybe they just shouted at each other. I can't remember the details."

The woman was truth-challenged. If it hadn't been for Bryndis' distress over Ragnar's arrest, I'd walk away right now, but I'd made a promise and intended to keep it.

I decided to leave the subject of the airport altercation for later. "Out of curiosity, what explanation did your husband give for being out so early in the morning at Vik?"

"Oh, that. Yeah, he told me he was walking around outside enjoying the fresh air, but I'm pretty sure he was lying. Ben hates the cold. I mean, *really* hates the cold. That's why we live near Phoenix. Frankly, I was surprised when he agreed to come on this trip, although it isn't all that cold, is it? But it was over a hundred and fifteen when we left Sky Harbor, and Ben was loving it. Me, when this mess is over and I get my divorce settlement, I'm moving to La Jolla."

"Nice town, I hear."

She gave me a wicked smile. "And plenty of handsome men, some of them even millionaires." Then, as if regretting that last comment, she erased her smile and pasted on a mournful expression. "But I don't want anything bad to happen to Ben. He's still my husband."

As if she cared. I heard a noise—something other than the wind—and turned toward the sound. The eagle had finally flapped away from the lighthouse. With a great rush of wings, it flew straight over our heads, then wheeled around to the west and flew toward an island in the distance. Their camera subject flown, the other Geronimos started walking toward us. Time to wrap up this conversation.

"Okay, so we're best buds from school. Now tell me, and quick, before your friends get here. Do you think it's possible that your husband really did kill Simon Parr?"

She watched the eagle as it dwindled into a black speck against the blue sky. "Well, you know what they say."

"What, Dawn? What do 'they' say?"

"That anything's possible."

Before I could renege on my promise to Bryndis and get the hell out of Stykkishólmur, the other birders arrived at our side, making appreciative noises about the island's abundant bird life. When they wound down, Dawn introduced me to them, proclaiming that her dear friend Teddy had promised to find out who murdered their wonderful benefactor. To hear her tell it, her old school chum was a private detective who possessed the combined investigative powers of Hercule Poirot and James Rockford. All I could do was stand there on that windblown rock, wishing I were somewhere else.

I did notice something interesting, though. When I'd seen Dawn's husband across the room in the Vik hotel, I'd been impressed by his movie star looks. His features were so impossibly perfect that I'd put them down to the work of a skilled cosmetic surgeon. But now the bright sunlight revealed the truth. His cheekbones, nose, and chin were indeed surgeon-sculpted, but for reconstruction purposes, not vanity. Tiny scars crisscrossed the left side of his face, and his left ear didn't match the right because it had also been rebuilt.

When he smiled, his teeth proved as falsely perfect as the rest of the face. "Wonderful to meet you, Teddy. Dawn's told me a lot about her childhood in San Francisco and how much she loved it there. But I'd been under the impression she didn't have many friends."

Dawn jumped in, her voice anxious. "Quality, not quantity, is what counts. Isn't that what you've always told me, Honey?"

His smile dimmed. "I remember saying something like that, yes. You didn't appear to be listening at the time."

She hooked her arm around his and looked up at him with fake adoration. "Oh, you know me, Ben. Regardless of what else is going on, I hear everything."

"I'm sure you do," burgundy-haired Adele said. There was no love in her voice, either.

The sixty-something man who had been introduced to me as Perry Walsh, the group's new president, cleared his throat. "Dawn, Adele, you both missed Oddi's great talk about that island out there." He pointed out to sea to a bump on the horizon. "That's Flatley. He says it's pretty much deserted now, but it still houses Iceland's oldest library. I was thinking we might take the ferry over. Anyone else interested?"

A discussion ensued about the virtues of Flatley as opposed to a visit to something called Helgafell. In the middle of it, Adele, who had already cast her vote for Helgafell, sidled up next to me.

"Are you really a detective? Or is that another of Dawn's tall tales?"

So Dawn was known for her lies. "A bit of a tall tale, I'm afraid. I'm only a zookeeper. My boss sent me to Iceland to take possession of a polar bear cub, and I decided to get in a little birding while I was here."

"But you knew Dawn when she lived in San Francisco, right? You were friends?"

Hating the false position I'd put myself in, I answered, "Yes, I've known her for years."

Adele gave me a pitying smile. "Poor you."

I couldn't agree more.

Chapter Ten

Continuing to play up my fake friendship with Dawn, I spent the rest of the morning tromping with the birders around the gentle hills near Stykkishólmur, making approving noises about this bird and that. Accompanied by two friendly border collies from a nearby farm, we climbed Helgafell—translation, Holy Mountain. Oddi, who like all the other Icelanders I'd met, spoke flawless English, told us that in Viking times the mountain was considered an entrance to Valhalla. In the thirteenth century, it became the site of a small chapel, which now lay in ruins at the summit. In accordance with local legend, we ascended silently, and once at the summit, turned east and, still in silence, made three wishes. Supposedly, wishes made in this manner were always granted if they were made with a pure heart. But whose heart was truly pure?

Still, after I'd finished three quick certain never-to-be-granted wishes, I looked around at the Geronimos, as they insisted I call them, and saw eyes shut and lips moving, with only two exceptions: Adele Cobb and Lucinda Greaves, a thin, fiftyish woman with a perpetual sour expression. Instead of wishing, she surveyed the extraordinary scenery. In one direction a string of bright green islands dotted Breithavik Bay, while in the other direction, glacier-topped mountains provided passage to Iceland's fjords. Above, more eagles sailed the flawless sky.

"I've seen better," Lucinda said, breaking the awed silence. Her eyes were narrowed against the bright day, and hastily applied lipstick bled along the lines radiating from her mouth.

The comment elicited mass scowls from the others, even the good-natured Oddi.

"Where?" Adele challenged.

"San Diego, for instance. Or any place with a beautiful shoreline. If you ask me, this place isn't even second-rate."

Adele looked at her with disgust. "Why don't you let yourself enjoy something for a change instead of trying to ruin everyone else's good time?"

Lucinda gave her a withering smile. "Unlike some people I could mention, I prefer to look at life without blinders on."

"Meaning what?"

"Meaning you, for instance. You knew what Simon was like before you started up with him, but you kept kidding yourself that he'd make an exception in your case. But that didn't happen, did it?"

I never found out what Adele was going to answer because Oddi shouted, "Ptarmigan! They're all over the place!"

In other words, grouse.

Now, grouse aren't rare—not even the white Icelandic type— so from the lack of shushing that followed the noisy pronouncement, it was obvious the "discovery" was no more than a ruse to break up the imminent brawl between Adele and Lucinda. For my part in the peacekeeping process, I grabbed Adele by the arm and said, "How exciting! I haven't seen ptarmigans since…since…"

"Yesterday?" But she smiled and allowed me to lead her to the closest ptarmigan hangout, while Lucinda remained behind looking at the "not even second-rate" scenery.

I'd left the grouse and had spotted a black-tailed godwit perched on an outcropping when a woman's voice behind me said, "Sorry about that. I'd like to say Lucinda means well, but she doesn't."

Turning, I recognized Enid Walsh, wife of the Geronimos' new president. Like her elderly husband, she had that too-lean, dried-prune look of people who'd spent too much time out in the desert sun. But it hadn't dimmed the warmth in her eyes. Somewhere in her late sixties, she looked as kindly as Lucinda looked sour. "This trip has been rough on her."

"Oh?"

"She's worried about her daughter." Enid gestured toward a waifish young woman who looked nothing like her mother. "Judy's had so many health problems of late that I was surprised Lucinda encouraged her to come along on this trip."

I studied Judy more carefully. She was thin, but her cheeks were pink, and she was talking animatedly with a beautifully groomed young man who had the bland good looks of a male model. His pants were perfectly creased and his Ivy League shirt was pressed within an inch of its one-hundred-percent cotton life. Even his fingernails were manicured.

"Nothing serious, I hope," I said in response to Enid's statement.

"Asthma, for starters. On top of that, she always catches whatever bug's going around. A few years back she took up yoga and even began teaching a few classes, but it only helped a little. Perry, that's my husband, thinks her problem's psychosomatic, and who knows, he could even be right. Twenty-two years old and still living at home. Heck, living with Lucinda would make anyone sick." She paused for a moment, watching an Arctic tern and a golden plover join the black-tailed godwit. Then she asked me a question I wasn't prepared for. "So tell me, Teddy, speaking of youth, what was Dawn was like as a little girl? It's hard to envision her as young and innocent."

I thought fast. "Dawn as a little girl? Hmmm. Not that different than the rest of us, I guess. Prettier, of course."

"Perry and I lived in San Francisco years ago." Enid sounded sad.

"Really? Which district?"

"Sunset."

"Nice area. I lived, uh, Dawn and I, we lived in Noe Valley."

"Lots of nice families there."

"Yep."

"What were Dawn's parents like?" Enid's eyes were as sharp as a bird of prey's, making me realize that what had appeared to be a friendly conversation was a fact-finding mission. I needed to be careful.

"Dawn's parents? I hardly knew them." I figured it was the safest thing to say. "You know what girls are like at that age, we both avoided our parents as much as possible."

"Myself, I suspect there was something off there, what with them dropping everything to concentrate on her modeling career. Adults generally have lives of their own, don't they? It's not like all that moving around from San Francisco to Los Angeles to New York and then to Europe was in her best interest in the long run. The girl received no education to speak of, not even financial counseling. God only knows what happened to the money she supposedly made. And now that she's showing her age, well…" Enid raised her eyebrows, as if expecting me to join in her forecast for Dawn's bleak future.

Instead, I excused myself and hurried to join the others as they oohed and ahhed at the ptarmigans.

Lunch was more enjoyable. For a while, anyway.

We ate at the restaurant across the street from the hotel, where I enjoyed a superb, caught-this-morning cod filet in a dill-sprinkled white wine sauce. Most of the other Geronimos welcomed me at their long table without hesitation, and although they knew more about birds than I, allowed me to join the conversation about terns, redshanks, and snipe. The only awkward moment came when Lucinda said, "You say that you're interested in birding, but you admit you don't belong to any birding clubs, not even the Audubon Society. Why not?"

Another person to watch out for. "I'm on the membership committee of the American Association of Zookeepers, and my volunteer work with that and the various animal rescue organizations I belong to, keep me busy. Not to mention my full-time job at the Gunn Zoo." Uncomfortable with her cross-examination, I added, "As you can see, I'm making time for birding now."

"Then what about that polar bear cub you're here to pick up?" Lucinda asked. "Why'd you leave him?"

Good question, but I couldn't give a truthful answer, so I waffled. "Magnus is in quarantine and is being well taken care of by another zookeeper. I'll have plenty of time to spend with him when we get to the Gunn Zoo."

"I don't approve of zoos," She stared at me with cold, hooded eyes. "Imprisoning wild creatures in small cages is cruel."

Stung, I said, "Good zoos don't do that." I went on to describe the large, natural habitats at the Gunn Zoo and others, such as the San Diego, San Francisco, and even the zoo closest to Apache Crossing, the Phoenix. I finished with, "Modern zoos are the Noah's Ark for the animal world. Because of over-building and poaching, without zoos and their careful breeding programs, many more species would be extinct today than already are. Besides, most of the animals you see in zoos today were never 'wild,' as the term is commonly understood. They were born in zoos."

"Disgraceful!" she snapped.

"Not as disgraceful as extinction." Recognizing from her expression that nothing I said would make any difference, I turned to Adele Cobb. "This cod's delicious, isn't it?"

"Yes, but I seem to have lost my appetite. What with everything, it's been a stressful few days and I guess it's catching up with me."

"You're talking about what happened to Simon?"

She nodded.

"Losing a good friend is always hard."

"Friend? I guess you could call him that." Her shoulders slumped as she put down her fork and stared at her plate.

To my surprise, Lucinda reached across the table and patted Adele's hand. "Maybe you should go back to the hotel and rest for a while. You can catch up with us at the Library of Water." To me, she said, "We've all agreed not to talk about what happened at Vik and to carry on as if this were merely another birding outing. Simon would have wanted it that way."

I've always been baffled by people who claim to know the wishes of the dead, but I kept my mouth shut. My mention of the murdered man had cast a pall around the table, and everyone sat in silence as Adele murmured her goodbyes and left. Through the restaurant's large picture window, I could see her wiping at her face as she crossed the street.

"She seemed okay when we talked up by the lighthouse," I said, by way of apology.

Lucinda's moment of compassion vanished and she returned to her usual sour self. "Take my advice, Miss Zookeeper, and confine your conversation to birds." With that, she and Enid Walsh began discussing a recent sighting of a Eurasian woodcock.

After lunch, Dawn, who had been seated at the other end of the table, hooked her arm around mine. "Let's not go to some stuffy old library. Why don't you and me and Ben go over to the gift shop and check out the goodies?"

Eager to talk to the other Geronimos, I was about to decline when Ben saved me the trouble.

"Dawn, we're going with the others. And it's not 'some stuffy old library.' It's a modern art museum featuring Roni Horn's installation of Icelandic glacier water. When you're through buying trinkets, go back to the hotel and wait for us or you'll miss the trip to see the Snaefellsjökull glacier."

With that, he turned on his heel and left her standing there.

As Churchill once said about Russia, Ben Talley was a riddle wrapped in a mystery inside an enigma. He appreciated birds and art, yet had pimped out his wife to Simon Parr in hopes of salvaging a failing restaurant chain. What kind of man did that?

I got my answer a few minutes later, when Oddi drove us, sans Dawn, to a sleek modern building perched on the top of a hill overlooking the town's stunning harbor. As the tour guide explained the art installation of immense floor-to-ceiling tubes of water, Ben wandered among them, seemingly lost in contemplation. I followed.

Ben didn't mind my company, and seemed happy to show off his knowledge of the exhibit. "Did you know the artist is a woman, an American woman?" he asked, as I gazed at one of the tubes. "Horn's instillations are exhibited throughout the world, MOMA, the Whitney, the Tate…One of the reasons I like her so much is because her work is profoundly ecology-oriented. This particular exhibit, for instance, is set up to reflect climate change. As an Icelandic glacier melts, its tube here is drained in the same proportion as the actual melt." He pointed across the room. "See that one there? It represents the Solheimajokull glacier. It's disappearing so fast, the tube will be emptied out in a few years, like the glacier itself."

"Fascinating. And depressing."

He turned his too-perfect smile on me. "Dawn tells me you're a zookeeper. That you went to school together when she and her family lived in San Francisco."

Since I was on shaky ground here, I steered the conversation away from my childhood. "I'm a zookeeper, all right. I always loved animals, even then. At one time, we had three dogs, four cats, and two horses."

He frowned. "Horses? In San Francisco?"

Boy, was I a bad liar. "There are stables, but we, ah, we had some property further south, in San Sebastian County. Pasturage. The horses stayed there, and we'd drive down on the weekends."

The frown didn't lift. "Dawn told me you two went to the movies every weekend."

I gave him a feeble smile. "She might be exaggerating a bit."

"Yeah, she does that from time to time." With that, he turned his back to me and resumed his study of the water-filled columns.

Thus dismissed, I rejoined the others, deciding that as soon as we returned to the hotel, I'd have a talk with Dawn about how much to say about our fictional childhood outings. If she kept making up stories, we'd be uncovered as the liars we were and my usefulness to Bryndis and Ragnar would be over.

Chapter Eleven

The rest of the birders were almost as interested in the exhibit as Ben, which gave me a chance to make a hurried phone call. Muttering something about needing fresh air, I left them with the vanishing tubes of water and went outside. Earlier, I had put Bryndis on speed-dial, so within seconds I was telling her I'd managed to hook up with the birders who had been at Vik at the time of Simon Parr's murder. I also told her about my fabricated friendship with Dawn.

"You work fast," Bryndis said, admiration in her voice.

"I try. How's Ragnar? Have you been able to speak with him since his arrest?"

Trying hard to control the hitch in her voice, Bryndis said, "Yes, and he is doing as well as can be expected, considering he is under suspicion of murder. Regardless of that rough-tough persona, he is a sensitive man." Were those sniffles I heard? "You have to help him!"

"I'm doing the best I can, Bryndis. I plan on talking to as many of the other birders as I can this afternoon, but this evening I should drive back to Reykjavik."

"Why? You need to stay with those people and…"

"Remember, Simon Parr's widow has a signing at your friend's bookstore tomorrow, and that may be my one and only chance to talk to her. That is, if Elizabeth St. John isn't mobbed by too many fans, and if she'll actually consent to having a conversation with me. I can rejoin the birders on their next stop tomorrow, which is…" I searched my memory. "Gull…Gulls something."

"Gullfoss? The waterfall?"

"Yeah, that's it. I looked it up and it's not that far from Reykjavik, so depending on how long St. John will talk to me—if she does at all—I can meet them at the waterfall after the signing since it doesn't get dark until almost ten."

"I would rather you stay there tonight and find out everything you can and drive back tomorrow. Her signing is not until six." The desperation in her voice was almost painful to hear.

"But I need to spend more time with Magnus. It's the main reason I'm here."

"Magnus is fine. He does not like quarantine much, but he will perk up when he is released into that nice new exhibit at your zoo. Right now we are babying him as much as possible. He is so desperate for attention it is obvious he misses his mama." She lowered her voice to a whisper, as if afraid the cub was listening. "She probably drowned, you know. What with the disappearing ice and the bears having to swim so far without rest, a lot of carcasses have been washing up around Húsavik and Raufarhofn."

I winced. The image of hungry polar bears swimming for miles and miles until they sank beneath the waves was horrible to contemplate, but it dissolved as the door to the museum opened and the birders streamed out into the sunlight.

Ben Talley spotted me before I could disconnect. "You must be one of those people who're addicted to their phones."

While keeping the line open, I forced a laugh. "Just calling a pal at the Reykjavik Zoo."

"You have interesting friends in interesting places."

Was it my imagination, or did I see suspicion in his flint-gray eyes? I gave Bryndis a quick farewell and killed the call.

"I've been bunking with her since I arrived," I told Ben. "She's working with a polar bear cub that's being transported to California." While we walked back to Oddi's van, I kept up a running commentary on Magnus and the difficulty in moving animals between zoos, hoping to deflect his attention away from my fictionalized life in San Francisco. "Besides the disruption to the poor animal," I finished up, "you wouldn't believe the amount of red tape involved in the process."

Unlike the other Geronimos filing around us toward the van, Dawn's husband had listened to my rambling monologue with interest. "Sounds like a zookeeper's life isn't as idyllic as I'd believed. But being around all those magnificent animals must make it worth it."

"Oh, it does." What a relief to be finally able to tell the truth.

Oddi drove us back to the hotel, where we picked up a sulking Dawn, then set off toward the Snaefellsjökull glacier. Ben ushered Dawn into the back of the van, leaving me sitting toward the front, close to Perry Walsh, his wife, Enid, and Tab Cooper, the young man I'd seen Lucinda's daughter talking to earlier. Tab kept us entertained during the drive by teasing the group's new president that he was so old he'd birded with Audubon.

"Don't lie, Perry," Tab said, straightening his shirt's already-perfect collar while we drove toward a range of mountains to the west. "I know you helped Audubon identify the ivory-billed woodpecker."

Perry didn't mind the teasing and actually played off it.

"Since you've discovered my little secret, that I'm an immortal masquerading as human," Perry said, with a wink toward me, "I might as well fess up to the rest. I once netted him a couple of passenger pigeons and a slender-billed grackle."

"I was with him at the time," Enid Walsh said, gleefully joining the conversation. "And I once made a try for a great auk but it waddled away so fast it escaped. They were speedier than they looked."

Enid tapped me lightly on the shoulder. "And what extinct species have you seen, Teddy? Not many, I'll bet, you're so young."

Taking up the challenge, I played along. "Carolina parakeet."

She nodded in approval. "Last known specimen died in 1918 at the Cincinnati Zoo. So you do know your birds! After hearing some of Dawn's blather, there was some doubt about that."

"Really? Yes, I'm a 'mainly mammals' zookeeper and don't

have your depth of avian knowledge, but some of my finest friends are feathered."

The Walshes tested me with a game of Name That Bird all the way to Snaefellsjökull, and thanks to the Gunn Zoo's big aviary and my habit of watching *Animal Planet*, I scored a reputable seventy-five percent. By the time we exited the van, I had regained some of my lost credibility. However, I reminded myself to catch Dawn alone soon and deliver a stern warning.

Snaefellsjökull, a dormant volcano covered by a glacier, was described in Jules Verne's *Journey to the Centre of the Earth* as the portal to Middle Earth, but the path to the summit was steep and dangerous, even with the proper equipment. After allowing the birders to take a multitude of photos of its menacing beauty, Oddi, who had no doubt ascended many an ice-capped volcano in his time, explained we would skip the five thousand-foot climb and keep to the safer trails at its base. Not surprisingly, no one argued.

Eagles flew above us as we began our hike, and it would have been a perfect outing except for Dawn's lack of common sense. Having ignored her husband's instructions to wear sturdy hiking boots, she wore strappy leather sandals, and before we'd gone less than a hundred yards along an easy trail, her whines could no longer be ignored. After a short discussion, Ben half-carried, half led her back to the van with me following, happy for the chance to talk to her without the others listening in.

She bid a sullen goodbye as Ben hurried to catch up with the others. "He should have stayed and kept me company," she complained.

Not wasting any time, I said, "Dawn, you need to quit talking so much about our supposed childhood together."

Her perfectly-shaped mouth made a perfect O. "But I need to convince everyone we're longtime friends. That's what you said to do, right?"

"You're getting it all wrong, and so some of them have stopped believing a word you've said."

"Like who?"

"Like your husband, for one. Then Lucinda Graves, second, and even the Walshes."

Those startling green eyes went saucer-big, feigning a naiveté it was obvious she didn't have. It wasn't attractive. "I'm only trying to help, Teddy."

"Then stop trying. Stop discussing me. Stop discussing our so-called shared childhood. The next time someone asks about it, deflect their curiosity by moving to a different subject. Or have you changed your mind about wanting me to help Ben?"

She returned to her earlier sulks. At least they weren't an act. "No, I haven't changed my mind. Regardless of how it looks, with Ben always arguing about something with Simon, he's probably not capable of murder."

Probably not? "Good to know. By the way, what happened to your husband's face, if you don't mind me asking?"

"Car accident." She said it with a total lack of sympathy.

I wondered when she'd started hating her husband. After he'd coaxed her into having an affair with Simon Parr, or before?

Leaving her to her sulks, I slid open the van's door and stepped outside. The Geronimos were long out of sight, but that didn't mean I couldn't take in some of the scenery. I wandered down one of the well-marked trails to an expanse of odd lava formations that reinforced Icelanders' belief in the gnome-like Hidden People. At a distance, a double mound—one large, one small—could easily have been mistaken for a mother leaning over to tend to her child. Another could have been an old man walking with a cane. Still another looked like a troll lying in wait for unwary hikers.

I took out my phone and snapped some pictures. As I was about to put it back into my pocket, a slight movement at the side of one of the formations caught my attention. Looking more closely, I saw that what I had earlier mistaken for a small lump of lava was in actuality a juvenile Icelandic fox, its dark gray coat almost the same color as the rocks.

The fox stared at me, pointed nose quivering as it took in my scent. I stared back, desperately wanting to ruffle its soft fur, breathe in its warm breath.

Instead, as the fox tentatively approached, I reached down and grabbed a small piece of lava. With a shout, I threw the rock close enough to alarm the fox but not close enough to hit him.

The fox scampered off, cutting a zigzag path between lava formations.

Mission accomplished.

Here's the problem with "friendly" wild animals. If a species known for its reclusiveness—such as the Icelandic fox—suddenly appears friendly, it might be sick. Sick, as in rabies. But if the animal isn't sick and still wants to come close, it has learned to equate human beings with food, never a good idea. Back in the States, bears have been known to attack campers in their tents, lured there by the smell of food. Some of the campers wound up dead, a tragedy repeated almost yearly at parks like Yosemite and Yellowstone. If caught, the bears responsible for human deaths were always euthanized.

Given its small size, the Icelandic fox presented no great danger, except to itself. And here's why. Some humans, most of them meaning no harm, like to befriend small, cuddly-looking animals, partially taming them with food and gentle voices. This seeming kindness signs the animals' death warrant. Because there's nothing a hunter appreciates more than an animal that won't flee when encountering a human.

Thus the shout. Thus the rock.

A little more than an hour later, the birders trickled back, tired but happy.

"We saw some lovely birds," Enid said, climbing into the van with her husband. "And eagles all over the place."

"Not to mention a boatload of varietals," Perry said. "A pair of bramlings, a whinchat, and a yellow-browed warbler."

"Don't forget the coup of the day, Perry," said Lucinda, her usual waspish expression relaxed into a smile. "The sanderling! Bold as brass, standing right there on that lava outcropping as if he owned the thing." Her smile vanished when she turned to Dawn. "And how are your feet, dear?" She sounded like she didn't care if Dawn's feet fell off.

"I'll live. I guess."

"See that you do!" Lucinda snapped. "We don't need another fatality on this trip."

The other birders gasped. Ben Talley, who sat next to his wife, looked thunderous. "That's a bit insensitive, Lucinda, considering what happened at Vik. I thought we'd agreed not to talk about that."

"Well, your wife…"

With an alarmed look on his face, Perry intervened. "Now, now, folks" he soothed. "Let's not squabble. I'm sure Simon wouldn't have wanted that."

The mention of Vik had changed the atmosphere in the van, and little more was said on the way back to Stykkishólmur.

Fortunately, everyone's raw nerves had eased by dinner and the conversation proved less testy. Of course, the calmer atmosphere might have been the result of Dawn—still sulking—announcing she wasn't hungry, that she preferred to stay in her hotel room.

My closest table companions were Adele Cobb and Judy, Lucinda's daughter. Adele appeared less depressed than earlier, but a thin veil of sadness still shadowed her face. She had loved Simon Parr, and it showed. Watching her, a thought struck me. That nude picture of her on Parr's camera, when had it been taken? Inspector Haraldsson hadn't given me that information, and there was no time stamp on the printouts, but the fact that Adele's picture was on the same memory card as the hoopoe made me believe Simon had snapped it recently. But that created a puzzle. If Simon had ended his relationship with Adele that night at the Viking Tavern, which was what I believed, when had he dumped Dawn?

The more I thought about it, the more I began to suspect that Simon had given Dawn her walking papers *before* he took the nude picture of Adele, which meant he'd either had two mistresses at the same time, or had exchanged a more beautiful mistress with an older and less attractive one. Despite what Dawn had told me, her drooping butt had nothing to do with their breakup. I also had to wonder if, with two mistresses assigned to the proverbial garbage can, if Simon had already found a replacement.

I looked down the long table and scored each woman's mistress potential. Enid Walsh, Perry's wife, was in her late sixties, and seemed quite fond of her husband, so I counted her out of the running. The age factor didn't work against Lucinda Greaves, who although little older than Adele, was too crabby to warm the cockles of any man's heart, or any other body part. That left Lucinda's daughter, Judy. With her willowy build and honey-colored hair the young yoga instructor was certainly attractive enough, but Simon's death appeared to have made little impact upon her. Then again, she might have been a good actress.

Considering the Geronimos' strictures against talking about the murder, quizzing Judy about a possible relationship with Simon proved difficult, but I was determined to try. My attempt was made easier by the fact that due to the enjoyable afternoon hike, everyone was in a loquacious mood.

"If we'd had crampons on our hiking boots, we could have gone further up the volcano, but we didn't, so Oddi wouldn't let us. Not that I blame him," Judy said. "He doesn't want to lose another…"

"Judy, I thought we all agreed not to talk about Simon," Lucinda said, a warning note in her voice.

"Oh. Right. Sorry. Anyway, the hike was really beautiful. I felt at one with the earth." She sighed happily.

Tab Cooper, who'd seldom strayed far from Judy's side all day, grinned. Either his parents had had the wherewithal to afford him great dental care while he was growing up, or all his perfect teeth were capped. "You're always at one with the earth, Judy."

She blushed so hard her ears turned red. "You would be, too, if you learned how to relax. When we get back to Arizona, why don't you drop by my yoga studio and I'll give you a free lesson?"

"If I relax too much, I won't be able to act. I'm up for a part in a new reality TV series, and if I get it, I'll have to play against type."

"But, Tab, you'd be so much happier!"

"Not in the unemployment line, I wouldn't."

Judy's comment about having a yoga studio surprised me. Given the supposed poor state of her health, I hadn't envisioned her involved in any kind of business. Yoga wasn't my thing, but the more I could get her to open up, the easier it would be to bring up the subject of Simon Parr.

"Why does bending themselves into pretzels help people relax?" I asked.

She rewarded me with a long lecture on the dangers excess cortisol has on the body's immune system, which could be avoided by the healing benefits of something called the para-sympathetic state. Or the parasympathetic system. Despite my science degree, I couldn't understand a word she said. As far as I was concerned, she could have been speaking Old Norse.

"Fascinating," I said. I was getting pretty good at lying, these days. "But tell me, besides this trip to Iceland, what other birding adventures have you and your mother gone on?"

"Cape May, New Jersey, lots of migrating seabirds there. Then Florida, for the swamp-waders. But this is the first time we've ever left the States."

"Not the last, I'll bet." I glanced down the table and saw Lucinda watching me.

"And after Iceland, anything else would be a come-down," Judy continued. "We flew first class, our hotel in Reykjavik is a five star hotel, Oddi's the most perfect tour guide imaginable…"

At this, Tab theatrically cleared his throat. "Careful there, or I'll get jealous."

Judy giggled and another flush rose to her cheeks. She was so rosy I found it difficult to believe she had any health problems at all. Maybe living with Lucinda interfered with her parasym-pathetic system, whatever that was, and being in Iceland had realigned it. Or was it chakras that got realigned?

"Oddi is nice," I said, glancing over at him. The big Icelander had been chatting up the Walshes, but was now speaking to Lucinda. Good. Once he turned her attention away from me, I had my chance.

"First class all the way," I said to Judy. "That's really something. Simon must have been a wonderful person to do something like that for his friends. I wish I'd known him."

At the mention of the forbidden name, Judy's smile dimmed for a moment, but she recovered quickly. "Wonderful, yes, and I'll always be grateful to him. This is truly the trip of a lifetime. But...but it's so horrible, what happened. Who could have done such an awful thing?"

"Some hunter who's too scared to come forward, I'll bet," Tab interjected. "It happens all the time."

"Not in Iceland," I said.

He shrugged. "People are people, wherever they are."

"How well did you know Simon?" I asked.

"My father was briefly in business with him."

It occurred to me then that I didn't know what Simon had done for a living. "What business was that?"

"He ran an accounting firm, nothing big. They dissolved the partnership not long after he married Elizabeth, so Dad signed on with a bigger outfit."

"Simon wanted to strike out on his own?"

Tab shook his head. "He began managing Elizabeth's career full time. To hear him tell it, her career was going nowhere until he took over. Next thing you know, she was on the best-seller list. When it came to business, Simon was one sharp guy."

"Simon was kind of cute, too, what with those sideburns," Judy said.

"Judy!"

Lucinda's voice rang out, so much so that several other diners in the restaurant stared at her. She didn't care. "We don't talk about that, remember?"

Caught using the forbidden name, Judy blushed. "Sorry, Mother."

Before I could steer the conversation toward a Lucinda-approved topic, we heard a commotion at the other end of the table. Then Dawn rushed past, her face pale.

Judy stood as if ready to go after her, but Lucinda motioned her back down. "Ignore her. She's after attention again."

Dawn's distress looked genuine to me. After throwing down enough Icelandic krona to pay my bill, I excused myself and hurried after her. I caught up with her in the foyer of the hotel.

"What's wrong, Dawn?"

"Everything." She strong-armed me aside and ran toward the stairs, while Leifur and the rest of the hotel staff looked on in alarm.

Taking the stairs two at a time, I reached her as she entered her room. "Maybe I can help. That's what you wanted me to do, remember."

"Not with this. But…But…" She took in a big gulp of air, which appeared to calm her. "There's something important I need to…But not now. I'll tell you tomorrow."

She closed the door in my face.

Sighing, I walked downstairs and approached the reception desk.

"Your friend, is she all right?" Leifur asked, concern in his voice.

"Dawn's fine. She…" *Involved in a murder case? Unhappily married?* Opting for diplomacy, I said, "Just a migraine."

"Ah. Then she will feel better in the morning. Our guests always find Stykkishólmur's clear air quite healing."

After agreeing that the air in Stykkishólmur was most definitely clear, I started to turn away, then stopped. I'd planned on driving back to Reykjavik this evening, but Dawn's promise to tell me something important tomorrow made me change my mind. If possible, I could spend the night here, talk to Dawn over breakfast, then make it back to Reykjavik in plenty of time to work with the polar bear cub before heading to the bookstore to talk to Simon Parr's widow.

"Do you by any chance have another room available, Leifur?"

He replied in the affirmative, and after scanning my credit card, escorted me up to a small but beautifully appointed room on the second floor. "We are known for having the most comfortable beds in Iceland," he said, "so you are assured of a good night's sleep. But just in case, you are welcome to borrow any of the books from our library." Noting my lack of luggage, he went on to inform me that Hótel Egilsen also kept a stock of emergency toiletries, and if I needed access to a computer, the hotel could even loan me an iPad. "We have a strong Wi-Fi signal," he finished.

Since I'd brought along my laptop, borrowing a hotel iPad wasn't necessary, but following Leifur's suggestion, after I'd fetched the laptop from Bryndis' Volvo, I availed myself of a battered copy of *Njál's Saga,* written in English. I'd forgotten my new copy back at Bryndis' apartment, and was eager to start it. Considering the fact that the ninth-century Icelander wound up being burned alive as the result of a blood feud, it promised to be an exciting read. Not that I would have time to finish the book.

Once settled into my room, I called Bryndis to tell her I was following up a promising lead in the case, and that I'd return to Reykjavic early the next morning. Then I cranked up the laptop and got to work, searching for any mention of the individual members of the Geronimo County Birding Association. The first hit was for the original article I'd found—"Powerball Winner Treats Birders to Iceland"—but when I typed in the birders' names, other interesting newspaper articles popped up.

For starters, Benjamin Talley, Dawn's husband, he of the Talley Restaurants chain, had a prison record. Ten years earlier, he had been convicted of vehicular homicide after his car ran a red light and hit a man in the pedestrian crossing. According to the article, Talley swerved at the last second and rammed his classic 1972 Corvette into a utility pole, but not soon enough to spare eighty-three-year-old Douglas Grey Hillman, who died on the way to the hospital. When Tally regained consciousness the next day—he'd hit the light pole going one-ten in a forty-five mile zone and was hurled through the windshield—he claimed not to remember a thing. He was sentenced to eight years. Due to good behavior and an even better criminal attorney, he wound up serving only a year and a half.

During Talley's incarceration, a fight with his cell mate added to the mess the trip through the Corvette's windshield had made of his face. According to another article, the cell mate—one James Edward Petovski—subsequently won a one-point-two million-dollar civil lawsuit against Talley for damages received to his own face during the fight.

Talley wasn't the only Geronimo with an eyebrow-raising past.

Of all people, charming old Perry Walsh and his equally charming wife Enid had narrowly escaped a fraud conviction in a scam revolving around fake gemstones. In charges brought against them and other franchisees of Hope Diamond Enterprises, they successfully convinced the jury they were unaware that the "gemstones" shipped to their customers were zircons, not diamonds.

Nothing on crotchety Lucinda Greaves, but her daughter Judy had once been arrested and fined for breaking someone's car window with a rock. As for Adele Cobb, Simon's ex-mistress, she had once been arrested for stalking.

If people realized how easy the Internet made it to find out their peccadilloes, maybe they'd behave better. The only people who emerged from my online snooping as prospective saints were the murder victim; writer Elizabeth St. John, his widow; ex-model Dawn Talley; and actor Tab Cooper.

I never felt good about prying into other people's dirty secrets, so after shutting down the laptop I took a long, hot shower to wash off my guilt. It didn't work. Still feeling sleazy, I crawled into bed. Leifur had told the truth; the bed was amazingly comfortable. Not yet ready to go to sleep, I opened up *Njál's Saga* and began to read. I had reached the part where wise Njál was warning his friend Gunnarr about the perils of bigamy when I fell asleep.

A little after two a.m. someone pounding on my door pulled me out of a dream where I'd been climbing a glacier only to have a volcano erupt beneath me.

"Teddy! Teddy, wake up!" A man's voice.

After pulling the hotel's fleecy white robe around me, I staggered to the door and opened it to find Ben Talley, his scarred face twisted in concern.

"Is Dawn with you?" Coming from him, it sounded more like a demand than a question.

"Huh? Dawn? She was at…" She was at dinner, I was about to say, but he interrupted me.

"She's gone!"

"Gone? Gone where?" Fuzzy-headed from sleep, I couldn't understand why he was bothering me at this hour.

He shoved me aside and barged past me into my room. While I stood in the doorway staring, he searched the bathroom, the closet, then squatted down and looked under the bed.

"Ben, what the hell are you…?"

"I thought…I thought…" Whatever he'd been about to say ended in a low moan.

My brain finally clear, I asked the obvious. "Did you two have a fight or something?" Which would come as no surprise, since according to Dawn, they were already headed to the divorce courts.

He stood up, apparently not caring that one of his pants legs remained crumpled at knee-length. He wasn't wearing socks. "No fight. She…she…at ten, she told me she was going out for a walk. But she never came back."

Chapter Twelve

Once Leifur was certain Dawn was nowhere on hotel premises, he and Oddi organized a hasty search party composed of hotel guests and nearby townsfolk, since Stykkishólmur was too small to have a police outpost. For the next couple of hours we walked the dark streets calling out her name. By the time the sun rose, the size of our search party had quadrupled, with more of the townsfolk and fishermen joining in. At no point did anyone articulate what some of us were thinking.

The night had been cold and the water in the harbor—less than two hundred miles south of the Arctic Circle—was even colder.

If Dawn had been foolish enough to walk along the narrow causeway in the dark to the tiny island of Súgandisey, she might have slipped and fallen into the harbor. Then the tide…Well, there was no point in thinking the worst. I hoped we would find her hunkered down somewhere warm, enjoying the drama she'd purposely created.

But by six, we'd found no sign of Dawn so I called Bryndis and alerted her to the situation. Shortly after I ended our conversation, several policemen arrived to organize the search in a more effective manner. With my services no longer needed, I exchanged cell phone numbers with Perry Walsh and Adele. Both promised to keep me updated. Then I checked out of the hotel and headed for Reykjavik.

The sun shone all the way, and I made the trip in what had to be record time. But when I entered Bryndis' apartment, Ragnar was exiting the bedroom, buttoning up his shirt. Before I could censor my mouth, it blurted, "Aren't you supposed to be in jail?"

Ragnar gave me a puzzled look. "Why?"

"Because you were…" I couldn't quite bring myself to say "arrested."

Bryndis appeared behind him, wearing a surprisingly feminine pink robe. "Oh, Teddy, forget everything you've seen on American TV. In Iceland, the police can't hold a suspect more than twenty-four hours unless they prove to a magistrate they have enough evidence to convict, which of course isn't the case here. Because Ragnar didn't kill anyone."

Using her vast knowledge of American law gleaned from watching reruns of *Monk* and *Criminal Minds,* Bryndis explained the major difference between her country's judicial procedures and the U.S.'s. Any suspect of a crime, even murder, could be picked up and questioned, but once that was accomplished, he was automatically released without bail. The concept of bail didn't exist in Iceland. Later, if enough physical evidence was found that would render a guilty verdict probable, the suspect would be re-arrested and kept in a cell until the trial.

"Ragnar's still under suspicion, then?" I asked, as I followed the two into the kitchen, where, after we'd settled ourselves at the table, Bryndis poured out big mugs of hot tea.

She nodded. "Only because he was in the wrong place at the wrong time. Say, is there any news the news on that missing woman?"

I shook my head. "When I stopped for gas, I called Perry Walsh, he's the president of the birding club, but he said she hasn't been found yet." Suddenly remembering Ragnar's painting of the puffin with the white streak across its head, I said to him, "Wait a minute, Ragnar. Did Bryndis just say you were in Vik when Simon Parr was murdered?"

He averted his eyes. "Um, yes. I heard about the hoopoe sighting and drove down there first thing that morning. I only stayed for about an hour, so when it did not show up, I came back. While I was there, I did not see any dead man."

I noticed that he'd averted his eyes when adding that last part.

"But Reykjavic to Vik, that's almost a three-hour drive," I said. "Each way. You're telling me you drove all the way to Vik looking for the hoopoe, and only stayed for one hour?" It wasn't unusual for dedicated birders sometimes to lie in wait for days hoping to catch a glimpse of their quarry, but this was a stretch.

"Well, I, hmm, I had to hurry back and get some canvases ready for my upcoming show. Artists have deadlines, too, you know."

Bryndis looked at him as if had delivered the Sermon on the Mount. Nodding, she said, "He swears he was back in Reykjavik long before the murder happened," she said. "Hours before." When she caught me staring at her, she added, "And I am certain the situation with the missing woman will turn out to be a misunderstanding. Iceland is a safe country. We do not murder tourists!"

There being nothing to say to that, I concentrated on my tea. It hinted of flowers and fire.

At nine-thirty, I arrived at the zoo with Bryndis. Putting my concern for Dawn aside, I made a beeline for Magnus. When I entered the quarantine shed, the cub looked up at me with his big dark eyes and squealed a hello. Lonely. He hadn't yet finished eating, so the zookeeper feeding him moved aside to let me hold the cub's bottle of fat-enriched milk. Still cuddle-sized, and only slightly gamey, the little bear squirmed around on my lap for a minute before snatching away the bottle with both paws.

"Delicious, huh?" I asked him.

Grunt. Slurp.

One of the reasons I like animals is because they are so uncomplicated. Eat, poop, sleep, play, mate—that was the sum total of their existence. Animals didn't muddle their lives with plotting and planning or dreaming of vengeance and murder. They killed for food or territory, but without malice.

"Teddy loves you, Magnus," I whispered, once the other zookeeper exited the shed.

Grunt. Slurp.

"Do you love Teddy back?"

Grunt. Slurp.

Although no great conversationalist, Magnus enjoyed being cuddled as he fed, so we spent a happy few minutes together until he finally batted his bottle away.

"Finished?"

Grunt. Belch.

I knew what was coming next, so I gently rolled him off my lap and moved away as he trundled into a corner, squatted, and defecated.

"Good bear!" I praised, picking up a pooper-scooper. "So neat! So tidy!"

Big black eyes blinked at me while I worked. Once he nosed at my leg, but since it didn't seem to be the source of any more food—he was too inexperienced to know that humans are yummy—he wandered away and began playing with his Boomer Ball.

Puffins Sigurd and Jodisi were nesting quietly in another quarantine shed near Magnus'. They'd been given an old cat carrier partially covered by a thick rug which mimicked one of the underground burrows I'd seen at Vik. As I approached, Jodisi stuck out her white-streaked head, stared at me warily for a moment, then went back to sleep. Her mate never roused at all.

My next stop was at the foxes' enclosure, where Loki and Freya were busy entertaining each other playing Attack, a common fox game which involved pouncing, biting, and rolling around in a two-fox bundle of fur. They yipped and snarled, and were having a grand old time. Once, at the end of a roll, Sigurd looked up at me, curiosity and intelligence radiating from his eyes and in that instance, I recognized the same curiosity accorded me by the wild fox near Snaefellsjökull.

People who believe animals have no souls have never looked into their eyes.

Deciding that I was no threat, Sigurd dismissed me and nipped at Ilsa's tail. She returned the favor.

I spent the rest of the day helping Bryndis with various tasks around the zoo. In between cleaning out one enclosure after another, I pestered Perry Walsh and Adele for news about Dawn, who by early afternoon, hadn't yet been found. Ben denied the two had fought, but I suspected he was lying. Given his history, I wouldn't have put it beyond him to say something so hurtful that she'd decided to travel back to the U.S. on her own. I consoled myself with the belief that a woman as beautiful as Dawn would have had no trouble hitching a ride from a helpful Icelander. The airport at Keflavik offered several U.S.-bound flights per day, and all she needed was a passport and a credit card.

I refused to ruin the rest of my day worrying about a woman who might already be buckling her seatbelt in preparation for a landing at Sky Harbor Airport in Phoenix. Shaking her out of my head, I headed over to the quarantine shed to give Magnus another bottle feeding.

At five, Bryndis and I returned to her apartment to clean up. Knowing how eager she was to see Ragnar, I turned down her offer for a ride, and instead, enjoyed a leisurely walk to the bookstore to see Elizabeth St. John.

The streets of midtown Reykjavik were surprisingly crowded for a Sunday, but I enjoyed the walk, weaving my way through window-shoppers, tourists, and sidewalk musicians. I had been concerned that given Elizabeth St. John's popularity the store would be so crowded with her fans that getting close enough for a conversation might prove impossible. That turned out not to be the case. If anything, the bookstore was less crowded than it had been the day Bryndis and had I visited, and Kristin, the store manager, looked concerned. Especially since some of the attendees seemed more interested in the refreshments she had laid out than they did in availing themselves of one of St. John's books. After buying a copy of *Tahiti Passion* for the author to autograph and helping myself to cheese and crackers, I was still able to find a seat in the first row.

At six on the dot Simon Parr's widow emerged from the back room and stepped onto the podium. With her long raven hair, she was still attractive, but those unusual dark blue eyes were reddened, and the ravages of grief made her appear far older than the photograph on the back of her book. Her designer dress, a blue Anotonio Berardi, hung on her as if she'd lost weight since its purchase, and her makeup looked hurried. A slash of coral lipstick accentuated her pallor, and clumpings of lashes caked in black mascara flaked onto her unrouged cheeks. When she adjusted her lapel mike with a shaking hand, I saw that her fingernails were bitten to the quick. I doubted she would make it through her talk.

Kristin introduced her to the audience, giving a brief summary of the author's accomplishments, but making no mention of the recent tragedy. She ended with, "Now here she is! Elizabeth St. John, the fabulous creator of the best-selling Jade L'Amour books!" Then she stepped away and let the writer take over.

Despite my misgivings, St. John's voice was strong as she spoke, although while giving the history of her fictional heroine, every now and then she appeared to lose her train of thought. Once she even misidentified the location of her latest book as Samoa instead of Tahiti, and found herself being corrected by a woman in the audience.

She tried to laugh it off. "Oh, well, Jade has conducted archaeological digs in so many different countries that I sometimes forget where she is! But as I was saying, in *Tahiti Passion*—not *Samoan* passion—Jade finally meets the man she thinks is the love of her life. Dr. Lance Everington runs a free vaccination clinic for the island's at-risk children, but as those of you who have already read *Tahiti Passion* know, he has a dark and tortured past."

I looked around and saw a chorus of nodding heads. The crowd was small but warm and enthusiastic. No matter how often the author bumbled and misspoke, they gave her a standing ovation when she finished, then lined up to get their books signed and personalized. I positioned myself at the end of the line. The short wait proved convenient, because when I handed her my copy, I had figured out the best way to start the conversation.

"Just make the personalization read, 'To Teddy Bentley, a fellow birder,'" I said, handing over my copy.

She gave me a startled look, then added my requested personalization above a flowery signature. When finished, she eyed me quizzically. "A fellow birder, you say? And your name, it sounds familiar." Before I could explain, she continued, "Oh. The article in *The Reykjavik News*. It said that you and another woman were the ones who found...who found..." Her voice, already hoarse from her talk, grated to a stop.

I nodded and told her I was sorry for her loss. "After what you've been through, it took grit to show up today."

"I wouldn't dream of disappointing my fans." Then she stood up, took hold of my arm and pointed me toward the exit. "I want to talk to you, but not here. Not with everyone watching." She shuddered.

After a quick goodbye to Kristin, she led me two streets over to the Hótel Keldur, a brand new glass-and-steel hotel facing the harbor. When we arrived, she guided me through the dramatic black, gray, and white marble lobby into the elevator, and finally to a sleekly appointed suite on the fourth floor. Lit mainly by two tall windows facing the bay, the suite's motif was also black, gray, and white, but like the rest of the elegant hotel, it somehow avoided looking cold.

Elizabeth—she refused to let me call her Mrs. Parr or even Miss St. John—sat me down on a white leather sofa and pulled up a black suede chair across from me. "Coffee or tea?" Her voice, now recovered, was stronger than it had been back at the store.

"I don't..."

"Please let me do this. I have so much to ask you."

"Coffee, then."

"The Keldur makes a lovely cappuccino."

"That'll be fine."

She picked up the phone and ordered two cappuccinos along with two helpings of *lagkaka,* which she explained was a traditional Icelandic cake layered with fruit and cream. She hadn't lost all her weight on that.

I cleared my throat. "Look, I meant to tell you I'm so sorry about your husband and…"

"Yes, yes, you've said that and I'm sure you are, but I have to ask you—how did he look? Had he…?"

She couldn't finish, but I knew what she wanted to know. The same thing Adele had wanted to know: Did Simon suffer before he died?

"He looked peaceful, Elizabeth," I lied. "He never knew what hit him, just died doing what he loved. Looking at birds."

She stared at me for a long time through those red-rimmed eyes, then said, "You'd have told me the same thing if he died in agony, wouldn't you?"

"I'm telling you the truth."

A weak smile. "Writers are good judges of character, Teddy. As such, I have to say that you come across as a woman who would go out of her way to avoid hurting anyone, even if it meant telling a lie."

"I wouldn't. I swear."

The smile grew warmer, giving me a hint of the woman she was when not grieving. "That was your biggest lie yet."

"I…"

We heard a discreet tap on the door. "Room service," a male voice called.

For the next few minutes we concentrated on our cappuccino and *lagkaka*, which was as delicious as described, but when we finished, she launched into a recap of her marriage to Simon Parr. Listening to her was unsettling, but she'd been left alone in her hotel suite for days with no one to talk to except the police, and for the first time in days she had the chance to unburden herself. Grieving people tend to do that in one of two ways: they either sob on your shoulder, or they become loquacious, wanting you to know what a saint their dearly departed had been. Elizabeth was the latter, with one exception. Her husband was no saint, she admitted, and neither was she.

"Ever since that awful Barbara Walters interview, I've been deluged with letters decrying some of the choices we made, but our marriage worked," she said, after giving me a half-hour of the standard biographical material (they'd met at a birding convention, married a year later, tried to have children but failed, traveled the world in search of rare birds, etc.). "It worked because we were able to make accommodations."

"Oh?" I pretended nothing more than slight interest.

"Over the years there were other women, and in my case, a man or two." She looked away, seemingly to study the large black-and-white abstract painting on a charcoal suede-covered wall. "None of our dalliances were serious, and they certainly didn't interfere with our love and respect for each other. If anything, they added to it."

"Ah."

"Compared to the Europeans, Americans are quite backwards on the issue of marriage."

"I've heard that." But I promised myself Joe and I would never wind up "European."

When Elizabeth turned away from the painting, her face had brightened, but her eyes were still red. "Besides, no one could do for me what Simon did. He *made* my career."

"Really?"

"He was a CPA, you know, but after we married, he closed his office, took a few courses in marketing and public relations, and became my business and PR manager. At that time, I was what you would call a mid-list writer, someone who, although enjoying a certain level of success, had never really broken through to the big-time. Simon's attention to detail and talent for research made all the difference. After sitting down and studying the entire *New York Times* best-seller list, he advised me to take Jade, my archaeologist protagonist, away from obscure digs in Wyoming and have her oversee digs in exotic locations like Egypt, Mykonos, and Fiji. And to put more sex in the books. Lots more sex. Even kinky sex, the kinkier the better. When my sales increased exponentially, he talked me into changing publishers. Next thing you know, I moved from mid-list to the *New York Times* best-seller list!" She beamed. "All due to Simon."

"Amazing."

The sorrow returned to her eyes. "Simon was generous in other ways, too. You see this suite?" She waved a hand at the black, gray, and white elegance surrounding her. "First thing he did when he won the Powerball, was plan this tour. He booked everyone into a suite similar to this, and footed the bills for the entire trip." She managed a wobbly smile.

I decided to dare a question. "That's generous, all right. But are you sure you didn't mind about the other women? Most wives would."

She shrugged her bony shoulders. "Oh, Teddy, you're a sweet girl, but you sound so old-fashioned. I'm not 'most wives.' I have my own successful career and my own interests. And my own diversions."

"Ah."

"Besides, Simon was no cad. He made certain the women he got involved with knew it was only a temporary thing. When their relationship had run its course, he ended it like a gentleman."

Like many recently widowed women, Elizabeth was over-romanticizing her husband. Yes, maybe the man had his good points, but each time I saw him in action, he was behaving like a lout. Ergo the scene on the plane, the one in the Viking Tavern with Adele, and the more private dismissal—thank God for small favors—of poor Dawn.

Which reminded me. Hoping Elizabeth would buy into it, I gave her a version of the same story I had told the others, that I'd run into old school friend Dawn at Vik, and joined her yesterday for a bout of bird-watching at Stykkishólmur.

"But now she's missing," I finished.

Elizabeth blinked. "Missing? What do you mean, 'missing'? Wasn't she with the rest of the group?"

"She disappeared sometime during the night, and last time I checked, she still hadn't turned up."

The blood drained from Elizabeth's already pale face.

"My God. That means…" She raised her hand to her mouth, as if trying to keep her next words from spilling out. "That means she was telling the truth. For once."

"I don't understand."

"She…she…"

For a second I thought she might faint dead away—she'd been through so much in such a short time—but showing the same resolve she'd shown at her book signing, she pulled herself together. "It's just that…" She took several deep breaths. "It's… it may be my fault."

"What do you mean?"

A tear streaked down her gaunt cheek. "Last night, Dawn called me just after ten, I think, because the sun had finally set. You've known her a long time, Teddy, so you must know what she's like. She loves drama, so when she called and started in with one of her tall tales, I'm afraid I didn't pay much attention. I humored her and told her to drink something strong or take one of her pills, and get some rest, because everything would look better in the morning. Sometimes that's all it takes to calm her down. That's why I…"

I knew the woman was grieving and that my visit had added to her distress, but I couldn't help being impatient. "Elizabeth, please. What, exactly, did Dawn tell you?"

"She told me someone was trying to kill her."

Chapter Thirteen

I had almost recovered from my shock when we heard another knock at the door.

Elizabeth rushed to answer it, and the next thing I knew, Inspector Thorvaald, all six-foot-five of him, loomed over me, flinty eyes narrowed into slits. "Well, well, Miss Bentley. So we meet again. I could say it is a surprise to see you here, but then I would be lying, would I not?"

"I...I..." My mouth was too dry for me to do anything other than stutter.

Fortunately, Elizabeth's own anxieties took over. Her voice trembled as she plucked at his sleeve. "Inspector, have you figured out who killed Simon?"

Haraldsson's voice gentled. "The investigation is ongoing, Mrs. Parr," he said, using her married name, not her more famous one. When he turned back to me, his voice resumed its former ferocity. "I told you not to get involved in this case."

Thinking fast, I waved my autographed copy of *Tahiti Passion* at him. "I went to Elizabeth's signing, and when she discovered I was into birds, she invited me up here for some..." I looked over at the table. "Some cappuccino. And *lagkaka*. I've never had *lagkaka*, before, so I..."

He waved me silent. "Do not insult me with your fibs. I have only now returned from Stykkishólmur, where I heard all about your so-called interest in birds. As well as your interest in other things, such as who was where and when were they there." His eyes narrowed even further. "Keep it up and I will find a good reason to put you in the Reykjavik city jail."

"No, you won't," I snapped back. "Since I've been here I've learned a little about your legal system and you can't."

"Oh, be quiet." He sounded more exasperated than angry.

Still plucking at his sleeve, Elizabeth entreated, "Tell me what you've found out, Inspector. I need to know who hurt my Simon!"

He gently pried her fingers away. "I am sorry, Mrs. Parr, but as I have said, the investigation is ongoing. Now, please, you ladies take your seats. There is something I must tell you."

"But…"

"Wait, Elizabeth." There had been something about the Inspector's tone and phrasing that raised the hair on my neck. "Why don't we find out why the inspector is here, since it obviously isn't to join us in cappuccino and *lagkaka*."

Elizabeth sat.

Haraldsson remained standing, looming over us like some forbidding Viking stele. He got right to the point. "Mrs. Parr, it pains me to tell you this, but earlier this evening the body of Dawn Talley was discovered floating in the bay."

Elizabeth's face lost all its remaining color. So, I imagine, did mine.

Giving us no time to recover from our shock, he continued, "So, Miss Bentley, I need to ask where you were between ten last night and seven this morning. And you, too, Mrs. Parr."

Elizabeth looked like she was about to faint so to give her time to pull herself together, I answered first. "Inspector, since you were in Stykkishólmur, you must know exactly what I was doing during those times; looking for Dawn, along with everyone else. Now tell me. Was it an accident? Or did she commit…?" I couldn't quite bring myself to say the word: *suicide*.

"She was found underneath a fishing boat, her hair entangled in the propeller. There were abrasions to her head."

"You didn't answer my question, Inspector. Was it an accident?"

He raised his eyebrows. "Our medical people are currently looking into the exact cause of the abrasions, but I am the one who is asking the questions here, not you, Miss Bentley."

"But..."

When Elizabeth finally spoke up, her voice was clogged with grief. "Dawn was my *friend*!"

The inspector's voice gentled again. "So I understand, Mrs. Parr. But I also understand that the relationship between you two was rather complicated, that she and your husband were, ah, involved in an affair. Which is why I must also ask you to tell me where you were between ten last night and seven this morning."

Her grief gave way to anger. "That relationship was over. And I was right here! If you don't believe me, you can check the mileage on my rental car. And its navigation system. It'll prove I've never been anywhere near Sticks...Sticks...what's-its-name."

"Stykkishólmur. I am sure you understand the gravity of the situation, two deaths in four days among the same small group of tourists."

"Of course I understand. But as for what you term a personal involvement between Simon and Dawn, I'd like to remind you this is the twenty-first century. Their affair was brief and meant absolutely nothing. I'm the one Simon always comes home to, and Dawn understands..." Her voice broke as she corrected herself. "...she *understood* that."

Late afternoon light streamed in from the tall windows facing the bay, bathing the stark black and white furnishings in a warm, golden glow, but the warmth didn't extend to Inspector Haraldsson's face. "That is a broad-minded way of thinking."

"Oh, please!" Disgust trumped the sorrow on her face.

"All the same, Mrs. Parr, I would appreciate your stopping by the police station sometime in the next few days to give us a formal statement. Your group is not due to return to the U.S. until Friday, am I correct?"

Elizabeth nodded.

"Excellent. And since you were so good as to bring up the odometer and navigation system on your rental car, yes, I would like my techs to look at it."

"Right now?"

A bland smile. "I will send someone out first thing tomorrow, so please refrain from using it before then. May I have the keys now? I will make certain you get them back."

Looking perplexed, Elizabeth disappeared into the bedroom, and when she returned, two sets of car keys were in her hand. After giving them up, she said, "I'd appreciate it if they're returned as early as possible. Except for my signing at the bookstore today, I've been cooped up in the hotel since Simon was…since Simon died, and I'm not sure I can take the isolation anymore. I need to be with my friends. I was thinking about driving to Gullfoss tomorrow, where the tour is scheduled to be next. Unless they've changed their plans, that is." As if suddenly exhausted, she resumed her seat on the leather sofa and picked up the iPhone resting on the chrome and class end table. "I'd better call and find out."

"What time did you plan to leave?"

"Before noon."

"The techs will have been here and gone by then, and you will have your keys back. I can also save you that phone call. When I was at Stykkishólmur, I spoke to Mr. Perry Walsh, who I understand is the president of the group. He told me that everyone had voted to continue the tour, that they were certain Mr. Parr would have wanted it that way. So! You will enjoy Gullfoss, Mrs. Parr. The waterfall is spectacular. And I hope you will see many pretty birds."

When Haraldsson turned to me, his voice could have dropped the suite's temperature by at least twenty degrees. "As for you, Miss Bentley, I repeat my warning. Pay more attention to your own business, which, I understand, is a polar bear cub named Magnus, not an Icelandic homicide investigation."

With that he left, closing the door softly behind him.

"What an interesting man," Elizabeth said, rising from the sofa. "Maybe I'll write him into my next book. Jade would go crazy for him. In the meantime, how about another slice of *lagkaka*?"

Although her voice was steady, her hands trembled. In four days she had not only lost her husband, but also a friend, and I could only imagine how she felt. Anxious to return to the comparative peace of Bryndis' apartment, I turned down the cake and announced my own departure.

Before I reached the door, something occurred to me. "Elizabeth? Why didn't you tell Inspector Haraldsson about the phone call."

"Mmph?" Her mouth was full of *lagkaka*. She swallowed, then said, "What phone call? You mean the one I started to make to Perry Walsh? The inspector said…"

"No, the phone call you got from Dawn last night, saying she was afraid someone was trying to kill her."

With that, Elizabeth looked at her plate of *lagkaka* as if it had been poisoned.

Bryndis had told me she would be spending the night at Ragnar's, so I was left alone in the apartment on Baldursbrá. In order to distract myself from the distressing events of the past few days, I watched a few television programs, including an Icelandic soap opera with English subtitles. A handsome young man from Akureyri had moved to Reykjavik, angering his sheep-farming family who'd wanted him to take over the family business, but delighting his Reykjavik girlfriend, a sculptor, whose parents weren't thrilled about their talented daughter dating a mere sheep farmer. I watched long enough to realize that—except for the lack of heavy makeup and neuroses—Icelandic soap operas were no different than their American brethren. Bored, I picked up Elizabeth's book and began to read.

To my surprise, I found myself fascinated by the adventures of Jade L'Amour. By the eighth chapter, the plucky archaeologist had saved a child from drowning in a tsunami, been clubbed over the head by an irate village shaman, and had fallen down a hidden well, all of which played merry hell with the Zac Posen evening dress she'd worn to a diplomatic reception an hour earlier.

Using her impressive martial arts skills Jade had also disarmed a knife-wielding art smuggler, hot-wired his treasures-packed van to escape the lava flow from an erupting volcano, romped through a passionate night with a French diplomat, and uncovered a relic at her dig the next morning that proved the Vikings had visited Tahiti in the early tenth century. It was only when I reached chapter eleven, which took place during a fire walk, that I remembered something odd.

Benjamin Talley had woken up everyone at hotel at two in the morning, panicked that his wife had left for a walk at ten and hadn't returned.

He'd never explained why it took him four hours to sound the alarm.

Chapter Fourteen

The next morning, I informed Bryndis that my plans for the next few days were complicated enough for me to need my own car. She argued, of course, insisting that she could always find a ride back and forth to the zoo, but I put my foot down, pointing out she had been generous enough.

"I might be gone for a couple of nights, and you shouldn't have to scramble at the last minute to find rides."

She grumbled some, then gave in and told me the name of a car rental place. An hour later, I was following her to the zoo in a brand new Volvo, this one a bright red, the better to find it in a snow bank—if there'd been any snow.

Magnus appeared thrilled to see me, but I suspected the little bear would be thrilled to see anyone who arrived with food. He burrowed through his breakfast, grunting and smacking his lips. After he'd finished his meal of fortified milk and fresh fish, I spent the rest of the morning caring for the foxes and the puffins. Skipping lunch, I bade farewell to Bryndis and the other zookeepers and headed for Gullfoss. The waterfalls were approximately seventy miles from Reykjavik, so I arrived at the bend of the glacier-fed Hvítá River around two.

When I pulled into the crowded parking area I couldn't see the falls, but I could hear them. The roar was so loud I almost wished I had brought along earplugs. Walking through the parking lot, I spied Oddi's blue van, which meant the Geronimos had already arrived. A few steps further and the famous double falls came into view. To my surprise, they weren't fenced off by safety railings. Apparently Icelanders weren't as litigious as Americans.

The falls were magnificent, but at the same time, terrifying. Set at seemingly impossible right angles to the river itself, they stair-stepped over an avalanche of boulders into a vast canyon before rejoining the lower reaches of the Hvítá. Their almost unearthly beauty was even more enhanced by a double rainbow arching over them. Although I hadn't come here to boggle at scenery, I couldn't help myself, and for several minutes I simply stood there taking in the view, enjoying the caress of the fine mist rising over the cliff edge.

Finally, after being jostled one too many times by enthusiastic tourists flocking around the cliff-edged overlook to snap selfies, I came to my senses and started looking through the crowd for the Geronimos. They were nowhere to be seen. Guessing they had trekked up the hill to the gift shop or cafeteria, I climbed the stairs to the visitors' center.

The Gullfoss Café was a large glassed-in dining hall under a two-story, beamed ceiling. The aroma from a big vat of the cafeteria's famous lamb stew reminded me I hadn't eaten lunch, so I got in line, loaded my tray with soup and big chunks of bread, then wandered through the crowded restaurant until I found the Geronimos ensconced by the window closest to the waterfall. Elizabeth St. John had also beaten me here, but she was too engrossed in a conversation with Adele to notice my entrance.

The moment he spotted me, Perry Walsh invited me to join them.

"Have you heard about Dawn?" he asked, as soon as I'd settled myself at the table.

Since Dawn had supposedly been an old friend, I tried to act more grief-stricken than I was. "I…I only found out yesterday, and it's, well, it's all so horrible. At least I have all those happy memories of her." God, I felt like a hypocrite.

Perry's wife Enid looked so distressed I suspected she'd been crying. "Poor Benjamin, he went back to Reykjavik with her…" She cleared her throat. "With her body. I've never seen a man so complexly undone. Regardless of the trouble those two have had lately, there was never any doubt in my mind he was crazy about her."

"No doubt at all," her husband echoed. "Well, I'm glad you're here, Teddy. Our little group has been dwindling, so it's nice…"

Lucinda interrupted his welcoming words. "Ah, the mysterious zookeeper turns up again," she said, acid dripping from her voice. "Tell me, Miss Bentley, to what do we owe the questionable pleasure of your company?"

Perry's shock rendered him speechless.

Not so Elizabeth St. John, who rose to my defense. "Mind your manners, Lucinda. Teddy was a great friend of Dawn's, and I, for one, don't blame her for not wanting to be alone right now. Grief shared is grief halved."

"Sounds like something from one of your books," Lucinda grumbled, but after a hard stare from Elizabeth, she fell silent.

Judging from their empty plates and bowls, they had been in the cafeteria for a while. I'd eaten nothing but a packet of trail mix before leaving the zoo, so despite the tension at the table, I picked up my spoon and started in. The soup was as delicious as the guidebook promised, and I was so starved that I went back for seconds. When I returned to the table, much of the tension had dissipated, but the sadness remained.

"That poor child," Enid was saying, her old eyes red. "Yes, she was foolish to go walking alone in the dark so I guess we shouldn't be surprised that she slipped and fell into the bay, but oh, what a loss. So young, so beautiful."

"Not quite so young and beautiful anymore," Lucinda ventured, after a nervous look at Elizabeth.

Possibly thinking the same thing, Elizabeth said nothing. After all, Dawn had once been her husband's mistress, and "European" marriage or not, she must have been relieved when Simon sent the former model packing.

Ironically, Adele showed a sympathy similar to Enid's. "Beauty is no guarantee of happiness," she said. "Myself, I wonder if what happened was really an accident."

The table fell silent.

"What do you mean?" I asked, when it because obvious no one else would.

"Dawn and Ben had a big fight last night. I know, because my room was right next to theirs. I couldn't make out what they were yelling about but whatever it was, it was serious enough that she slammed out of the room and took off. Then, when that Inspector Haraldsson asked Ben why she'd gone for a walk alone so late, I heard him say he thought she was getting some exercise, and since Iceland was so safe, he figured he didn't have to worry. He never mentioned the fight."

Elizabeth frowned. "You mean Ben stayed in the room? Didn't go after her?"

"I didn't hear him leave," Adele answered, "so he must have let her go by herself. In retrospect, a big mistake."

But doors weren't always slammed. They could be closed so quietly that the person in the adjoining room might not hear a thing. As it was, Ben's story about that night had been bothering me, too, and I wondered if it had bothered anyone else.

"Adele, did Ben explain why he took four hours before he sounded the alarm?"

She shrugged. "Maybe he did later. The inspector talked to him twice. The first time, Ben was so broken up he wasn't making much sense. The next time the inspector talked to him in his room."

Like me, Elizabeth remained troubled. "Dawn could be a handful, but do you really think Ben would do anything to hurt her?"

Adele looked at her in shock. "That's not what I'm saying! It's just that I think…I think maybe what happened to Dawn wasn't an accident after all, that maybe she committed suicide."

A few minutes later, Oddi, the tour guide, eager to turn the conversation away from murder and suicide, ushered us down the stairs for a final look at the falls. The crowd had thinned somewhat, but the jostling back and forth still worried me, so I positioned myself several feet back from the cliff edge. Not that it made any difference. One heavyset man bustled toward me, apparently intent upon taking a selfie with the falls as backdrop. As he passed, he knocked into me, shoving me closer to the edge than seemed safe. Before I could return to my original position, he swung his camera around, inadvertently slamming his elbow into my head. This final blow tipped my balance and I began to reel backwards. If Elizabeth hadn't grabbed me and pulled me back, I might even have gone over and been smashed on the rocks below.

"Watch what you're doing, you idiot!" she bellowed at the man.

He didn't hear, or pretended not to, and snapped another selfie.

Unnerved, I let Elizabeth lead me to the foot of the stairs. "You okay, Teddy? You're white as a sheet."

I tried to make light of the incident. "Oh, I always look like this when almost falling off a cliff."

"People!" she fumed. "There should be a law against such stupidity. C'mon, let me take you up to my car. I've stashed a flask of tequila in the trunk to help me over the rough spots, and you look like you could use a good belt yourself. It's El Conde Azul Blanco. Potent, but smooth as butter."

Smooth or not, the thought of tequila on top of the lamb soup turned me off. "Thanks, but no thanks. I…"

"What's going on?" It was Lucinda Greaves. She'd left the group and was walking toward the staircase. "You look like a ghost, Teddy."

"Didn't you see?" Elizabeth asked.

"See what? So many people were in the way I could hardly see the waterfall."

"Some fool almost knocked Teddy off the ledge."

A mean look at me. "She must be exaggerating."

"Lucinda, for your information…"

Eager to avoid a catfight, I interrupted. "I've changed my mind, Elizabeth. That shot of tequila sounds terrific."

Maybe the El Conde Azul Blanco was as good as Elizabeth claimed, but after two bowls of lamb soup and a heap of fresh-baked bread, one sip of tequila proved it made a lousy dessert. I was still tasting it when I climbed back into the Volvo. Elizabeth, in a generous mood, had talked me into following them to Haukadalur, famous for its geysers, and even to Thingvellir, whatever that was, the next day.

"Poor Simon shelled out so much money for this trip and the hotel room would only sit empty now that poor Dawn is, ah, no longer with us, and Ben's gone back to Reykjavik. Since you and Dawn were old school friends, I'm sure she'd want you to enjoy yourself."

Yet another person who professed to know the wishes of the dead. Still, I was happy to accept Elizabeth's offer since it furthered my goal of proving Ragnar innocent of Simon's murder.

From Gullfoss, I followed Oddi's van and Elizabeth's leased Mercedes to Haukadalur, where two famous water spouts put America's Old Faithful to shame. The larger one—Great Geysir—had lent its name to similar geysers the world over, but for the past few years, the smaller one, Strokkur, had begun to spout more frequently. After Gullfoss, watching a couple of geysers rise into the air seemed less impressive, so while Oddi and the birders stood around waiting for another eruption, I wandered down the well-marked path that led past numerous geothermal springs, one of them a bright turquoise blue. Given the boiling waters, I found it amusing to see signs warning tourists not to dip their hands in the springs, but the guidebook informed me that every year numerous hand-dunkers had to be treated for burns.

Like most of Iceland's landmarks, no opportunity had been lost in attracting money-bearing tourists. During my walk, I passed a golf course, a museum, a souvenir shop, a clothing store specializing in Icelandic sweaters, a snack shop, a more formal restaurant, and a plethora of signs pointing the way to good fishing spots on the Hvítá River. For the ice-walking crowd, there were directions to the nearby Langjökull glacier.

An hour later, my sight-seeing finished, I caught up with the Geronimos as they were checking into Hótel Geysir, which despite its name, was actually a series of small chalets set alongside the Hvítá.

My room was small but bright and afforded a nice view of the hot springs. Spaced a distance from the others, it gave me more privacy than I'd expected. A good thing, because I had phone calls to make and free Wi-Fi to utilize.

After glancing at my watch, I discovered it was almost six, which meant that it was around ten in the morning in Gunn Landing. Joe always held a conference with his deputies at ten, and the chances were good my mother would be out shopping, so I decided to text everyone. Given my lack of experience with using my phone as a keyboard, I'm a lousy texter, but I was finally able to send off a message. I knew the text might alarm Joe, but it couldn't be helped. He hated it when I snooped around crime scenes, but I hoped he would come through for me if only for the chance to deliver a warning and/or refer me to the proper authorities. I would deal with the fallout when I made it back to Gunn Landing.

PLZ RUN CK ON LUCINDA GREAVES & JUDY MALONE & BENJAMIN TALLEY & TAB COOPER & ADELE COBB & PERRY WALSH & ENID WALSH. ALL LV N GERONIMO COUNTY AZ PSBLE MURDR SUSPCTS BT NO WORIES IM BEING V CARFL & AROUND PEPL ALL TIME. NO SOLO STUF I PROMSE. MUCH LUV & XOXO!

My mother was a different matter. She hated texting but she hated having her shopping interrupted even more.

SRRY NOT CALL EARLIER BUT LVLY TRP 2 GULFOS, BG WATRFAL, NOW GYSIR WIT FRENDS & FMUS WRTR ELIZBT ST JOHN. NO WORIES. ALWYS WEAR BRA & SUNSCRENE & CREAM ON FACE EV NITE. XOXO!

Most of that text was a lie. I can't sleep in a bra, I hate sunscreen, and my freckles are allergic to night cream.

Next up was a text to my boss, Aster Edwina.

TEDDY HERE, MAGNUS A DOLL, EVRYTHNG
OK, THX FOR WONDERFL VACAY.

Romantic, familial, and work-related duties taken care of, I set up the laptop and started typing in last night's events and today's conversations. Only when entering my conversations with Perry Walsh did I remember my old friend Cowgirl Spencer. A real classmate instead of a made-up one, whose parents ran a large Angus cattle ranch a few miles outside Apache Crossing. She had always loved reading Agatha Christie mysteries almost as much as she loved competition. Back in school, she'd been dubbed Cowgirl Spencer not only because of her background, but because she and her horse, Big Mac—yes, we were allowed to board our own horses at Miss Pridewell's Academy—won more blue ribbons than the rest of us put together. I vaguely remembered hearing that after graduation Cowgirl finished up her education at the University of Arizona, married, divorced, and was now running her aging parents' spread.

What was the name of that ranch? I should remember, because we used to make fun of it. Oh, yeah the Lazy S, and teenagers being teenagers, we'd promptly reduced that to its lowest common denominator.

I wondered if, by any chance, Cowgirl had ever run into any of the birders. She didn't seem the birding type, but it was worth a try. And given her love of one-upmanship, if I worded a message in the right way, she might bestir her lazy S enough to help me out. The fact that I had already texted Joe for the same information made no difference; gossip can be more revealing than police records.

A quick search of the Internet brought up the Lazy S website, where I found a picture of Cowgirl Spencer wearing a Stetson and as good-looking as ever, albeit slightly weathered. She must not apply night cream on a regular basis, either.

As with most websites, this one offered a contact button. I clicked on it and wrote an email:

Howdy, Cowgirl!

Theodora Iona Esmerelda Bentley here, emailing you after all these years from the icy reaches of Iceland. Somehow I've gotten myself involved in a murder investigation up here, and remembering how much you love mysteries, I was wondering if you can help me out. Do you know anyone who belongs to the Geronimo County Birding Association? I've looked them up on the Net but can't seem to find out any information at all. You know me—I was never good at that sort of thing.

Big fat lie there, but knowing Cowgirl Spencer, she'd jump at the chance to show me up.

The people I'm most interested in finding out about are Simon Parr, Elizabeth St. John (yes, the famous writer!), Adele Cobb, Benjamin and Dawn Talley (she's a model and used to be known as just "Dawn," you might have seen her picture on the cover of Cosmo), Lucinda Greaves, Judy Malone (she's Lucinda's daughter), Perry & Enid Walsh, and an actor named Tab Cooper. If you know anything about them, especially anything dastardly, email or text me back or give me a call if you're not too busy shoveling manure. My cell number is 1-831-555-7691.

P.S. Even gossip will be appreciated!

Your old Pal,
Freckle Face

After reading the message several times, I hit "send" and returned to my typing. I had finished typing the conversation I'd had with Elizabeth prior to Inspector Haraldsson's appearance when my phone rang the opening bars of "Born Free."

I looked at the phone and saw a 520 area code. Arizona.

I snatched the phone off the bed and answered it. "Freckle Face here. Could that possibly be Cowgirl Spencer, calling me all the way from what she used to refer to as Butt Hole, Arizona?"

A familiar cackle. "Don't forget much, do you, you little snit? Yeah, it's me, and yeah, I'm still living in Butt Hole, but you had me the minute you typed the word 'murder.' So which one of my ex-husband's fine feathered friends did you kill? If you need bail money, count me out. I'm broke. You wouldn't believe how much cows eat. When you emailed, I was online doing my accounts, and believe me, they're not pretty."

I had to smile. "No bail money necessary since I didn't do the deed myself, but did you just say 'fine feathered friends'?"

"You didn't know?" Another cackle. "The ex-Mr. Cowgirl Spencer was a charter member of that stupid birding club, which is one of the many reasons I divorced him. Somehow I'd got it in my mind that he'd help me out with the ranch, but, no, every weekend he took off with those idiots. The day he came home and told me about the breeding habits of the friggin' sandhill crane and started mimicking their pre-coital arias was the day I threw him out."

Well aware of Cowgirl Spencer's irascible temperament, I suspected there was another side to this story, but truth is irrelevant when you're coaxing information from an old friend. I gave her the rundown on what had happened since my arrival in Iceland, beginning with Simon Parr's death and ending with Dawn's.

"Can't say I'm surprised about Dawn," Cowgirl Spencer sighed. "All she ever cared about was money, and not even Ben had enough for her. Hell, there's not a millionaire in the county she didn't go after at one time or another. But Simon! I'm really sorry to hear about that. Weird hair and a bit of a wimp, but a real sweetie. We're all jealous of Elizabeth down here."

I looked at the phone in disbelief. "I'll give you the weird hair, but wimp? Sweetie? Are we talking about the same Simon Parr? I've seen him in action and he was about as far from being a wimp or a sweetie as you can get." I gave her the details of

Simon's loutish behavior on the plane and in the Viking Tavern, finishing with, "The poor woman left in tears."

"Which woman was that?"

"Adele Cobb."

"Oh, yeah, the dark-side-of-forty redhead. A mere case of bad timing there, I figure. Simon always did love his liquor, although I never saw him get mean when he was drinking. If he had, Elizabeth would have done something about it. Strong woman, that. But, yeah, come to think of it, his behavior did start to change after he won all that money, or I might have made a run at him myself! For a fling, you understand, nothing permanent. He'd never leave Elizabeth. She's his meal ticket. Was, anyway. God, the poor woman! She must feel crushed. Those two were so perfect together, almost like honeymooners, they were…they were…" Her voice caught and she snuffled.

I gave her time to blow her nose then steered her back on course. "You thought about having a fling with Simon Parr?" Weathered-looking or not, the naturally blond Cowgirl was total man-bait.

Outside, I could hear one of the geysers spouting again and imagined the patter of droplets as they fell on the roof of my cottage. I was in a country so foreign it might have been another planet, and yet the phone connection was so clear Cowgirl could have been in the next room.

"Why so surprised at the idea of me going after Simon?" she said, recovering. "Freckle Face, it can sure get lonesome out here among the rattlesnakes and lizards, and the word through the Geronimo County Grapevine is that the man had incredible stamina, if you get my drift. Must've been all those long hikes cross country to see the purple-winged nebbish or the fork-tailed flipflop or whatever." Her tone suddenly changed. "Not that it helped Roscoe any."

"Roscoe?"

"My ex. A banker. Don't ever marry one. Once they seal the deal, it's over. I'm thinking about a personal trainer next or a marathon runner, maybe even a boxer. They say boxers are…"

Not wanting to get bogged down in Cowgirl's sexual fantasies, I pretend-sneezed, excused myself, and got back on subject.
"Happy hunting, then, Cowgirl. Now what can you tell me about
the other birders? Dawn's husband Ben, for instance. I found
a newspaper article that he did time for vehicular homicide."

A silence for a moment. Outside, another geyser hissed away.
"Cowgirl?"

Her sigh carried perfectly all the way from Arizona to Iceland.
"Don't believe everything you hear about Ben, Freckle Face. He's
not the one who ran that man down. Everyone knows Dawn
did that. She was driving that night, speeding like crazy, doing
one-ten in a forty-five mile zone. Before the cops arrived on the
scene, Ben made her change seats with him. Not that he had
to do much forcing. Dawn never takes responsibility for her
actions. Er, *took*."

In my experience, the phrase "everyone knows" is often the
prelude to a stint of unfounded gossip, and maybe that's what
I was after, but it didn't sit well with me. Dawn was dead, and
there was nothing to be gained by slandering her memory.

Out of necessity, I controlled my irritation. "Why would he
do such a stupid thing?"

"Because as flighty as Dawn could be, Ben was crazy in love
with her, and he figured—rightly, I must add—that while he
could deal with prison, it would destroy her. No Dior dresses,
no two-hundred-dollar-an-ounce eye cream."

It sounded noble enough, but if true, wouldn't the police have
noticed that the car's windshield was cracked on the passenger's
side, not the driver's? And that Dawn had no injuries? Then I
remembered the faint remnants of a scar on her forehead. The
original injury must have been more expertly repaired than Ben's
face.

"What else do you hear on the Geronimo County Grapevine?" I asked.

Plenty, it turned out. She started with Adele Cobb. "As they
say on the cop shows, no wants, no warrants, as far as I know.
She's a perfectly nice woman. Volunteers at the Geronimo

County Women's Shelter, a homeless pet sanctuary, charitable stuff like that. Oh, and a couple of times she's helped me out with our horses."

"She rides?"

"No, just likes animals. You ought to see her own menagerie—something like seven cats, four dogs, and a Ukrainian-speaking parrot. God only knows how she was able to find a house-sitter to take care of them while she's in Iceland, but I do know that Simon covered the cost."

I'd learned the hard way that someone liking animals doesn't necessarily mean they're pure at heart. Or won't commit murder. "I hear she was arrested once for stalking."

"Sounds like you've got your own little grapevine twining nicely up there in the frozen north. I hate to burst your bubble, Freckle Face, because that so-called stalking incident eventually came to nothing because it wasn't really stalking in the first place. Cops dropped the charges. What had happened was, a couple of teenagers burgled Adele's condo. Some guard dogs those rescues of hers are, huh? Anyway, the kids took her big screen TV and some jewelry Simon had given her. He was always generous to his playmates. Anyway, Adele suspected the neighbors—real punks—were behind the break-in, and decided to play detective on her own.

"The kid's parents, potheads the both of them, caught her following them around, peeping through their window, stuff like that, and were stupid enough to call the cops. Adele was held for a few hours, fingerprinted, had her picture taken, the whole deal, but the upshot of it was that the TV and jewelry mysteriously reappeared on her front porch a few days later. Charges were dropped against everyone, even the punk-ass kids. So, nah, the only thing I can say against Adele is that she fell too hard for Simon. She should have known better. I mean, everyone who knew the man knew that once the thrill was gone, and it always did, he'd go back to Elizabeth."

"Elizabeth told me she and Simon had what she called a 'European marriage,' not that any Europeans I know would agree with that description."

She laughed. "The woman confuses her plots with real life. If it's something her heroine would do, Jadine or Jala some such phony name, Liz would try it, too. And in those books, Jadine screws around with any good-looking guy she comes across."

"Jade. Jade L'Amour is the heroine's name."

A snicker. "You read that trash?"

"Just her recent book."

"Total garbage."

Cowgirl Spencer might have been quick to condemn certain types of literature, but she was quick to pardon the supposed sins of Perry and Enid Walsh. "Those claims that they knowingly sold fake gems? Lies! Those two are as honest as summer days are long. They were suckered by their supplier, which even the most imbecilic jury could see, so if anyone told you they served a day in jail, they're lying. I bought a ring from them, myself, four-carat princess cut, platinum setting. Had it appraised last year, could buy eighty more acres with it, not that I'd want to. God knows I've got enough work on my hands as it is."

She was less charitable toward the acidic Lucinda Greaves. "Horrible woman, everyone knows that."

I nodded, then remembered we were on the phone. "She's unpleasant, all right."

"She has trouble keeping a job, too, because of her mouth. The rumor around here is that she's about to lose her house. As for Judy, her daughter, I tried a couple of yoga classes at her studio and nearly dislocated my shoulder. Never went back. Other than that, I don't know much about her. I did hear from someone that Judy suffers from asthma, but I never saw an inhaler in her studio, so I don't know if it's true. She looked healthy enough to me. Although maybe a bit too thin. 'Course, that might only be jealously on my part, since I'm a bit too *un*-thin."

"Do you know anything about her getting arrested once? For breaking someone's window?"

She made a dismissive sound. "Can't help you there, Freckle Face. When it happened, I was going through my divorce. All I know is that she got arrested and there was some kind of lawsuit. But since I was experiencing my own courtroom drama, I didn't pay much attention."

Swallowing my disappointment, I asked, "Why do Judy and Lucinda have different last names? Is there an ex Mrs. Judy somewhere?"

"Nah, Judy's never been married. But Lucinda's been married three or four times."

I yipped in surprise.

Cowgirl Spencer laughed. "The first unlucky man was Judy's father, hence her last name."

I was still reeling from shock. "How in the world did such a harridan snag so many men?"

"Feminine wiles, m'dear. Lucinda always starts off like Miss Sweetie Pie, but once the ring's on her finger, she reverts to her old self, you know, like a rattlesnake crossed with a scorpion. But none of those guys, even Judy's father, were worth anything. Not in the financial department or the ethics department. For instance, Lucinda's second husband, Jim, he was a commercial real estate broker, supposedly brought in big bucks for a while. Then there was some financial hanky-panky and his license got taken away. And as for the home front, there was a rumor Jim made a move on Judy, and the kid was only thirteen at the time. Lucinda went damn near homicidal over it, took after him with a butcher knife before he could say, 'But, honey, it's not like it looks.'"

My dislike for Lucinda slipped a bit. "Good for her."

"Exatamundo. Even harridans have their good points."

"How about Tab Cooper? Know anything bad about him?" As a zookeeper who spent three-quarters of her waking life up to her knees in muck, I'd grown to be suspicious of anyone who was obsessively neat.

A brief silence, then, "Oh, no real scandals there unless you consider bad acting a crime. He shows up on TV sometimes, either as a walk-on or as some airhead's dim-witted boyfriend, which believe me, is total type-casting because that boy couldn't find his well-pressed bee-hind without a map. But Judy really fell for him. 'Course, she's not the brightest star in the firmament, either, so I guess they're a good match."

"They're engaged?"

"Were. Past tense. Lucinda threw a wrench in the works."

"She didn't approve of Tab? Why not? He seems nice enough, even if he may be a lousy actor." And too clothes-conscious for my taste.

"It wasn't that Lucinda disapproved of the kid so much as that she'd her sights higher for her darling daughter."

My own mother had spent half her life shoving eligible bachelors at me, and to her, "eligible" always meant "moneyed." So with some sympathy I asked, "Did Lucinda have a prospective husband in mind for Judy?"

"Simon, of course, but only *after* he won that obscene Powerball payout. If Judy had married him, or played house with him, her and Lucinda's money troubles would vanish. But now that Simon's pushing up daisies, it sounds like Judy's gone back to her pretty boy. Bet that's got ol' Lucinda's knickers in a knot! Listen, Freckle Face, I'm tired of talking about those crazy birders. What about you? Married and settled down with two-point-three kiddies and a golden retriever?"

It was fun setting Cowgirl straight on my life, and to give the devil her due, she sounded impressed when hearing about my work at the Gunn Zoo. She had always liked animals more than people.

While I was thinking about the other things we had in common, she said, "Hey, the ranch house has a nice guest room with an ensuite, so there's no need to be a stranger. I've got a couple of horses I'd like to see you try to ride. Besides the Angus, the ranch is a sanctuary for rescued mustangs."

"You want me on a mustang?"

"For as long as you can stay on, Freckle Face. Or are you chicken?" She made clucking noises.

Intrigued by the thought of riding a mustang across the Arizona desert, I promised to visit someday.

In the middle of adding how pleased she was about that, she gave a yelp. "Oh, crap! One of the horses got his hoof stuck in the wire fence. Gotta go!"

The phone went dead.

It was only later that I realized that I'd asked Cowgirl Spencer everything but one important question.

Which of the birders did she think was most likely to commit murder?

Chapter Fifteen

Despite my frustration at not having asked that important question, I slept dreamlessly through the night and awoke feeling refreshed. Iceland's pollution-free air had performed yet another miracle. Before stepping into the shower I checked my phone. No messages or texts from Joe, no surprise there, since it was still the middle of the night in California.

After a quick shower I wandered over to the restaurant, where I found the birders lingering through breakfast. As I approached, I heard Oddi speaking about the benefits of Iceland's geothermal energy. When I joined them at the table, he broke off to welcome me, but Lucinda cut his warm greeting short.

"With your 'old school chum' dead, I can't see why you're still hanging around," she sniped.

Some scientific studies claim that the ozone produced by running water is mood-enhancing, but Lucinda apparently hadn't heard about them. "I'm sure Dawn would have wanted it this way." Like the others, I could speak for the dead, too.

Lucinda opened her mouth to say something else, but Elizabeth interjected. "I'm the one who invited Teddy to accompany us on the rest of the tour. I find her knowledge of animals most interesting."

"She doesn't know a tern from a titmouse," Lucinda muttered, but after a glare from Oddi, fell silent.

Elizabeth looked less haggard today, so reuniting with her friends must have helped. She even smiled once as I reeled off a list of birds I'd seen on the way from my cottage to the hotel.

"In addition to the Arctic terns..." this, a snipe at Lucinda... "I saw a blackcap, several mallards, and a scaup."

Elizabeth's eyes lit up. "I'm hoping for a dotterel, myself. I saw a couple in Ireland, once, and they sometimes make it to Iceland like the hoopoe Simon..." Her eyes dulled momentarily, but after a pause, they brightened again. "Everyone laughed when Simon said we might see a hoopoe before the trip was done, but Inspector Haraldsson showed me some of the pictures Simon took before, well, before what happened, and there it was, big as life. Simon was a wonderful birder. That's how we met, you know. But I'm sure you're not interested in that."

Fleetingly, I wondered if Haraldsson had shown Elizabeth the other pictures, such as the one Simon had taken of a nude Adele Cobb, but nodded politely when Judy Malone interjected, "Elizabeth, go ahead and tell Teddy how you two met. It's such a romantic story!" The young yoga instructor was sitting so close to Tab Cooper that their shoulders touched. Despite the frown Lucinda directed at them, neither moved away.

I noticed several other restaurant patrons who appeared to be eavesdropping on our table. Fans of romantic suspense, perhaps?

Elizabeth seemed pleased at Judy's prompt. "Well, if you insist. Twenty-seven years ago almost to the day, I was in Wyoming doing research for *Mesozoic Passion*, when this handsome young man wearing binoculars around his neck came up to me and said he recognized me from my book covers. I was flattered. What author wouldn't be when a good-looking guy says he reads your books? But then he went on to say I'd made an error in *Jurassic Passion* that, to date, no large flocks of seagulls had ever been spotted swooping up fish from Wyoming lakes. I wasn't a birder then, you understand. After informing me about a few rare sightings of solo lesser-black-backed gulls, he offered to buy me lunch and I accepted. Long story short, a year later, I moved from Laguna Beach to Arizona to be with him. As they say, the rest is history."

Simon Parr? Handsome? I'd only seen him dead, with a chewed-on nose and a bullet through his head, but the idea of him as handsome was a new one.

My surprise must have showed on my face, because Elizabeth said, "Oh, Teddy, you should have seen him then! Thick black hair—yes, this was before his Elvis sideburns phase, which believe me, I didn't approve of—bright blue eyes, and a wonderful physique. He was built like a marathon runner, slim and fit. For his fortieth birthday, he even ran, swam, and biked all the way through the Iron Man to prove he could! People were always telling him he should have been an actor. Like you, Tab."

Here Elizabeth looked across the table at the young man, who up to that point hadn't been paying much attention to the conversation. Tab, wearing yet another perfectly ironed ensemble, beamed.

"Tell Teddy about the name thing, too," Judy urged.

Elizabeth's smile held a hint of wistfulness. "A romantic suspense writer can't use a name that sounds golf-related—*Parr*, get it?—so when we married, I kept my maiden name. I'd discussed it with Simon, and he didn't mind. Why, at parties he always introduced me by my still-legal maiden name, by saying, 'And my wife, here, is Elizabeth St. John. The *famous* Elizabeth St. John.'"

"Reflected glory," Lucinda sniffed.

Irritated, Judy turned to her mother. "Women don't have to take their husband's last names. Think of all the trouble keeping your maiden name would have saved you."

The ensuing silence gave me time to wonder: was it my imagination, or had Judy become bolder recently? When I'd first met her, she'd seemed shy and deferential, especially around her bullying mother. Maybe her behavior had been camouflage for a more independent mind.

Tab saved the awkward moment. "Anyone want to join us for yoga before we leave for Thingvellir? Judy's giving a beginner's class this morning at her cottage. Oddi, Adele, and Enid Walsh are coming. How about you, Teddy? And Lucinda?"

"Count me out," I said. After last night's conversation with Cowgirl Spencer, I needed time to think. Contorting myself into Downward Dog would be distracting.

"No yoga for me, either," Lucinda snapped at her daughter. "Since you've taken it upon yourself to ask everyone over to *our* cottage without my approval, I'm going to take a walk. Birds make more sense than that om-om gibberish." She pushed her chair away and left the restaurant in a huff.

Her outburst signaled the end of breakfast, and we filed outside, where Oddi and others headed for yoga class, leaving me standing in front of Geysir with Elizabeth. Lucinda had already disappeared down the marked trail.

After a long silence, Elizabeth said. "Mother-daughter relationships can be stressful, can't they?"

"So I've noticed."

Lucinda might have caused considerable familial disruption by marrying three times, but my own mother, with her five marriages, had her beat by two. The constant changing of the guard at home hadn't always been easy.

Elizabeth's voice broke into my trip down Memory Lane. "Penny for your thoughts."

Here was my chance to find the truth about something that had been puzzling me. "I was thinking about Judy. A sweet person, but someone told me—sorry, I can't remember who— that she once broke someone's car window with a rock. Some kind of road rage incident?"

Elizabeth shrugged her bony shoulders. "That sounds like something Dawn would say. Pay no attention to anything that poor girl ever told you, Teddy. I was fond of her, but she and truth were not exactly close friends. There was no road rage incident. Judy has always been a considerate driver, and as far as temper, she's quite peaceful. All that yoga, I guess. Here's the real story about that broken window. You know how hot it gets in Arizona in the summer? One day when Judy was crossing the parking lot at the Geronimo Mall, she spotted a puppy locked in a car. It had to be something like 115-degrees outside, which meant that the temperature inside the car was even hotter, so she did what any decent human being would do."

"Called 9-1-1?"

"That, too. But first she ran back to her own car, got a tire iron, and broke the car window to drag the little thing out. He was in bad shape. Dehydration, heat stroke, the whole nine yards. Then, before the cops arrived, its owner showed up, some dunderheaded woman who saw no problem leaving an animal in a car in the middle of July while she was in an air-conditioned mall buying shoes. Judy was beside herself. There was a fight, and by the time the cops pulled up, she'd bloodied the woman's nose. Both cops being animal lovers themselves, they didn't arrest her, but she did get a ticket. And later, she got sued."

"For hitting the woman or breaking the window?"

"Dog theft. Judy refused to give it back, still has it, too. Named it Shiva. Ugliest creature you ever saw, some kind of pit bull/great Dane mix, grew to the size of a donkey. But loyal? God help any burglar who tries to break into that house!"

"Lucinda didn't mind her bringing a rescue home?"

A wry smile. "She would have have preferred a rescued eagle instead of some dehydrated mongrel, but she wasn't about to turn it away. On that front, she's the same as her daughter. She's like that inscription on the Statue of Liberty, 'Give me your tired, your poor, your huddled masses, et cetera,' only applied to animals instead of people."

Since I had to resort to my Icelandic guidebook to find the place, the birders arrived at Thingvellir ahead of me but I caught up with everyone in the crowded visitors' center at the top of a steep hill. While hordes of vacationers milled around them, the birders listened as Oddi explained the area's significance. I was so entranced by the spectacular view outside the center's large window that only now and then did I catch a few words of the tour guide's well-practiced spiel.

"Beginning in the tenth century, the Vikings held their national assembly, called the Althingi, here and…"

Having already read about Thingvellir's significance, I moved closer to the window and further away from the history lesson. In the distance ran the deep rift of Almannagja, where two active geological plates literally split Iceland in half. Running northeast to southwest, the eastern side of the canyon marked the end of the Eurasian continental plate. On the western side, the beginning of the North American plate. Each year the two tectonic plates moved further apart by almost an inch, which may not sound like a lot, but to geologists and science nerds like myself, it meant Iceland would eventually become two separate land masses divided by the North Atlantic. I couldn't wait to get outside and study the rift more closely, along with the birds that flew above it, of course, but I didn't want to be rude and leave the others behind.

"...and it's rumored that the Vikings actually practiced human sacrifice here," Oddi continued, to the oohs and ahs of his appreciative audience.

Weren't the Geronimos here to see birds? Flocks of various species were winging their way through the Almannagja, swooping down to pluck up a snack, then back aloft in an aerial dance. Gulls, terns, puffins—you couldn't go anywhere in Iceland without being surrounded by puffins—warblers, goldfinches... Wait! Wasn't that red bird with the black wings a scarlet tanager? Impossible. A tanager's habitat was too far south. Then I remembered the African-based hoopoe Simon had photographed at Vik before he was murdered, so anything, however improbable, was possible. I wouldn't know for sure unless I heard the bird's distinct *chip-durr, chip-durr* call, but from in here, with Oddi yammering...

"...while the law-giving assembly conducted its business, merchants displayed their wares in booths all along the Almannagja. You can still see the remains of..."

Oh, the hell with it.

"Scarlet tanager!" I yelled, dashing out the door.

It took only a few minutes to reach the Almannagja, and from ground level, it was even more impressive than it had been from above, yet somewhat claustrophobic. The cliff walls between the two sides of the chasm loomed forty feet above me as I hurried along the trail below in pursuit of the red bird. The tanager didn't make it easy, darting back and forth from both sides, stopping every now and then to scoop up a bug. Finally, about a quarter-mile from the hubbub of the visitors' center, it came to rest atop a moss-encrusted outcropping on the North American plate and began preening its feathers. I moved into the shadows of the Eurasian side, not wanting to frighten it away.

Chip-durr, chip-durr.

Yep, a scarlet tanager.

Although the bird's grating call was considerably less beautiful than its plumage, it still thrilled me. iPhone at the ready, I crept closer to the preening bird. I managed to snap three shots before it cocked its head as if listening to something, emitted an un-tanager-like squawk, and flew further down the chasm.

Cursing under my breath, I followed, while the tanager increased its distance from me.

Now the claustrophobia I'd felt upon first entering the low trail between the two plates really kicked in. Those high canyon walls seemed to close in on me as I ran after the bird, while the flat plain of civilization above appeared to vanish. Down here in the narrow rock tunnel it was all too easy to imagine fierce Vikings above, throwing their sacrificed victims down to the chasm below. Scarlet tanager or no scarlet tanager, I was beginning to regret leaving the visitors' center by myself.

But there!

The tanager, spotting a tasty morsel atop a pyramid-shaped rock on the North American side of the chasm, swooped down. After landing and gobbling another treat, it stayed to scratch for more.

Perfect.

I stepped out of the shadow of the Eurasian cliff wall and moved forward to get another picture.

And that saved my life.

Chapter Sixteen

I heard the noise first, then a mini-second later felt pain as a bowling ball-sized rock roared down from above, grazing my right heel.

It missed my head by an inch.

Still, the impact knocked me off my feet. Momentarily stunned, I fell back on the Eurasian side of the chasm, staring at my ruined hiking boot. The rock had torn its leather heel away, exposing what was left of my thick sock. Now the beige sock was dappled with bright red polka-dots in the process of growing larger. As I studied the slow color change, I heard a clatter from above. Then a grunt.

The sound snapped me out of my stupor. Instinctively I rolled into the middle of the trail as another rock—this one only slightly smaller than the first—crashed down onto the very spot where I had been lying.

Ignoring the pain in my foot, I stumbled to my feet and dashed across the trail to the North American side, seeking shelter from the next Eurasian rock fall. I pressed myself against the cliff wall, praying that the western side of the separating plates was more stable.

Then I heard footsteps. Quick. Light.

A person on top of the Eurasian plate was running away, back toward the visitors' center.

Not a rock fall.

Someone had tried to kill me.

As his—or her—footsteps faded, I thought I could hear my heart pound and even the seep of blood through my sock. I looked down at my hands. They were shaking and dirt-encrusted, but empty. Where was my cell phone? I needed to call 9-1-1, or whatever passed for HELP ME in Iceland. What had the guidebook said it was? 2-1-1? 1-1-2? Whatever. I'd dial until some helpful Icelander answered. If I called quickly enough, the police might be able to catch my attacker. I'd been taking a picture of the tanager when the first rock fell…Scratch that. When my attacker threw the first rock at me.

Heart still pounding, I limped back to the Eurasian side and scratched around in the debris, finally finding my phone lying face-up beneath the second rock. Its screen had been crushed, and when I tried to punch in a number, nothing happened. No light. No sound. Dead as a dodo.

Regardless, I put the ruined cell in my pocket and began what now appeared to be a painfully long and uphill trudge back to the visitors' center. Hobbling along on a flapping piece of leather that used to be a boot didn't help.

Luck was with me. As I limped past several large stones arranged in a rough rectangle—the remnants of one of an ancient sacrificial altar?—I saw a group of sightseers walking toward me. I recognized none of them, but they, too had a tour guide, this one a woman.

"…and remember, this is the same place where the Icelanders, who up to this point had remained pagan, voted to accept Christianity as their official relig…Oh, my goodness, Miss! Are you hurt? Yes, of course you are. You are limping and there is much blood all over…"

I waved away her concern. "I'll live, but I'd appreciate it if someone could lend me a phone. I need to make a call."

They all, including the tour guide, reached into their pockets, backpacks, and/or handbags, but Tab Cooper surprised me by emerging from the back of the mob and handing me his Android.

"Holy crap, Teddy! Do you need an ambulance?" His voice and face radiated concern. At least it sounded and looked like concern.

"I need the cops more." Then I raised my voice, addressing the rest of the crowd. "Anyone know their number?"

"Try 1-1-2," their tour guide answered.

I limped far enough away from the group that they couldn't eavesdrop. After a brief conversation with an emergency operator, I found myself transferred to a police sergeant, who after hearing my story, transferred me yet again, this time to Inspector Thorvaald Haraldsson. I wasn't happy about that, and neither was he.

"I am dispatching local officers immediately, but in the meantime, you stay put until I get to Thingvellir!" he ordered, after I'd repeated my story.

"Stay put? In between two separating tectonic plates?"

"Do not get smart with me, Miss Theodora Bentley. Go up to the visitors' center, have your leg attended to at the First Aid…"

"Foot."

"*Foot* attended to at the First Aid station and then sit there on your pretty a…ah, sit there until I drive over from Reykjavik. It'll take about forty minutes. You *can* sit still for that long, can't you?"

I was so irritated by his bossy tone that my foot forgot to hurt. "Oh, I dunno, Inspector. I'm an active gal."

"So I have noticed. In the meantime, whatever you do, do not—I repeat—do not allow yourself to be left alone with any member of the Wild Apaches, do you understand?"

Despite my aching heel, I had to snigger. "You mean the Geronimos."

"The what?"

"The birding group calls themselves the Geronimos, Inspector. But I read you loud and clear." I rang off. Haraldsson's warning had been unnecessary. Those tectonic plates would be a hundred miles apart by the time I trusted any of the birders again.

After returning the phone to Tab Cooper, I announced that I needed to visit the First Aid station, which further complicated my situation, because Tab immediately offered to help me get there. Ordinarily I would have accepted, because he was a strong-looking guy and I could lean on him as I limped along. However, when he'd loaned me his phone, I'd noticed that for such a perfectly groomed man, his hands were filthy.

So filthy that he could have been playing in the dirt.

Or throwing rocks.

The awkward moment was saved by a muscular Icelander who offered his own services. "The history of this place is quite interesting," he said, "but this is my fourth time at Thingvellir and I already know everything our beautiful guide is telling us. I will help you to the First Aid station, Miss, and catch up with my group later."

Before Tab could protest, I accepted the big Icelander's steadying arm, and off we went.

Along the way, we passed other Geronimos. With the exception of the Walshes, who were photographing a dowdy chaffinch together, each was alone. After professing dismay at my condition, they all denied hearing me scream "Scarlet tanager!" and explained that after Oddi finished his lecture on the area's history, they had each gone their own way. The only excuse that seemed suspect was Judy's. She had paused beneath a rocky overhang to use her inhaler. When the big Icelander paused to ask if she needed assistance, she waved us away.

But not before I noticed that her hands were as dirty as Tab's. And her face was as flushed as if she'd just finished running a four-minute-mile.

Time may fly when you're having fun, but it drags when you're limping along on a sore foot. Thanks to my Icelandic crutch, we eventually reached the First Aid station, where he handed me over to an equally compassionate attendant. After cutting what remained of my hiking boot and sock off my blood-soaked foot, the attendant cleaned the wound, salved it with a pain-easing ointment, and wrapped it in bandages to keep it clean.

My foot would heal, he said, but my boot was toast. "Unless you know a skilled cobbler, Miss?"

I shook my head. Like most Americans, I seldom repaired shoes or boots when they became old or damaged; I bought new ones. Since these old boots had been with me for years, I felt no pang of loss, and decided to simply buy a new pair when I got back to Reykjavik. While being helped through the visitors' center to the First Aid station, we'd passed through the clothing section, where I'd spied a backless pair of clogs with the Icelandic flag emblazoned on the vamp. I tried on a pair and discovered they were not only cute, but perfect for my wounded heel. Even better, when I limped up to the checkout counter with them, the solicitous clerk gave me a twenty-five percent discount.

God bless Icelanders.

Sporting my new pair of shoes, I went over to the book section and bought the new Yrsa Sigurdardóttir mystery. Book in hand, I settled onto a bench and waited for Inspector Haraldsson.

What with the traffic getting out of Reykjavik, the inspector had been somewhat optimistic about the time it would take to get to Thingvellir, and he and an accompanying officer didn't show up for almost an hour. By then I'd made it to page forty-seven and the discovery of a fourth murder victim, killed horribly in a machete attack. Iceland may have averaged less than a murder per year, but its authors loved wholesale slaughter.

When Haralsson saw the book I was reading, he frowned, but instead of playing literary critic, said, "The local police radioed they were unable to find your assailant."

"That's what they told me, too."

At the clip my assailant was running away, he—or she—probably made it back to the visitors' center or even the parking lot long before the local police had shown up. When the two officers had interviewed me, I was unable to even give them a description. It was a relief knowing they accepted my story without question, but it was also alarming. They, too, were convinced someone had tried to kill me.

For that reason I repeated my story again, adding a few details I hadn't been able to give Haraldsson over the phone. Neatness freak Tab Cooper's soiled hands, for instance, Judy's red face and inhaler for another, not to mention the fact that the birders had wandered along the pathway individually, not as a group, and that Oddi, their tour guide, said he had lost sight of them all.

"Each of them split off to photograph birds. Different birds. Perched on different rocks."

Haraldsson's frown grew deeper. "I will interview them. Did you say they were in the restaurant?"

"Your officers told them not to leave until you'd talked to them, so they decided they might as well enjoy an early lunch. Elizabeth promised to bring me a sandwich." She had, too. The ham and cheese was dry, but at least it kept my stomach from growling.

While customers milled around the store buying plush toy puffins, Icelandic flag key rings, and tee-shirts emblazoned with phrases in Old Norse, I continued my story, adding that when they found me in the gift shop, each of the birders, even crotchety Luncinda, had acted distressed over my injured foot.

"They took it for granted the rock fall was a natural occurrence," I said. "At least that's what they said. Shifting tectonic plates and all that. The only one who differed was Elizabeth. She thought the rock fall was too much of a coincidence."

I had seen alarm leap into the author's eyes. Tellingly, perhaps, she had directed a hard look at Tab Cooper and Judy Malone. She also had no trouble understanding why I preferred to wait for the inspector in the gift shop and not with the others in the restaurant.

"Writers are trained observers," I told Haraldsson, "She might have noticed something I didn't."

His grim expression became even grimmer. "I will interview them all. By the way, I spoke to the magistrate this morning, stressing the fact that this small group had already been involved with two murders and one murder attempt in only four days, and he has given me the authority to relieve you all of your passports. Do you have yours on you, Miss Bentley, or is it back in Reykjavik?"

"At Bryndis' apartment. But I'm supposed to fly back to the States on Saturday! And I think the Geronimos are leaving the day before."

"Not any more. Considering everything that has happened, we would be remiss not to demand you all stay in Iceland until an arrest has been made."

"You mean *another* arrest." I wasn't about to let him forget he'd first arrested Ragnar. "What if you can't solve the crime?"

"That is unlikely."

"But if you can't? What are we all supposed to do? Rent an apartment? Get jobs and hang out together until the killer finally confesses out of sheer frustration?"

Or commits more murders, as per the plot line of Agatha Christie's *Ten Little Indians*.

"I doubt it will come to that," Haraldsson said.

Further argument proved futile. Giving up, I said, "Oh, all right. I'll go back to Reykjavik, get my passport, and drive it down to the police station." I stood up and managed to totter a few steps away before he caught me by the arm.

"You cannot drive in your condition."

"Sure I can. The Volvo I rented is an automatic, not a stick."

"Your right heel is injured, and unless rental cars have changed their design in the past year, your right foot will be the one pressing the accelerator as well as the brake. Therefore I will drive you back to Reykjavik myself."

"But my rental…"

He didn't let me finish, only nodded toward the young officer who had accompanied him. "Eymundur will return your car to the rental company. There will be no more driving for you."

"But…"

"Give Eymundur your car keys, Miss Bentley."

"You can't…"

"I certainly can. Hand them over or I will take them from you."

Grumbling, I surrendered my keys. For his part, Officer Eymundur accepted them with a sheepish look. The two then headed toward the restaurant to interview the others, but before leaving, Haraldsson managed one final comment.

"Cute shoes," he said. "The Icelandic flag looks good on you."

Chapter Seventeen

The trip back to Reykjavik with Inspector Haraldsson wasn't as uncomfortable as I had feared. Instead of lecturing me, he pointed out sights that amused him. Smoking volcano; tourists snapping pictures. Ancient sheep farm buried by lava; tourists snapping pictures. Steaming hot springs; tourists snapping pictures. Film set on lava-strewn beach; tourists snapping pictures. Roadside horses begging for handouts; tourists snapping pictures.

Which reminded me. "My phone's ruined. Why are you keeping it?" We were passing yet another spectacular waterfall and the inevitable camera-snapping tourists.

"Because our crime lab can work wonders. There is a possibility that after you dropped it, it continued snapping pictures before breaking, maybe even taking a picture of your assailant."

"Before breaking? *Squished* would be a more accurate term."

"Squished? Good word. I will add it to my English vocabulary." When he smiled, he looked almost handsome. "But you must stop poking your nose into places where it does not belong or your nose also might become squished."

And here I'd thought I'd escaped another lecture. "I had to 'poke my nose,' as you put it, because you arrested the wrong person. Ragnar didn't kill Simon Parr."

"This I know."

I looked at him in surprise. "When did that revelation strike you?"

"Our medical examiner discovered that Mrs. Talley—whom you told everyone was your old school friend, but was a lie—did not drown. She was killed by a blow to the head from that blunt instrument your American mystery writers are so fond of when they are not shooting their victims to death with big guns. There was no water in Mrs. Talley's lungs, none at all, the poor lady."

So Inspector Haraldsson had a heart, even if he took pains to hide it. "Yes. Poor Dawn."

We passed another volcano and more tourists taking pictures.

"As to your roommate's boyfriend, Ragnar," Haraldsson continued, "when Mrs. Talley died, he was with a group of artist friends in Höfn, helping them set up a new art collective. He has many, many people who will swear to his presence. We believe them, although they are artists." Was it my imagination or did that grim mouth twitch into a grin?

"Where's Höfn?"

"More than three hundred kilometers east of Reykjavik." While I was still converting kilometers to miles in my head, he added, "That would be approximately two hundred U.S. miles. I also do not find it credible that one person killed Mr. Simon Parr and a different person killed Mrs. Talley, do you?" Not waiting for my answer, he continued, "Of course you don't. You can act foolishly, but you are no fool. Now, Miss Bentley, I do not want your head squished like Mrs. Talley's or shot like Mr. Parr's. Do you understand?"

Another hot spring, more tourists. "You've made that perfectly clear, Inspector."

"Then give me your promise you will cease your snooping."

"Promise," I said, hiding my crossed fingers with the other hand.

A chuckle. "Now promise again, Miss Bentley, this time with both hands where I can see them."

There's nothing more irritating than an observant cop. "Only if you promise to listen without arguing while I tell you everything I've found out."

"I promise, and not with crossed fingers. So now it is your turn to promise. For real."

After I complied, he listened intently while told him everything I'd discovered over the past few days. I'd expected him to look impressed, but he didn't.

He looked worried.

Bryndis hadn't returned home from the zoo by the time we drew up to her apartment, but since she had given me a key, it created no problem. After I unlocked the door, Haraldsson followed me to the desk in the living room where I'd stashed my passport.

"You may want to alert Icelandic Air to your possible cancellation," he said, stashing the passport in his suit pocket. "I have said the same thing to the other members of your group."

"They're not *my* group."

He shrugged, made me renew my promise not to stick my nose in police business—both hands showing—then left. Annoyed, I limped toward the kitchen. I needed coffee.

Chamomile tea would have been a better choice, because after a few sips my hands, steady enough earlier, started trembling. After I sloshed away half the contents of my mug, I gave up and poured the rest down the sink. While wiping up the coffee I'd spilled on the table it occurred to me that I should have asked Haraldsson to drop me off at an electronics store—there was one on almost every block in Reykjavik—so I could replace the phone I'd lost. Well, not lost, exactly…

My hands shook so hard the dishrag I was holding fell to the floor.

That's when I realized the problem wasn't caffeine. I was having a delayed reaction to my near-death experience at Thingvellir. Haraldsson had been right. What was I thinking, playing detective in a strange country more than four thousand miles from home? Hunting for a two-time killer, no less!

I needed to talk to someone, and that someone was no frosty Icelandic police inspector. Fortunately, the clock on the stove read almost six, which meant it was around ten a.m. in

California. Or eleven, since the state's switch to Daylight Savings Time, which never ceases to confuse me. Whichever, Joe would be be at his desk in the San Sebastian County sheriff's office. If I hurried, I could make it to the electronics store down the block before it closed.

Halfway there my foot reminded me how sore it was. Despite the pain and a warning trickle of blood, I soldiered on, reaching the store at the same time the proprietor was hanging up the CLOSED sign. Being a typical Icelander, he took pity on my frantic state and opened the door. A half hour later I was back at the apartment with a new phone and a newly throbbing foot. Five minutes later, after chugging two aspirins, I was on the line to Joe, who luckily, was finished with the morning briefing. He was usually even-tempered, but not today.

"Just what do you think you're doing, Teddy?"

Feigning innocence, I said, "Why, I'm talking to the hand-somest county sheriff in California."

I've known pit bulls with friendlier growls. "Don't play the innocence card with me."

"You're worried about that text I sent you last night, aren't you?"

"Oh, gee. What makes you think that? Why should I be worried, finding out that the woman I love to distraction has gone and immersed herself in another murder case, this time in a place where I can't come galloping to the rescue? Why should I be upset about that? Huh? Huh?"

I winced. Joe seldom got mad, but he was boiling now. It was a good thing there were four thousand miles between us or he'd shoot me. In a manner of speaking, of course. Twenty years on the job and Joe had never shot anyone, although I knew there were times when he'd been tempted. Like now.

"You think it was my fault I was out horseback riding and stumbled across a dead guy?"

"Knowing you, yes!"

"Really?"

I could hear him draw a deep breath. "Well, you didn't have to get involved in the case." The growl diminished to a soft rumble.

"Joe, I didn't have any choice. The police questioned me like they did everyone else."

Another deep breath. "Teddy, did you know that the *Gunn Landing Reporter* ran an article this morning about that homicide and your name was mentioned? As a witness?"

"I was not a witness. He was dead when I got there."

"Ha ha." But he wasn't laughing. "I must have called you a dozen times and left a dozen messages! And nearly texted my fingers off! Why haven't you returned my calls?"

Because in the morning I was busy talking to murder suspects, and after that, whoever killed Simon and Dawn tried to kill me, and in the attempt, squashed my phone to smithereens. But I had better sense than to tell him that. "My phone went kablooey this morning when I was hiking out in Iceland's version of No Man's Land, and I've only now returned to the Land of All Things Electronic. Your number was the first one I dialed on my new phone, which is quite nice by the way." I left out the fact that I was delivered back to Reykjavik via police escort.

"Oh."

"Yeah, *oh*." Now that he was on the defensive, it was time to make my move. "But I'll admit I'm curious about the people who knew Simon Parr, the dead guy, and I was wondering if you had any information on them. Reykjavik's a small place. In fact the whole country's kind of small, and it's hard to avoid anyone here, so it would be good to know if any of them are dangerous so I can stay far, far away."

A suspicious silence. Then, "Are you playing me, Teddy?"

"No, no, I'm not, I swear." Hoping to distract him, I said, "I'm just tired, Joe. I've been working with the bear cub, some Icelandic foxes, and a couple of puffins."

"Puffins?" A native Californian, Joe had never seen a puffin in his life, except while watching *Wild Kingdom* with me.

"If you want, I'll give you a private tour as soon as they're settled in at the Gunn Zoo."

For a minute I didn't think he was going to answer. When he did, it had nothing to do with animals, at least not the four-legged kind. "Teddy, listen to me carefully. I want you to stay far away from Benjamin Talley. He's done time."

"For vehicular homicide, I know."

"That, too."

It took me aback. "What do you mean, 'that, too?' Was there something else?"

"Your boy's been in more fights than Mike Tyson, but unlike Tyson, he loses most of his. He starts them, though. You know that Talley's Restaurants chain? Like the one here in San Sebastian?"

"And formerly one in Gunn Landing."

"Soon-to-be-formerly here, too. The chain's filing for bankruptcy. But that's besides the point. A few years back, Talley worked as bouncer in the flagship restaurant's bar—they're Kansas City-based—and he was always getting in fights. His specialty was blowing trivial incidents into major ones, something a good bouncer never does, but from reading his sheet, I got the idea he liked the action. The biggie was the time he decked some guy from Topeka for mouthing off, and put him in a coma for a week. The guy sued, and the money the Talley family attorneys threw at the other attorneys couldn't make it go away. The guy eventually got a big cash settlement, and Talley wound up doing six months. After he was released, the family gave him the title of VP, along with a monthly stipend, but that's it. He's officially persona non grata as far as they're concerned. You stay away from that man, hear me?"

So much for the accuracy of Cowgirl Spencer's gossip-mongering. Not that I could blame her. She could only tap into the scandals around Geronimo County, not events halfway across the country. This new information make me look at Ben in a new light. Dawn, too. Had he ever gotten physical with her? And that so-called "shoving match" at Sky Harbor International Airport before the birders departed for Iceland? From the information Joe had given me, Ben might have been the aggressor there, not Simon Parr.

"Agreed. I won't go near him." Good thing he couldn't see my crossed fingers.

"Now, as to the rest of your buddies…"

"I told you, they're not my buddies."

"The rest of your *buddies* don't smell like roses, either! Perry and Enid Walsh are under investigation for…"

"I know all about that," I interrupted. "The charges were dropped."

"First time around, yeah. But my information is that they're back at it, fobbing off fake jewelry as real."

"They're nice people!" I protested.

He actually laughed. "The best con artists always are. Don't buy anything from them." He laughed again.

Since I liked her, I was almost afraid to ask about burgundy-haired Adele Cobb, Simon's ex-mistress, but I did anyway, adding, "Please don't tell me she's an ax murderess."

His voice turned serious. "No, she used a Colt .38."

"What!?"

"Teddy, one of these days you're going to learn not to place your trust in people because they seem 'nice.' Point in fact, for a few years there was a string of domestic violence calls from the Cobb residence…" He paused. "You do know she'd been married, right?"

"Uh, no." I was so focused on Adele's relationship with Simon Parr that I hadn't thought to ask.

"Reece Cobb was a bad actor, no doubt about it. He put Adele in the hospital twice, but she would never testify against him, so the case always went away. Then one night he broke her jaw, and I guess she'd had enough, because she popped him one with his own handgun. But she was a lousy shot and got him high in the forearm. Flesh wound. Went right through, so he's fine. Re-married and from what I could find out, is busy battering the second Mrs. Cobb. Nothing happened to Adele, because it was an obvious case of self-defense."

Why hadn't Cowgirl told me? I asked the obvious question. "This didn't happen in Geronimo County, did it?"

"Florida. She moved to Arizona twelve years ago. Why do you ask?"

"Just wondering. Other than her shooting her husband, who as far as I'm concerned deserved it, was there anything else?"

"Well, there was this one time she played detective over a theft at her house and maybe went a little too far in pursuit of justice, but what the hell. As far as I'm concerned, she saved the local law trouble and money. Crime-fighting doesn't come cheap, you know. Another thing. She volunteers at a shelter for battered women, and every now and then feeds the folks at a homeless shelter. Can't help liking a woman like that." He paused, then added, "Or wondering, maybe, if she's too good to be true."

The article I'd found on the Internet said that when Simon won the Powerball, he had donated a large amount to a battered women's shelter. The one Adele volunteered for, I bet. Their pillow talk must have entailed something more substantial than the standard billing and cooing.

"Is that about it?" I asked. "No more tales of terror and/or wickedness re the people you keep referring to as my 'buddies'?"

"Nope. Tab Cooper, clean as a whistle. Almost suspiciously so, you might say, not even a parking ticket. As for Elizabeth St. John, her life's an open book, ha ha." He waited for my laugh, which I duly gave him, then continued. "Well-respected, well-liked, yadda yadda yadda. Donates to various charities, local and national. As for Lucinda Greaves, several marriages and some financial troubles—looks like the bank's going to foreclose on her house—but no overt law-breaking I could find. Her daughter Judy runs a small yoga studio in a strip mall, and once got into some minor trouble over a semi-violent animal rescue but that's about it."

Myself, I wouldn't call a bloody nose "semi-violent," but where an animal's safety is concerned, I wouldn't have cared if Judy had ripped off the woman's ears.

I'd saved my most important question for last. "Look, Joe, I know you're telling me all this to warn me away from the group, and believe me, it's working. But I am curious. Did you find out anything hinky about Simon Parr? Why would someone want to kill him? His wife's already loaded, so she wouldn't do it for the money. From what I hear, Arizona's a community property state, too, so she'd have been paid out half the Powerball winnings when they showed up to collect the prize."

His voice lowered to growl again. "Aren't you forgetting about the *second* victim, one Dawn Talley? The newspaper article mentions her, too."

"Yeah, but given what you told me about her husband…"

"He's top suspect there, for sure. But back to Mr. Megabucks Parr. I'll admit I did a little digging around on him and I discovered that he led an exemplary life. Until…" he paused for effect. "Until he won that obscenely large Powerball. Then, in the short space of two months, he racked up three DUIs. The only reason he's not in jail now—besides being dead, of course—is because his ever-so-expensive attorneys keep getting the court date pushed back." He paused again. "You know, Teddy, I shouldn't have told you any of this. At the worst, I'm aiding and abetting. At best, I'm enabling. Know what an enabler is?"

Just then, Bryndis came through the door, her arms full of groceries. She bustled past me, leaving a faint trail of Eau de Zoo, and set the bags on the counter. It gave me the chance I needed to avoid another lecture.

"My roommate just got home!" I said. "She brought groceries, and I need to help put them away."

Bryndis shook her head fiercely, not wanting to interrupt my phone call, but I ignored her. "After everything you told me, Joe, I promise to mind my own business from here on. Bye! Love you!" Over his protests, I made kissy noises and killed the call.

"I thought you said you were staying with the birders through tomorrow," Bryndis said, as she set a bag of sugar onto a pantry shelf. "Say, isn't that a new phone?"

I updated her on what had happened so far, ending with the reason for the new phone. I also mentioned my confiscated passport. To her credit, she looked every bit as alarmed as Joe had sounded.

"Do not worry about Thor confiscating your passport, Teddy. You can bunk with me as long as necessary and it will be a pleasure. This is all my fault because I should never had have asked you to help Ragnar. As it turns out, Thor has already dropped him from their list of suspects. Ragnar called me this morning and told me."

Thor, meaning Inspector Thorvaald Haraldsson. I still found it startling that Icelanders referred to everyone, from their police to their president, by their first names, but I guess that's how it works in a small country where everyone is related to everyone else.

"Did the inspector say Ragnar is off the hook because there's been another killing and he was nowhere near the scene of the crime this time?" I asked.

"He didn't have to. What happened in Stykkishólmur is all over the news. It is a lucky thing Ragnar was in Höfn, isn't it?"

"Very lucky."

Maybe too lucky.

Chapter Eighteen

My first day in Reykjavik, I'd learned about Valkyrie, Bryndis' rock band, but I hadn't yet had a chance to see them in action. The night I'd spent at Stykkishólmur had been the night for their regular gig at Hávær Tónlist, an arts district hard rock bar whose name meant "Loud Music." As soon as Bryndis had showered off the gamey smells of the zoo, she informed me that I could see them tonight, if I wished.

While someone had been trying to kill me in Thingvellir, the Valkyries had been experiencing better luck. They had received an offer to sub tonight for Of Monsters and Men, a popular Reykjavik band now opening for U2 in Brussels. The night club Myndavél—Icelandic for "Camera"—was larger and more well-known than the Hávær Tónlist, so it was a great opportunity.

"This will be your last chance to experience Valkyrie in action before you return to the U.S. on Saturday."

"If Inspector Haraldsson doesn't cut my passport loose, I'll never make that flight," I mourned.

"Then you can stay here and be our official groupie."

I smiled. "And help you take care of more polar bear orphans. Not a bad deal."

The thing to know about Icelandic night life is that it happens late. Very late.

When we arrived at Myndavél at eleven, Bryndis was already in her stage costume. Brass breastplate lined with fleece for

comfort; skimpy leather loincloth, brass arm and wrist brace-
lets, brass helmet, hammered brass shield, and laced knee-high
leather sandals. She resembled the shield-maiden Lagertha, on
the *Vikings* TV series.

Three similarly attired Valkyries were waiting for her in the
Icelandic equivalent of a Green Room, except it was painted
black. The rug and sofa were black, too. To lighten the mood,
black-and-white photographs of other bands who had played
the venue hung on the walls. Some I even recognized: The
Sugarcubes, Beck, Sigur Rós, Arcade Fire, Kings of Leon, and,
of all people, Kanye West.

As fierce as the Valkyries appeared, each displayed childlike
joy at the prospect of playing a major venue. Most of the time
the women were polite enough to speak in English so that I could
understand them, but so high was their level of excitement they
kept breaking into frenzied Icelandic soliloquies.

Leaving them to their ecstasies, I mouthed a "See you later"
to Bryndis and wended my way through a tightly packed crowd
to sit at the table reserved for the band; it was the only empty
table in the entire place. The Green Room's color scheme continued in the club itself. Black floor, black walls, etc. When the
waitress, dressed in black, natch, came around I ordered a bottle
of Black Death in honor of the occasion.

I was taking my first sip of the strong brew when someone
tapped me on the shoulder and a man's voice said, "Can we
join you?"

I turned around to see Tab Cooper, dressed like an editorial
spread in *Ivy League Quarterly*, holding hands with Judy Malone,
resplendent in a colorful sari-print dress. They stood out from
the rest of the black-clad crowd like sunshine at midnight.

"Sure," I answered, "but since this is the band's table, you'll
have to find another spot when they go on break."

"No problem," Tab said, pulling back a chair for Judy.
"How's your foot, by the way? You were limping pretty badly
at Thingvellir."

"Much better, thanks." My heel hadn't swollen as much as I'd feared it would, and luckily, it still fit into my Nikes. And my limp was manageable enough that I would be able to continue my work at the zoo.

Once Tab and Judy had ordered their drinks, I explained how I came to be in the tavern that night, hoping they would do the same. They did. After Inspector Haraldsson took possession of everyone's passports, the group voted to return to their Reykjavik hotel for a breather. Although their tour hadn't been physically strenuous, the loss of two members had taken an emotional toll on everyone.

"When we left the hotel, Mom and the others were with Elizabeth," Judy said. "She'd seemed fine all afternoon, but while we were at dinner, she started crying, so Enid Walsh helped her to her room. You know how solicitous she is."

Solicitous for a crook, yeah. "Did Ben Talley have dinner with you, too?"

Tab shook his head. "Nobody's seen him since we left Stykkishólmur."

Grieving, maybe. Or gloating. Mistrusting my own growing cynicism, I looked at my watch. The Valkyries weren't due onstage for another ten minutes and this was a good chance to clear up a few things.

"How'd you get involved in birding, Tab?" I asked. "It seems like an unusual hobby for an actor."

He smiled his perfect smile. "Dad was one of the Geronimos' founding members, and every chance he got, he'd take me with him when he went on their trips. Birds were the only thing we had in common, and I guess that's one of the reasons it stuck. I'm grateful we were able to share that, because he passed away last year. Everyone in the club turned out for the funeral."

After expressing sympathy—there was so much of that going around these days—I said, "You say you two didn't have much in common, so I take it he wasn't an actor."

"CPA. He was actually in business with Simon for a while."

I'd like to say fireworks blazed into the sky. Instead, the light show was more of a slow dawning. "Your father was Simon Parr's partner?"

"Fifteen years ago. Burlingame and Parr, that was their company." By way of explanation, he added, "Cooper's my professional name. And I'm not 'Tab,' either. It's Jim. James, actually, but my agent said there were already too many of both."

No wonder Joe hadn't found anything on "Tab Cooper." Remembering Tab's dirty hands at Thingvellir, I made a mental note to run a web search on James Burlingame as soon as I got back to the apartment.

I looked at my watch again. Five more minutes. Enough time for a few more questions. "Boy, it's sure close in here," I said, dabbing fictional sweat off my face with my beer napkin. "Hot. Stuffy. I can hardly breathe. Doesn't this bother your asthma, Judy?"

She frowned. "Who told you I had asthma?"

"Your mother, I think. She worries about you." Not that Lucinda had ever showed it in my presence.

"Mom's more of a control freak than a worrier, but to answer your question, I'm fine these days. Yoga has done wonders for me."

"No flare-ups?"

"Only when I overexert myself, which I've learned not to do."

Except, possibly, when throwing around boulders at Thingvellir, then running as fast as possible to get away from the scene of the crime.

"Now I'm regretting not taking you up on that free yoga lesson at Gullfoss," I said.

Her face relaxed. "You could always drop by the hotel. Just call ahead." She reached into her handbag and took out a card. White lettering on a dark blue background said, "Be at one with the Universe." Beneath that rather ambitious saying was her name and her cell phone number.

"I'll do that. By the way…"

My next question was interrupted by an announcement in Icelandic over the loudspeaker, and a second later, the Valkyries sprang onstage, ready for battle. After a shout in Old Norse from Bryndis, they began to play.

Imagine a blend of heavy metal bands Metallica and Megadeth, overlaid with harmonies that would do any gospel choir proud. Flying in the face of probability, this bizarre mixture of styles worked for the Valkyries, and the few people in the audience who had been lucky enough to find seats, rose to their feet, fannies waggling, fists pumping in time with the beat. Judy, Tab/Jim/James, and I rose with them, shaking fists and waggling our butts along with everyone else. I hadn't felt so energized since I'd been in college and attended a Pearl Jam concert at the Fillmore.

The highlight of the Valkyries' set was a speed-metal version of "Hey, Jude," sung in a mixture of Old Norse and English, and dedicated to "Our great American friend and defender of the environment, Teddy Bentley."

After what seemed like a too-short set, the band left the stage and made their way through the still applauding crowd to our table. Tab and Judy stood, ready to give up their seats, but Bryndis told them to sit back down, that they would drag up another couple of chairs. At first Tab could hardly keep his eyes off the musicians' skimpy outfits, but after Judy jabbed him in the ribs a couple of times, he settled down. The ogling ground to a stop when Ragnar, who'd been standing unseen against the back wall, walked over and joined us.

"How did we do?" Bryndis asked him, her eyes shining.

It takes an artist to know how to really praise other artists, and Ragnar let 'er rip. By the time he was through extolling the band's various and sundry virtues, all of it true, the Valkyries looked more like love-struck maidens than fierce warriors.

As the night wore on, the Valkyries played two more sets, and in between each, returned to our table to chat, interrupted every now and then by fans who stopped by to have their Valkyrie CDs autographed. Every now and then I noticed Bryndis sneaking looks at Tab. Girls will be girls, right?

When we finally made it back to the apartment in the wee hours, I learned how wrong I was.

"Do not trust that man," she said, unbuckling her breast plate.

"Are you talking about Tab? Or Ragnar?"

She placed her forefinger alongside her cheek and cocked her head. "Hmm. Let me see. Could I be talking about Ragnar, who has always been honest about his roving eye, or Mr. Tab Cooper, he of the two different names?"

"Well, he's an actor…"

I sat down on the bed while she peeled over the rest of her costume. All that brass and leather had left red marks all over her body. Stripped to her undies, she wrapped herself in a terry robe, then sat down on the bed across from mine.

"Tab Cooper is an actor, you say? So, to a certain extent is Ragnar, as you will find out when *Berserker!* is released."

"Berserker?" I'd heard the legend of the fabled Viking warriors who behaved like madmen in battle, spurred on by large amounts of booze and a mysterious drink that was the Dark Ages version of crystal meth.

"Ragnar begins filming the battle scenes tomorrow. He is always on call for movies, especially when they're about Vikings. Or bikers."

I had to laugh at that, but rather than let myself be dragged into a conversation about the similarities between the two groups, brought her back to the subject. "What has Ragnar's film work got to do with Tab Cooper, and his untrustworthiness thereof?"

She gave me a sly look. "Little, other than the fact that both Ragnar and Tab are actors and are therefore skilled liars. But given Ragnar's faults, and they are legion, he has never lied to me, whereas I am certain Mr. Two Names spent most of the evening telling us what you call whoppers."

"Examples, please."

"Regardless of his big fake smile, Mr. Two Names is an angry man. We Icelanders get to know one another by discussing family, and to a certain extent, you Americans do, too, so I asked him about his."

"I don't remember this."

"At the time, you were in the ladies room, getting rid of the beer you love so much."

True. I'd drunk two bottles of Black Death, and its effect on my bladder had been considerable.

"While you were gone, Mr. Two Names told me he was an only child, that his mother worked in an office she hated, and that her boss was rude to her. He also talked more about his father dying, and kept saying, 'It shouldn't have happened, it shouldn't have happened.' As he told me this, his eyes were trying to look pitiful, but he is not the actor he thinks he is. He was more angry than sad."

My opinion of Bryndis' astuteness rose even higher. But she was a zookeeper, after all. Our charges can't talk to us so we become experts at reading body language.

"What do you think Tab's angry about?"

"I have noticed that Americans get emotional about money. Especially its loss."

She wasn't wrong there.

"I also talked to Judy," Bryndis continued. "When I first met her at Vik, which was for only one short conversation, she seemed as angry as Mr. Two Names. But now she is happy."

"Young love makes pussycats of us all."

"Perhaps. But I will say this one thing, and then I must go wash off the grime of the night. I sweat a lot under that breastplate. So here it is. Mr. Two Names' mother continues to work at a job she hates, so therefore she must need the money. Her son, being an actor, probably has little to contribute to her welfare, yet when he discussed her with me, he seemed fond of her and concerned about her well-being. As a son should! Now I will discuss Mr. Two Names' girlfriend. Like her boyfriend, Judy makes little money and is two months behind on the rent of her yoga studio. Her mother is between jobs and the bank is going to take her house away."

I had to interrupt. "You learned all this while I was in the bathroom?"

A smug expression. "I knew from past experience there would be a long line waiting to get into one of the stalls, so I worked fast. Besides, Judy was drunk."

True, at the end of the night, Tab had had to pretty much carry Judy out of the bar. I was still smiling at the memory when Bryndis added something else.

"Consider this. Two pretty people with little money, one being pushed forward by her mother to be the wealthy Simon Parr's new girlfriend—or wife, if she played her cards right. If I were a detective, I would ask myself, how successful was that push? Was Judy having an affair with Simon even though she loved another man? I read a lot of American books, many romances and mysteries, and there I find that rich American men are often generous with their girlfriends, sometimes even writing them into their wills."

With a final sly smile, Bryndis walked into the bathroom and turned on the shower. She was still singing an Icelandic version of "Hey, Jude," when I crawled into bed and immediately fell asleep.

Chapter Nineteen

Despite my few hours of sleep, five a.m. Wednesday found me huddled over my laptop scrolling through the Internet for any mention of James Burlingame, aka Tab Cooper. After ruling out the Burlingames I found elsewhere—they were all over Arizona—I finally hit pay dirt. Last July James Burlingame, Sr. had committed suicide-by-hanging in the garage of his Apache Crossing home. He left no note, but according to the newspaper article, an unnamed source said that after several failed investments, the family had been experiencing financial difficulties. A follow-up article two days later mentioned that James Burlingame, Jr., had been arrested hours later following a physical altercation with an unnamed male at the home of Elizabeth St. James, the famed romantic suspense author. Burlingame, Jr. "obviously intoxicated," the article stated, had been briefly arrested, but released on his own recognizance the next morning when he sobered up. The "unnamed male," almost certainly Simon Parr, refused to press charges.

Looking back on our conversation the night before, I remembered Bryndis telling me that Tab appeared angry when discussing his parents' situation. Perhaps in some way he blamed Simon for his father's death, although that would make no sense. Simon had split from the business years earlier.

It being still Tuesday night in Arizona, I punched in Cowgirl Spencer's number on my new phone. As soon as she answered,

I whispered, "Why didn't you tell me the truth about Tab Cooper?"

"Why are you whispering, Freckle Face?"

"Because it's five a.m. Wednesday here and my roommate's still in bed. Does the name James Burlingame, Jr. ring a bell?"

"Oh, that."

"Yeah, that." I waited.

"He changed it legally last year, when he started getting a few TV roles. Walk-ons, mainly, but…"

"Stop evading. Your boy Cooper or Burlingame or whatever you want to call him attacked Simon Parr the day after his father's funeral."

"Water under the bridge."

"Except Parr got shot in the head a few days ago while Cooper/Burlingame was less than a mile away."

"Don't be silly. We Arizonans don't carry grudges."

"And I'm the Sugar Plum Fairy. Why are you so determined to whitewash him?" The minute the words were out of my mouth I figured it out: her earlier comments about lonely desert nights and her unceasing quest for a significant other, whether suitable or not. "Ah, Cowgirl, don't tell me you were…" I paused, searching for a less blatant word "…uh, *dating* him?"

A chuckle. "At night it can get pretty chilly out here on the Arizona desert, especially around February, and there's nothing like hot young blood to warm things up."

"Cradle robber!"

"Don't judge, Freckle Face. Jimmy moved on a couple of months later, leaving me with happy memories."

Something ugly occurred to me. "Moved on to whom?"

"Judy Malone. I thought you knew. But that didn't last long, either."

"Because Judy 'moved on' to Simon, right?"

"Sho 'nuf."

"And this happened right after Simon won the lottery."

"As I told you, Lucinda was having money trouble and she talked Judy into…"

"Stop right there, Cowgirl. Are you certain that Judy went after Simon simply because her mother told her to? From what I've observed lately, she can be quite good at ignoring Lucinda. Perhaps the instigator of Judy's relationship with Megabucks Simon was someone else."

"Like who?" She sounded baffled.

"Like Jimmy/Tab."

She laughed outright. "Don't be silly. Why would he do such a thing?"

"From everything I hear, Simon had a habit of being financially generous to his girlfriends."

"And you think Jimmy…" She snorted. "No way, Freckle Face. That boy may be many things, but he was never venal. He—"

I cut her off again. "Any rumors around Apache Crossing about the contents of Simon's will?"

"That's a joke, right? The attorneys around here are as tight as a bronc's saddle."

"A half-billion dollars is no joke."

She sounded irritated. "Don't forget, Elizabeth got half, and with Simon dead, she gets the rest, not that she ever needed it, what with those stupid books of hers." She paused, then grudgingly said, "And minus what he might have left to various charities. And maybe a woman or two."

"Such as Judy Malone."

A sigh. "He did seem pretty taken with her."

I had no more questions to ask, so we spent the next few minutes chatting about horses. When I finally rang off, Bryndis was up and singing in the shower.

Later that morning, I stood in the quarantine shed at the Reykjavik Zoo watching Magnus eat his breakfast while I mulled over everything I had learned so far.

Tab Cooper wasn't the uncomplicated pretty boy he'd first appeared, and for some reason, held Simon Parr responsible for his father's suicide. The only question was if he had enough brain power to cook up a Machiavellian revenge scheme that culminated in murder. Not only would Tab have to be smarter than he appeared, but his powers of persuasion would also have to be good enough to talk Judy into going along with his plan. To accomplish all this, Tab Cooper aka James Burlingame, Jr., would need to be a better actor than Cowgirl Spencer believed.

But why kill Dawn?

The obvious answer might be that Dawn had seen him leaving the hotel the morning of Simon's murder, and being venal herself, attempted to blackmail him. Simon had dumped her, and she and her husband were on the brink of divorce. Her looks were fading and her own financial future looked bleak, so blackmail could have seemed like a reasonable solution to her problems.

However, as the old saying goes, "You can't get blood out of a stone." Like most actors, Tab was broke. Surely, given Dawn's limited brain power, she wasn't capable of figuring out his elaborate plan of sharing his girlfriend's theoretical inheritance. This made me question my earlier assumption that the murders of Simon Parr and Dawn Talley had been carried out by the same person. Unlikely as it seemed, there could be two murderers operating here, each killing for his—or her—own reason. And maybe one, or even both, of the killers was an Icelander. Take Oddi, for instance. The tour guide had been present at each…

Magnus sneezed, derailing my train of thought.

"You'd better not be coming down with a cold," I told the polar bear cub. "You'll never make it through Customs if you're sick."

Taking the temperature of a mature polar bear can be tricky; not so with Magnus. His reading of 98.6, the same as a human's, proved he was healthy. His eyes were clear and bright, too.

After assuring myself of Magnus' continued well-being, I tried to decide what to do next: visit the foxes or call Inspector Haraldsson to relay what I'd learned from Cowgirl. After some reflection, I decided that the smartest thing would be to stay away from both him and the Geronimos, but avoiding the latter might prove difficult. Although passport-less, the birders had been given permission to continue their sight-seeing tour, but instead were hunkered down at the Hótel Keldur in downtown Reykjavik. Too close for comfort for me. I felt safer with polar bears.

Especially since the bear in question was adorable little Magnus. I was already dreading the day Magnus grew to full size and I could no longer cuddle him. Right now he continued slurping down his breakfast, oblivious of my doting looks.

"He is a sweetie, isn't he?" Bryndis said, entering the quarantine shed. The last time I'd seen her this morning, she'd been cleaning the mink enclosure.

"Will you miss him?" I asked, noting a brief flash of sadness in her eyes as she studied him.

She nodded. "We zookeepers are cautioned not to fall in love with our animals but we do anyway. They are such individuals. Magnus there, he loves for me to hold his right paw while I scratch behind his left ear. Katrin, the last cub we rescued, the one we sent to the San Diego Zoo, she did not like her paws touched but she liked her belly tickled."

While we watched Magnus scarf up breakfast, I thought of the many animals at the Gunn Zoo I felt especially close to. Lucy, the giant anteater. Wanchu, the eucalyptus-loving koala. Alejandro, the rescued llama who had once saved my life. I loved them all. Then there were my personal pets: DJ Bonz, Miss Priss, Toby…Come to think of it, where was Toby now? Was the little half-Siamese still bunking with my friend Cathie Kindler, or had he returned to his bad old habit of roaming the marina, mooching off one gullible liveaboarder after another?

Just thinking about my animal friends made me homesick, and for the first time since I'd arrived, I longed to be back in Gunn Harbor. Iceland was a great place, but home is home. No matter how handsome Icelandic men were—even the grim Inspector Haraldsson—none could compare with Joe, whose warm brown eyes…

"Ah, I see you are thinking about your boyfriend."

I felt my cheeks redden. "How could you tell?"

"By the dreamy look on your face."

"You should talk. I heard you muttering Ragnar's name in your sleep last night."

Her turn to blush. "The thing between me and Ragnar, it is nothing serious."

"Right. I can tell."

Despite her embarrassment, she had to smile, and together we left Magnus' shed and walked toward the outbuilding where the foxes were quarantined.

Not only did Bryndis and I work well together, we shared what would surely be a continuing friendship. Since I was now not only passport-less but carless, I was back to commuting to the zoo with her, and on the way to work this morning, we'd discussed the possibility of her flying to Gunn Landing next winter to thaw out for a couple of weeks on the *Merilee*. I liked her "ex" boyfriend, too. Tonight Ragnar, who had returned from Höfn last night, was treating us to a night on the town. With the Geronimos out of the picture, I could relax and have a good time.

But halfway between the quarantine shed and the foxes, I saw something that stopped me in my tracks. Watching the seals being fed were Enid and Perry Walsh, Adele Cobb, Lucinda Greaves, and Oddi, the Geronimos' tour guide. Before I could scuttle behind an outbuilding, Oddi waved.

"Miss Bentley! Why don't you tell these lovely people the difference between seals and sea lions?"

Sporting a smile I hoped appeared genuine, I limped over and began the same spiel I'd heard Bryndis give earlier.

"For starters, sea lions bark, where seals—which we have here—mainly grunt," I said, as the seals' heads rose from the water to catch fish a zookeeper threw to them. "Sea lions have ear flaps, seals don't, and seals spend more time in the water than sea lions. Their diet is a bit different, too, because leopard seals will eat penguins when given a chance, whereas sea lions usually confine their diets to smaller prey, like fish and small octopi."

"Penguins!?" Adele Cobb looked shaken, the lines on her face deeper than ever.

"I'm afraid so."

"I like penguins." The bright morning sun made her maroon hair glow, but it also revealed her gray roots. Since I had first seen her that night in the Viking Tavern, she'd aged ten years.

"Most people like penguins," I commiserated. "They look something like us, only more dressed up. Plus, they have an adorable waddle."

Her wrinkles softened. "Can't help loving that waddle, can we?"

The other Geronimos moved on to the barn to see the goats, but Adele remained staring at the seals. "They don't look big enough to kill penguins."

"These seals aren't. Wrong hemisphere, too. Like I said, it's mainly leopard seals that do that." Along with orcas and other large ocean predators which had developed a taste for penguins, but there was no point in reminding her that among carnivores, someone's always eating someone else.

"How's your foot?" Adele suddenly asked, turning away from the seals.

I looked down at my Nikes. "Sore, but as you can see, I'm still hobbling around."

Since she showed no inclination to join the others in the barn, I dismissed my earlier qualms about the birders and decided to get as much information from her as possible. The sooner the murders were solved, the quicker I could get back to Gunn Landing. And Joe. If Inspector Haraldsson didn't like my meddling, too bad.

"Where are Tab and Judy?" I asked. "And Elizabeth. They're not with the group."

"Elizabeth was going to come with us, but she's having a bit of a relapse over Simon. She seemed okay at the beginning of breakfast, but then she started crying again and ran off to her room. Ben's in even worse shape. No one's seen hide nor hair of the guy since Dawn was killed. As for Judy, Lucinda says she's not feeling well and Tab stayed behind to keep her company." When she made a sour expression, I noticed that her hastily applied lipstick had bled into the lines around her mouth. She had dressed carelessly, and her socks didn't match.

"Outside of birding, do you know Judy and Tab well?"

Adele shrugged. "Not really. Given our age differences we don't share the same interests other than birding. But Apache Crossing isn't that large and we do run into each other from time to time. Judy seems okay. I'm even thinking about enrolling in one of her yoga classes. It might be good for my creeping arthritis. As for Tab, maybe it's just me but there's always been something about him that struck me wrong."

"In what way?"

She shrugged again. "He seems like he's always acting a part."

"That kind of thing can make you feel uncomfortable, all right." I flashed back to the day at Thingvellir, and Tab approaching me with a smiling face and dirty hands. Seizing on the parallel, I added, "I used to feel the same way about Dawn. When we were in school it was always hard to tell which was the real Dawn and which was merely the Dawn she wanted you to see."

"She didn't know the difference herself, poor girl."

"You sound sympathetic, considering everything."

Her eyes narrowed. "Everything? Everything *what*?"

Oops. "Her affair with Simon, for instance. I met you only days ago, but I could tell you loved him."

"Well, aren't you the Smarty Pants?" But there was more resignation in her voice than anger.

"Sorry if I upset you."

A bitter laugh. "After this past week, hearing someone state the obvious isn't going to upset me. Yes, I loved Simon. Up until recently, he was one of the kindest, sweetest men I'd ever known. Why, look at everything he did for Elizabeth! He gave up his own career to do her scut work, research, PR, hell, he even did her typing for her. Men like that are rare as snow in July. But Dawn didn't love him. With her, it was always about the money. Still, that didn't make her any less pathetic, did it? Sure, Simon played around with her for a couple of months, and at the same time he was playing around with me. The man was a polygamist at heart." Here Adele managed a smile. "But after he got that big Powerball payout, he dumped her, and rather cruelly. The poor thing came crying to me, saying it happened because of her declining looks, but I'm telling you there's no way that was the case. I've looked like hell for years and it never bothered him."

"Then why do you think he broke up with Dawn?" While I didn't think Adele, to use her own words, "looked like hell," at her best she could never have competed with Dawn in the looks department.

"Beauty can attract a man, but beauty alone will never keep him. Look at Marilyn Monroe. Men wanted her, but once they got what they wanted, they couldn't wait to get rid of her. Maybe Joe DiMaggio truly loved her, but after a few years even he couldn't put up with her neuroses. Dawn was like that, too. Every man wanted her, but she couldn't make them stick around. Not even her husband, who as broken up as he seems now, was still divorcing her. When I first found out about the divorce, I thought, 'God help her when she loses the last of her looks.'"

Since Adele was in a soul-baring mood, I took a chance. "Speaking of breakups, what caused the split between you and Simon?" I didn't bother asking why she had carried on an open affair with a married man, since none of the Geronimos—including Elizabeth—seemed to think there was anything was odd about it.

"Beauty had nothing to do with my relationship with Simon, not skin-deep beauty, anyway," she answered, in a matter-of-fact tone of voice. "We'd been together—I guess you can put it that way—for six years, which is longer than some marriages these days, but after Simon won that damned Powerball, everything changed. *He* changed."

Doctors say that the way a person lives his or her life can often foretell the way they would die, that life and death followed the law of cause and effect. Smoke too many cigarettes? Lung cancer or emphysema is in your future. Eat too much and exercise too little? Say hello to a heart attack. Murder sometimes worked that way, too. The two times I had seen Simon Parr alive he'd been drunk and churlish. Yet those who knew him best—his wife, his friends, and at least one of his mistresses—described him as considerate and generous. Which were they: broad-minded, naïve, or liars all?

"Adele, in what way did Simon ch—?"

"Adele!" Lucinda called, stepping outside the goat barn. "You said you wanted to see the horses!"

I looked over to see the Geronimos heading toward the corral, where three Icelandic horses stood looking bored. Still curious about Simon Parr's Dr. Jekyll/Mr. Hyde personality—and aware that I had only seen Mr. Hyde in action—I followed Adele over to the corral where the Icelandic horses were trying to pretend they didn't hear the Geronimos calling, "Here, horsey! Here, horsey!"

Behind the birders, Oddi rolled his eyes. I limped over to join him. "I'm surprised to see you here. I would have thought that given all that's happened, you'd have lined up another tour."

He glanced at my foot. "I am surprised to see you here, too. But your injury does not seem as bad today as yesterday. You are a tough girl. As to my own presence here, Mrs. Parr asked me to stay with them until they return to the U.S. so that is what I will do."

It took me a moment to realize he was talking about Elizabeth St. John, who never used her husband's name. "Who hired you originally? And how?"

"Mr. Parr found me on the Internet. I have a big website, with many generous recommendations. He closed his eyes and quoted, "'Oddi Pálsson showed us the Iceland that is seldom seen by the average tourist,' and 'Oddi Pálsson kept us safe even while glacier-walking.'"

Kept us safe? There's irony for you. "What do you think of them?" I asked. "The Geronimos?"

"Nice people."

"Any one in particular who's given you trouble?"

"No."

I tried again. "How about Lucinda? She can be rather difficult."

"Not with me."

"Tab Cooper?"

"He gives no trouble, either."

"His girlfriend Judy?"

"Also no trouble. And it is the same with the rest of them." Maybe it was my imagination but I could swear I saw the hint of a smile tugging at the corner of his mouth.

Since pumping the tour guide for information was getting me nowhere, I left him for a try at Enid Walsh. "Considering everything that's happened, I'm surprised to see you guys out and about," I said, sidling up to her.

She managed to tear her eyes away from the horses long enough to give me a wondering look. "I could say the same thing about you, Teddy. How's your foot?"

"All better," I lied. To keep the conversation going, I started talking about Magnus. After telling her about the care and feeding of orphaned bear cubs, I discussed the time and expense it took to transport them from one zoo to another across international waters.

"You can't simply put them in a crate and load them into the belly of a plane," I said. "Their crate has to be constructed just so, they have to have access to food and water....And there's a pile of paperwork to fill out, too, both in Iceland and in California. These days I'm drowning in red tape."

When she made a face, I realized I had struck a nerve.

"Red tape, ugh! It's given me and Perry nothing but grief. As far as I'm concerned, the market's being hamstrung by red tape and paperwork. Write this, write that, attach affidavit this to affidavit that, connect provenance A to provenance C...The whole thing's gotten to the point where red tape has made it almost impossible for small businesses to survive."

"I know what you mean." Writing up invoices that claimed fake gemstones were real had to be a major hassle.

Seemingly out of nowhere, she said, "Poor Dawn loved our jewelry. She bought several pieces from us."

"When was this?" Before or after the Walshes got caught pawning off fakes?

"Not long before we came here. A tennis bracelet and a necklace with matching earrings. Ben wants to bury her wearing them."

"When did he tell you that?"

"This morning. Perry and I stopped by his room to see how he was doing."

I put the idea of fraudulent gemstones aside for a moment. "I hear he's pretty broken up."

"He's a mess."

"Why do you think Ben…?"

Before I could finish, one of the horses farted in our direction. Whether done intentionally or not, the result was that the birders moved away from the corral. I moved with them.

"Disgusting creatures," I heard Lucinda mutter.

"What were you about to ask about Ben?" Enid said, as I followed the group toward the mink enclosure.

"If he was divorcing Dawn, why would he be so broken up about her now?"

Another wondering look. "Divorcing? Who told you that?"

"Uh, Dawn." And a couple other people.

Enid snorted. "Another one of her exaggerations. Sure, they hit a rough spot a couple of months ago, but that kind of thing happened with them all the time, threats of divorce, him moving out, him moving back in, then back out, etcetera, etcetera, etcetera. Next thing you know they were all lovey-dovey again, but what can you expect? No matter what kind of crazy stunt she pulled on him, Ben was always a fool about her. Now, excuse me, but I want to hear what Oddi's saying about minks in the wild." With that she turned away.

Properly shushed, I broke away from the group and headed toward the foxes.

Loki and Ilsa had been fed an hour earlier, so now the only thing they needed was a clean enclosure and fresh bedding, so as I worked, I considered everything I'd learned.

Other than jealousy, Ben Talley had no reason to kill Simon Parr—or at least I hadn't found one so far—but despite Enid's assurances, he could have killed Dawn. All you had to do was tune into the late-night news to see how often men killed the women they supposedly loved. Of course, it sometimes worked the other way, too, but Dawn was dead and Ben was still among the living.

Something else Enid said struck me. Dawn bought jewelry from Hope Diamond Enterprises. Had the stones turned out to be fake, and Dawn threatened to go to the police? Or, given her love of money, even tried a spot of blackmail? No crook with any common sense would knowingly sell fake gems to a friend who lived in the same small town, but crooks often displayed a lack of common sense. Look at my own felonious father. A wealthy man in his own right, he'd embezzled millions from his own company merely for sake of an adrenaline rush.

Crime could be as addictive as crack cocaine.

Chapter Twenty

Bryndis didn't like what I'd proposed on the way home from the zoo, but she grudgingly went along with it. After we stopped by her apartment to clean up, she directed me to a small shop where I could buy flowers. The bouquet of white and cream dahlias—they were out of lilies—cost a small fortune, but I couldn't show up at Ben's hotel room empty-handed.

"What do you think about this sympathy card?" I asked, showing her a pretty one with a picture of a sad-looking whopper swan on the front. The message inside was written in an elegant Icelandic script.

"That's a party invitation."

"Oh." I put it back and picked up a card with a pied wagtail on it.

She looked at the inscription. "My heart goes out to you for your loss. Are you sure you're up to this?"

"The card says that?"

"It says the stuff about the heart. I said the rest."

"Of course I'm up to it."

"Mmph."

A few minutes later, as she parked her Volvo in one of the visitor's spots at the Hótel Keldur, she said, "After what happened at Thingvellir, you would be wise to stay away from those people. Ragnar is no longer in danger of being arrested again, so you are taking a needless risk."

"Right, that's why this is the last time I'll talk to any of them, especially Ben."

"Mmph." She was beginning to sound like Inspector Haraldsson.

You could tell how expensive the hotel was from the high-end cars in its underground parking lot. In the guest spaces, Mercedes and Land Rovers—the better to drive on ice-covered mountains—ruled the day, with a few Saabs, Lexuses, and Acuras thrown in to keep things interesting. Their elegance made the cars in the staff parking spaces look shabby by comparison: older-model Toyotas, Suzukis, Volkswagens, Renaults, and a sprinkling of American subcompacts.

"I need to get this interview with Ben out of the way. Afterwards I'll treat us to that play you were telling me about." Deflection, deflection, deflection.

"It is a one-man show, not a play. You do not feel guilty, intruding upon the poor man's grief?"

My attempt at deflection having failed, I sighed. Yes, I did feel guilty, but I didn't want to talk about it anymore. As we walked toward the elevator, I made one final try. "Aren't you going to lock your car?"

"No one locks their cars in Iceland."

Right, because why would one cousin steal another cousin's car? I kept forgetting how closely related all Icelanders were and how much their blood ties affected their behavior toward one another.

"I will not go up there with you," she said, parrying my deflection again. "Instead, I will wait in the bar, where I might be able to afford a bottle of Perrier."

"My treat." I handed her five thousand kronur, courtesy of the Gunn Zoo. It sounded like a lot, but in actuality was less than forty dollars American. "Maybe it'll get you a beer."

"Not in the Keldar. Promise you will be careful, okay?"

"I'll warn Ben there's a Valkyrie waiting for me in the bar, and if I don't turn up within a half hour, she'll charge in to rescue me with her sword and shield."

"Smart mouth." But she smiled.

We parted ways in the lobby, me for the elevator, her for the bar.

Enid had given me Ben's room number, but due to the labyrinthian hallway, I took a couple of false turnings before I found it. Finally, standing in front of the black enamel door, I took a moment to get my courage up, and even then my knock sounded hesitant.

Ben opened the door almost immediately. He looked like hell and smelled like he hadn't bathed in days. "Oh. It's you."

"Were you expecting someone else?"

"Elizabeth said she'd stop by." He eyed the dahlias. "Well, you might as well come on in. The more the merrier, I guess."

He led me into a suite identical to Elizabeth's, all black and white and chrome. The only spots of color came from several vases of wilting flowers set around the room. He took my bouquet and stuffed it into a vase already filled with dying lilies.

"I'm so sorry…" I began.

"Yeah, yeah. Want a drink? The Chivas is gone but there's some Gray Goose left."

"No thanks."

"Suit yourself." He slumped down on the sofa and grabbed the half-empty glass off the table next to it. He took a sip of the clear liquid inside, made a face, took another sip. "I'm not really a vodka guy, but any port in a storm, right?"

He was drunk, which may or may not have been a good thing, so I took a deep breath and started in. "Ben, I'm confused about a couple of things."

"Join the club." More Gray Goose.

"Someone told me you packed a Glock in your suitcase on the way to Iceland."

"Then someone told you wrong. I thought about bringing it, but then I had a rare attack of common sense and left it at home."

"I also heard you got into a shoving match with Simon at the Phoenix airport."

He took another sip of vodka, this time keeping the glass in his hand, like he was afraid to let go. "Sounds like the same little someone who told you I packed my Glock. But yeah, I got a little physical with the guy. Served him right, too, him all of a sudden acting like a big shot just because he won a pile of money."

"The altercation—at least the story I heard—was about Perry Walsh being elected president of the Geronimos, not about money. Is that true?"

"Another small nugget of truth. Adele was running for president, but Simon rigged it so his good buddy Perry Walsh won. Adele's as straight as they come, but Perry's a crook. God knows what'll happen to our treasury when he and his Enid get their hands on it. So to an extent, the 'altercation,' as you call it, was about money, and its looming vanishing act."

Since he was being so cooperative, I decided to go ahead and ask the big question. *In vino veritas*, and all that. "Did you kill Simon?"

He made a sound somewhere between a growl and a bark. "Don't be an ass, woman! I know damned well that my dearly beloved wife is the one who pointed the finger at me." He finished the rest of the vodka in one big gulp, then stared mournfully at the empty glass.

"Dawn wouldn't do anything like that. She was a lovely person."

"Dawn was a lying bitch."

"Uh, well, she could be rather spirited."

"An unfaithful slut."

"Marriage can certainly be diff…"

"A narcissistic, thieving, ungrateful whore."

'You know, maybe I will have that drink." I hurried to the wet bar and poured myself a finger of vodka, which wasn't my thing, either, but as the man said, any port in a storm. "Thieving, did you say?"

"Greedy slag always went for the pot of gold, never mind the rainbows."

Keeping the wet bar between us—just in case—I took a not-so-wild guess. "You're talking about Simon Parr again, right?"

He toasted me with his empty glass.

I bolted my Gray Goose. "I've heard so many conflicting stories, Ben, so help me get this straight. Were you and Dawn going to get a divorce or not?"

"Yeah, but just think of the trouble I could have saved myself if I'd killed the bitch years ago!"

Ooo-kay. There was an ice pick lying next to the ice bucket. I picked it up. Again—just in case. "My friend's waiting for me downstairs. He's six-foot-six and knows karate."

"Lucky you. Did you know I went to prison for her?"

He certainly wasn't talking about Bryndis, so I took another not-so-wild guess. "For Dawn?"

Another toast.

"She ran that man down, not you, right?"

He began another toast, then noticed his glass was empty. With a determined look on his battered face, he stood up and staggered toward me.

I was saved from deciding what to do—run screaming into the hall or pour him another drink—when someone knocked at the door.

"Don't move, I'll get it!" I rushed to the door and threw it open before I realized I still held the ice pick in my hand.

"For chopping ice or self-defense?" Elizabeth St. John asked, gazing at the pick. She was carrying a large tray that held several covered dishes and a gigantic carafe of coffee.

My smile felt phony even to me. "Just refreshing my drink. Want one?"

"There's been enough drinking around here already." She entered the room and set the tray down on the chrome and glass coffee table. "What are you doing here, Teddy?"

"Just stopped by to extend my condolences." I motioned toward the dahlias.

"I'm sure Ben's grateful for your kind thoughts, but it would be better if you left him alone now. He needs food, not more vodka." With that, she snatched my ice pick away, grasped me firmly by the arm, and escorted me to the door.

"That did not take long," Bryndis said, when I met her in the bar. Ragnar had joined her and they were drinking Ölvisholt Lava.

"*Interviewus interruptus.*"

Bryndis snickered, but Ragnar didn't get it. "Isn't that Latin?"

After assuring Ragnar and Bryndis that my injured foot was almost back to normal, we walked from the hotel to Harpa, the concert hall, where they treated me to an English-language performance of *How to Become Icelandic in 60 Minutes*, a one-man show written and performed by one of Ragnar's friends. Bjarni Haukur Thorsson had spent enough time in the U.S. to realize how strange some Icelandic customs might appear to Americans, and did his best to explain them. Bjarni's take on Iceland's infamous "shower police," whose indignities tourists had to suffer before taking a dip in the Blue Lagoon, had everyone in stitches.

"But enough of high art!" Ragnar chuckled an hour later as we left Harpa. "Now we go get drunk!"

If I had known he was taking us to the Viking Tavern, I would have begged off, but I didn't, and so to my horror a few minutes later I found myself sitting two tables away from the remaining members of the Geronimo County Birding Association. Minus Ben and Elizabeth, of course.

Lucinda scowled at me across their table, but Adele and the Walshes gave me half-hearted waves. As for Judy Malone and Tab Cooper, they were too engrossed in each other to notice anyone else in the room.

"There is the woman Mr. Parr was so unkind to," Ragnar said, gesturing toward Adele. "Instead of looking sad, she should be happy to know he will be unkind no longer."

Seeing Adele, who was looking depressed again, I mentally congratulated myself on my luck in finding Joe: Joe the kind-hearted, Joe the faithful. Speaking of Joe, hadn't he once told me one of the main motives for murder was thwarted love? I studied Adele's face more carefully and came to the conclusion that she didn't look like a murderer. But neither had Ted Bundy.

Unsettled, I returned my attention to Bryndis, who after a brief glance at her iPhone, began questioning Ragnar about his latest job as a film extra on some big Hollywood production being filmed at Vik. It was still early in the evening—for Icelanders, anyway—and the noise level in the tavern was low enough that I could hear their conversation.

"Why do the producers think Americans will pay money to see a movie about berserkers?" she asked him. "They were a Viking phenomenon, and most Americans do not know what they are."

Ragnar shook his head. "Japan had their ninjas, America the lone cowboy, yet both are popular there. I am certain it will be the same with berserkers."

"The ninjas and the cowboys were not crazy. The berserkers were."

He shrugged his broad shoulders. "Not so crazy. When they went into battle they were under the influence of drugs and merely felt invincible. Do not forget, the berserkers' religion taught them that death in battle would guarantee their entrance into Valhalla."

Bryndis didn't look convinced. "I think Americans will much prefer their cowboys."

"It does not matter to me, because I get paid anyway." Giving her a sly look, he added, "Besides, there will most certainly be a big turnout of lonely American women to admire all those big, half-naked berserkers."

The image of a half-naked Ragnar flashed into my mind. Guiltily, I immediately replaced it with one of Joe.

Bryndis' voice jerked me out of my fantasy. "Look there, Ragnar, she is thinking about her boyfriend again!"

Caught, I felt myself blush. "It's just warm in here."

She grinned, then lowered her voice to an almost-whisper. "Now that I have your attention, I must tell you I just received a text from my friend Ulfur at Vik. He texted me that the hoopoe is back. Tomorrow I am scheduled to give a talk at the zoo about the changing migration routes of reindeer in Finland, but I have the next day off. A storm is due in sometime over the weekend, and Friday may be our last chance to see him. What do you say? I have never seen a hoopoe in the flesh."

Hoopoes and Vik brought back memories of Simon Parr's mutilated face, so my first instinct was to say no, but Bryndis' hopeful expression changed my mind. She had been such a kind and generous host I hated to disappoint her.

"That sounds great!" I lied.

Truth be told, and truth seemed an increasing rarity in my life, the idea of returning to Vik unsettled me to such an extent that after lying in bed for an hour without sleep while listening to Bryndis' soft snore, I gave up and tiptoed into the living room. Reading could sometimes act as an antidote to insomnia. At first I avoided Elizabeth's new novel because of its exciting, if over-the-top plot, but when Bryndis' technical journals failed to put me to sleep, I surrendered to *Tahiti Passion*.

Was there anything Jade L'Amour couldn't do? By chapter sixteen, in addition to her earlier heroics, the beautiful archaeologist had found a horde of Viking gold, changed a tire on a Jeep, unmasked a serial killer, and danced the night away with the handsome Dr. Lance Everington. She did this all while wearing a black lace Betsey Johnson frock and red, five-inch Jimmy Choo stilettos.

I fell asleep just as the good doctor unhooked her scarlet Faire Frou Frou bra.

Chapter Twenty-one

So far during my stay, Iceland had been blessed with perfect weather, and as Bryndis and I drove southeast toward Vik two days later, nothing had changed. The sky remained cloudless and blue, the moss-covered lava fields an eye-dazzling green. The only unsettling element was the sea, a blue so dark it almost looked black. Bryndis told me it meant the weather would turn by the next morning.

"A storm brought Mr. Hoopoe in and a storm will see him out," she said, as she pulled into the crowded car park near the beach. "Let us hope that pretty bird can at least hang on through today. By the way, did I tell you I like the tee-shirt you're wearing today? It's even cuter than your HONEY BADGER DON'T CARE one."

I looked down at the bright red shirt Joe had given me for my birthday. The black lettering across the front said, I BRAKE FOR REDHEADS.

"A gift," I explained. "Uh, why are all these trucks and trailers here?" I asked, looking around. "It's not even six yet."

"Film crews. Cinematographers like the early morning light. They pretend it to be a dramatic sunset, although with no clouds, they must feel disappointed. But the clouds will come, then everyone will be happy. Except for people who do not like wind and rain."

When we stepped out of the Volvo, I remarked on how much the wind had risen since we left her apartment, so we both reached back into the car for the windbreakers we'd brought along in case the weather turned.

"I feel like I'm being hit in the face with a wet dish rag," I said, shrugging into my jacket. In contrast to Bryndis' light blue jacket, which matched her eyes, mine was more the khaki color of my freckles.

Bryndis looked up at the sky. "The wind announces the storm will be here by sunset."

By which time, I hoped, we would be back in balmy Reykjavik. My heel had almost returned to normal, but given my near-sleepless night, I wasn't looking forward to the steep climb ahead of us. Since the farrier was visiting the horse farm today, a comparatively easy horseback ride to the puffin rookery via horseback had been ruled out. We could have taken the land bridge route, but that would have added another mile to our hike, so the serpentine route up the side of the cliff face remained the best solution. When an African bird rare to Iceland is in the offing, you do what you have to do.

When we rounded the base of the cliff and stepped onto Vik's famous black sand beach, an unusual sight came into view. A large crowd was watching several space-suited astronauts crawl out of a landing craft that had crashed in the waves just off shore. One astronaut was dragging another, who—judging from the amount of blood on his space suit—had suffered fatal injuries.

Was I, in my exhausted state, having what is referred to as a waking dream?

"Cut!" someone screamed. "What the hell, Jeff? You look like you're dragging a sack of potatoes!"

Oh. Just another film set.

The astronauts, including the dead one, duly sloshed their way back into the space craft, only to reemerge a few moments later with astronaut Jeff carrying the "corpse" like a groom his bride. No one yelled "Cut!" although the scene looked unintentionally humorous. But what did I know?

"Those aren't berserkers," I said to Bryndis.

"This is the set of *Death on Orion 12*. The *Berserker!* set is further down the beach, on the other side of the village, so we may yet get a glimpse of Ragnar in his costume. Or lack of one." She grinned. "But first, we find our hoopoe!"

With that, we turned our backs on the struggling astronauts and began the long trek up the side of the cliff to the puffin rookery. The trail's switchbacks had been terrifying enough on horseback, but without a sure-footed Icelandic horse under me, the climb seemed doubly so now. The increasing North Atlantic wind didn't help. The wind howled around us, tugging at our jackets and at one point, almost swept the hood back off my head. I re-secured it with trembling fingers, and as we wound our way upwards, tried not to look down. If only I had Jade L'Amour's courage!

"I see you back there, hugging the cliff wall!" Bryndis shouted, her words almost carried away by the wind. "You did not tell me you worry about falling from heights!"

"It's not the fall that worries me, it's the sudden stop!" I yelled back. An old joke, but given the circumstances, an apt one.

Once during the climb, a puffin flew by carrying several small fish in her beak. I thought I saw a white stripe running across her head, but she vanished so quickly I couldn't be certain. Flashing back to the similarly striped puffin in the Reykjavik Zoo, I wondered how long the mutation would carry down through the line. For a couple more generations, then die out? Or would the stripe remain permanent to the genetic line? It would be interesting to find out, so I made a mental note to keep track of the phenomenon. Maybe Mama Puffin would poke her beak far enough outside her burrow for me to snap a few pictures, something I had been too shocked to do when I first saw her pecking at...

Better not think about that. I returned my attention to the winding trail, finding its terrors preferable to memory. My sore foot helped provide a distraction, although my limp had disappeared. The heel was scabbed over nicely, and yesterday I'd managed a full shift at the zoo with no trouble. And what was a slight soreness compared to a seeing a real, live hoopoe?

After what seemed like hours but by my watch were mere minutes, Bryndis and I reached the top of the cliff, spooking several puffins as we stepped onto the level grassland. Unfortunately, the puffins weren't the only creatures annoyed by our sudden presence.

The Geronimo County Birding Association wasn't happy to see us, either. I should have known someone would give them the news about the reappearance of the hoopoe.

"Well, look what the cat dragged in," sniped Lucinda.

Enid Walsh merely frowned.

Perry Walsh proved his talent for diplomacy by stepping forward with a twinkle in his eye and an outstretched hand. "What a delight, Teddy!"

Shaking his hand, I smiled back. "You don't see a hoopoe every day, especially in Iceland."

"You missed him by seconds," said Tab Cooper, looking slightly cranky himself. "When he heard you two coming up the cliff—and you made a lot of damn noise—he flew off."

Before I could apologize, Perry said, "I'm sure he'll be back. All we have to do is wait."

Tab's scowl was eased by Judy Malone, who rubbed his arm in sympathy.

Lucinda, who had always hated seeing any display of affection between them, snapped, "If you two would just keep your minds on the birds…" The wind blew the rest of her words away. Just as well, I figured. They wouldn't have been nice.

"I took pictures of the hoopoe," Enid Walsh said, thrusting her camera at me. "Although it is too bad you…"

"Great shot!" I exclaimed, cutting off what was certain to be another comment about Bryndis' and my noisy trip up the side of the cliff. "Oh, look, in this one he's sharpening his beak on a piece of lava! And yellow? Such a bright, beautiful yellow! I didn't know you were such a good photographer, Enid."

Mollified, she took the camera back. "One of my prints, a close-up of a road runner eating a gecko, won Silver at the Geronimo County Fair."

"She should have taken the Gold," her husband said. "The winner was a shot of a toddler picking his nose. It was taken from a distance, but that's just another reason she should have won the Gold. The judges should have exercised some taste."

"You have to admit the toddler was cute." Enid said.

"Cute toddlers are a dime a dozen. You were robbed. You should have…"

Forestalling a litany of should-haves, I interrupted. "Actually, I'm surprised, ah, happily surprised, of course, to see you guys here. After everything that's happened, I would have thought you'd stay in the Reykjavik area." Where the police were just a short phone call away.

Perry harrumphed. "That's what Inspector Haraldsson suggested, too, but we weren't about to miss seeing that hoopoe."

I could see his point. Why stay holed up in Reykjavik when the spectacular countryside of Iceland beckoned? But the Geronimos' presence made me uncomfortable. After all, one of them had tried to kill me. Maybe even twice. I still remembered that near-tumble into the waterfalls at Gullfoss. Good thing Elizabeth had pulled me back.

Speaking of Elizabeth, she stood at the back of the group talking to a wan-looking Ben Talley. Apparently her ministrations the other day had worked, and although stress, grief, and booze had left their mark, he was at least upright and fairly focused.

"People, let's move further back!" Perry said. "The hoopoe won't return if we keep standing around in his favorite spot. And for God's sake, everybody stop talking!" This last was directed at Bryndis and me.

Obediently we all moved about twenty yards further inland, stopping just past the point where remnants of yellow police tape fluttered from the moss-covered lava. As we settled ourselves on the ground, I tried to forget what had happened there, but was unsuccessful. The only thing that halfway cheered me was the sight of Mama Puffin stuffing fish into her chick's craw. She was so intent on feeding her baby that she paid no attention to any of us.

I hauled my iPhone out of my pocket and snapped off a couple of shots. Bryndis, who had taken care to bring along her Panasonic Lumix, did the same. I heard a few clicks from the Geronimos' fleet of cameras, but the group was otherwise silent, waiting for the hoopoe.

The hoopoe didn't disappoint. Only a few minutes later he appeared in a shimmer of yellow, black, and white, alighting on a bare lava outcropping. After a few low calls of *poo-poo-poo*, he preened his feathers for a minute, then hopped off the outcropping and began to hunt. For an appetizer, he pecked up a crane-fly. A fat yellow dung fly became his entrée, and a wasp—caught on the wing—his dessert. During this buggy meal, camera clicks from the Geronimos continued without stop.

Maybe at some point the hoopoe had developed a taste for fish, because he then hopped toward the head-striped puffin, only to be growled away. Yes, puffins can growl.

Good Mama.

I could have stayed there the rest of the day watching Mama Puffin feed and protect her chick, but once the hoopoe flew away, the Geronimos rose as one and high-fived one another. The racket sent Mama Puffin scrambling further down into her burrow, where she was no longer visible.

"Well, we finally saw the impossible," Bryndis said. "Now it is back down the cliff to look up Ragnar. I am certain he will look handsome in his berserker costume. Is your foot still okay, Teddy?"

"It's good to go." God bless Nike and a layer of moleskin.

With relief I watched the Geronimos start over the gently sloped land bridge toward the distant hotel, then I dutifully followed Bryndis to the cliff-side path. At least the trip down would be less onerous than the climb up.

A few minutes later we found the *Berserker!* set on the expanse of flat marshland that separated the peaceful village of Vik from the rowdy North Atlantic. Clad in a variety of costumes, and up to their knees in mud, scores of film extras battled to the death. Historical accuracy was hardly the film's forte, because up against the Viking warriors raged a stew of ninjas, Mongols, Huns, and Visigoths. Maybe the production company was just trying to save money by using whatever costumes that just happened to be lying around, regardless of the era they represented. It wasn't hard to spot the six-foot-four Ragnar, who was going toe-to-toe with a black-clad ninja. Eye makeup intensified Ragnar's blue eyes, and the Runic symbols "tattooed" on his chest emphasized his manly pecs. His pseudo animal skin loincloth didn't leave much to the imagination, either.

While Bryndis and I stood in open-mouthed awe, Ragnar's double-headed ax made short work of the ninja, but judging from the nasty gash the berserker had received across his throat and the amount of fake blood flowing freely down his naked chest, his part in the film was over. With a mighty roar, the big berserker spit up a fountain of blood, then collapsed twitching, into the marsh.

"Ragnar is known for dying well," Bryndis said, as he delivered a final twitch. She had to raise her voice over the roar of the surf. The shoreline was less than a hundred yards away.

"That was a spectacular performance, all right."

The battle raged on for another couple of minutes—it looked like the berserkers were winning—when the director, who wore a New Orleans Saints cap, yelled, "Cut! Y'all take five!"

As one, the corpses rose from the dead and made their bloody way to the catering trucks parked on higher ground.

"Ragnar says that with this director, 'take five' can mean an hour," Bryndis commented, so he may come over to talk to us."

Spotting us, Ragnar bypassed the catering trucks and trotted over. For a dead man, he looked great.

"Ah, I am fortunate to be visited by the two most beautiful women in the world!" Close up, Ragnar's double-headed ax was an obvious fake.

Bryndis tittered, but I just smiled. Experience had taught me to never trust silver-tongued devils. Or berserkers.

"Did you see the way I twitched, Bryndis?"

Her eyes went limpid with admiration. "You twitched magnificently."

"Yep, those were some pretty good twitches," I said. "Very realistic. Just like that slash across your throat. That ninja got you pretty good, didn't he?"

"In real life Stefán is a fencing instructor, but you will notice I almost beheaded him. He died well, too, although not as well as me."

"No one dies as well as you, Ragnar." More limpidity. Bryndis leaned toward him. He leaned toward her.

If the canoodling lasted any longer, I'd have to tell them to get a room, so I threw some verbal cold water into the conversation. "Say, Ragnar, did you know that the Geronimo County Birding Association is back here in Vik?"

A scowl. "Are they here to look for that yellow hoopoe or to kill someone else?"

"Just the hoopoe. It returned and they were able to get off some great shots. Of the camera kind, I mean. Of the bird."

"They are your countrymen, Teddy, so you must play nice with them, but it would be wise for Bryndis to stay far away." He placed a protective arm around her shoulders, smearing her windbreaker with fake blood. From the adoring look she gave him, she didn't mind.

"I plan to avoid them, too," I said, miffed that he'd shown no concern for my safety.

"Then you are smart."

A whistle pierced the air, followed by a shout. "Places, y'all! Places! Berserkers A, C, and F, change wardrobes!"

With that, part of the rag-tag army of spear-throwers and ax-swingers slogged back into the marsh, while others headed for a big motor home parked near the catering trucks. Ragnar gave Bryndis a quick peck on the cheek. "I am F, so I go to die now as a Visigoth and then as a ninja."

We spent the rest of the morning watching Ragnar die.

He died quite well in his Visigoth garb of helmet, tunic, and pleather trousers, but I preferred his death throes as a ninja. Clad from head to toe in body-hiding black, he upped his physicality, flopping and thrashing long after he sank into the marsh. His screams and groans as he twitched into death added a fine texture to his performance. I could have watched the handsome hunk die all day, but when Nicolas Cage, the film's star berserker, arrived on set for his close-ups, the director let the extras break for lunch. As soon as Ragnar changed back into street clothes—leaving on his screen makeup, including fake blood—we clambered into Bryndis' Volvo and drove up the hill to Hótel Brattholt.

I had forgotten about the presence of the Geronimos until we entered the hotel's crowded dining room. There they sat, at a long table near the big picture window, looking oddly normal compared to the blood-spattered film extras enjoying an early lunch. After a quick glance around, I realized their table had the only unoccupied seats in the room.

"Perhaps we should eat somewhere else," Bryndis said. "There is another hotel a few miles east of here. Or we could go back to the catering trucks, where for once the food is better than it needs to be."

Ragnar shook his head. "If this is all right with Teddy, it is all right with me. It is of no consequence to me that because of the actions of one of those people, I spent many unhappy hours being questioned by the police."

"So should we stay or leave?" Bryndis asked. "It is up to you, Teddy."

"We didn't have much in the way of breakfast this morning, so my vote is to stay. I don't think anyone else will get murdered in a room filled with this many people."

"Famous last words," Bryndis muttered.

For himself, Ragnar put a good, if bloody, face on the situation and strode toward the Geronimos' table, shouting out greetings. With the exception of Lucinda, they all professed joy at our arrival. Elizabeth and Adele might have even been sincere.

"May we see the pictures you two took of the hoopoe?" asked Perry Walsh as I sat down, across from him, while Bryndis and Ragnar took the two seats at the other end.

I handed over my iPhone, saying, "These won't be as good as the ones Bryndis took with her Lumix, but at least I got the whole bird in the frame." I was a notoriously bad photographer, once having cut off the head of a rare white rhinoceros in a once-in-a-lifetime shot.

My pictures were amateurish, but Perry and his wife politely oohed and ahhed, then passed the phone along so the others could see. The praise sounded more sincere when Bryndis' Lumix passed around the table. While they were mooning over her pictures, I took my chance.

"How are you feeling?" I asked Ben Talley, who was sitting next to me.

After Wednesday's booze-a-thon, his skin still bore a green tinge and his facial scars appeared more obvious.

"How does it look like I'm feeling?" He stared down at his plate. He had hardly touched his fish.

"Not so great. But better."

He gave me a guilty look. "I must apologize for my behavior, and I hope you didn't take anything I said seriously. Not that I can remember much about it, just you coming over with flowers. They're nice by the way."

"Dawn was a lovely woman."

A dark chuckle. "Oh, yeah. Lovely." Then, as if he realized how ugly he'd sounded, he cleared his throat and said, "As I'm sure you know, none of us can leave the country until the police have finished their investigation. After that, I'm taking her back to California. Her parents have a family plot in Holy Cross Cemetery."

"That's in San Francisco?"

"Colma. It's not too far, so they can visit as often as they wish."

"Was she an only child?" The minute the question slipped out of my mouth, I knew I'd made a mistake. As a supposedly old school friend of Dawn's, I should already know the answer.

Ben gave no sign of noticing my blunder, but Elizabeth frowned and gave me a sideways glance. She'd noticed.

"Dawn had three brothers and two sisters," Ben said, obviously not as astute as the writer. "I spoke to them on the phone. They're devastated, of course."

"Of course. Ah, speaking of the investigation, does Inspector Haraldsson know you're in Vik?"

His mouth tightened. "I didn't bother to tell him. That damned cop's stopped by the hotel every day since it happened, sometimes more than once. God only knows what I told him the other day because I sure can't remember. He'll stroke out when he finds out I left the hotel, but Elizabeth insisted I get out of there for at least today."

Elizabeth had been right. As ashen as Ben looked right now, he looked a hundred percent better than he had the last time I'd seen him.

The busy hum in the restaurant continued around us as more tourists and film extras arrived, and every now and then I could hear snatches of conversation. The people at the table next to ours had taken pictures, too, and more cameras were being passed around. It all seemed so normal. The Geronimos, after their first initial shock at seeing me, were chatting like normal people, too. I wondered how long that would last.

Keeping my voice low, I said, "You know, Ben, I meant to ask you something the last time I saw you, but you were, ah, kind of under the weather, so I'll ask now. That night in Stykkishólmur when Dawn turned up missing, you didn't raise the alarm for four hours. Why wait so long?"

He didn't appear offended by the question. Maybe he'd given up caring about anything, even my curiosity. "Want the truth? Well, here it is. I didn't 'raise the alarm,' as you so subtly put it, right away because I thought Dawn was with someone else. If I'd panicked and called in the National Guard, or whatever it is they have in this damn country, to search for her, it could have been embarrassing for everyone, especially her. As it turns out, I was wrong. My wife wasn't with anyone. She was dead.

However crappy our marriage was, she didn't deserve that. But it doesn't matter now, does it? She's gone and it's all over except for the burying."

"Teddy!" Bryndis called, over the ongoing chatter at our table. "The waitress has asked you twice for your order."

I looked up to see the waitress, little more than a teenager, standing next to me with a notepad and pen. She bore a strong resemblance to Ulfur, the hotelier. His daughter? Come to think of it, where was Ulfur, anyway? Last time I was here, he'd been tending bar.

"Uh, I'll just have the fish and chips." I hadn't even looked at the menu.

With a nod, she moved on to the next table.

By then, Ben Talley had turned away from me and was talking to Lucinda Greaves, who for once, was treating him with kindness. No matter. I had already learned what I needed, that Ben suspected Dawn had moved on from Simon Parr to someone else. I could think of only one viable candidate.

Tab Cooper.

Chapter Twenty-two

Young and handsome, Tab Cooper could have served as a temporary distraction for Dawn until she found herself a wealthy man. But weighing against my theory was the fact that right now Tab was sitting so close to Judy Malone he was almost in her lap. Had he, too, moved on or had he been playing one woman against the other? The way some people arrange their so-called love lives these days, I shouldn't have felt shocked by the idea, but I did. If my theory was correct, I wondered if Judy had known about him and Dawn. More to the point, had Ben? If I could figure it out, he could, too.

Then I realized I'd forgotten another candidate for Dawn's sexual favors.

Oddi. The Geronimos' tour guide.

With his wrestler's bulk and graying hair, Oddi Pálsson might not have been anyone's idea of a Nordic god, but there was no denying his attractiveness to women. His experience as a tour guide lent him a somewhat slick, yet charming, persona but any woman who paid attention could also detect the rugged alpha male hidden under the slick veneer. On more than one occasion I'd seen Dawn and Judy sneaking looks at him. Even Lucinda and Enid had done the same. Just because a woman was north of fifty didn't mean she was dead blow the waist. And for a woman like Dawn, who in her modeling heyday had been every man's fantasy, only to wind up discarded by a birdwatcher…

Then again, Simon Parr wasn't just a birder. He was a *multi-millionaire* birder who, after years of living in his more successful wife's shadow, had finally come into his own. Dawn loved money, which explained her initial pursuit of her husband, then of Simon. After Simon kicked her to the curb, she might have consoled herself with the more experienced Oddi. I'd once read an article in *Psychology Today* about crimes of passion. The article claimed that when confronted with infidelity, a worldly man would kill his rival, but a less-worldly man would kill his wife. Yet this killer had opted for both.

Which begged the question: did I really believe Benjamin Talley had it in him to murder two people?

"Good God, Teddy, what is going through your head?" Bryndis' voice cut into my thoughts. "You look like you're chewing nails."

"Just thinking."

"About what, the end of the world?"

In a way I was, since the world *had* ended for Simon and Dawn.

The waitress arrived with my fish and chips, and I set to eating. As I'd hoped, it was delicious. In Iceland, you couldn't get bad seafood.

My gloom further vanished when the Walshes found a close-up of the hoopoe on Bryndis' camera and praised it loudly. From there, the conversation turned to other "vagrants," birds found in unusual places. Lucinda said she'd heard of a rock partridge nesting near a woodpile in Ireland. Perry told of a sandhill crane hanging out in a Shetland Islands farmyard, stealing corn from the pigs. But I was most riveted by Adele's account of a puffin spotted last year on the Spanish coast.

"The birder who saw the puffin said it had a white stripe across its head," Adele said. "He uploaded a picture on the Net and it looked just like the one we saw on the cliff this morning. The same one, you think?"

"If you believe a puffin would range that far south, you'll believe anything," Lucinda said. Her reservoir of sympathy for Ben run dry, she had returned to her old cranky self.

"Are you accusing that birder of faking his picture? Why would he?"

"Adele, I'm saying you're gullible, which is not an advantageous trait for any good birder."

"I am not gullible!"

Lucinda's laugh had spikes in it. "You believed Simon when he said he was leaving Elizabeth for you, when any fool knows he would never…"

She didn't finish the sentence because Elizabeth slammed down her water glass. "You know, Lucinda, I've had just about enough of your mouth."

As the other Geronimos held their collective breaths, the author threw her napkin across her plate and stood up. To everyone's relief, she headed not toward Lucinda (With a fish knife? With a fork?) but toward the ladies' room.

There was a mass exhale as she vanished down the hall.

Lucinda's mouth kept moving. "…leave his meal ticket. Say what you will about Simon, the man wasn't stupid."

Now it was Adele's turn to rush away from the table. Unlike Elizabeth, she headed outside. Looking through the restaurant's window, I could see her shoulders heaving as she wept.

It was more than I could take. After neatly folding my napkin and placing it on my plate, I followed in Elizabeth's footsteps. If there had been two of me, I'd have gone to comfort Adele, too.

When I reached the ladies' room, I heard Elizabeth blowing her nose in a stall.

"Lucinda's an ass," I called. "Don't let her get to you."

A sniff. "Easy for you to say." A honk, then a few more sniffs. "I told Simon he was making a mistake, inviting her along. She's a good birder, but all she's ever done is make trouble."

"What do you mean, 'make trouble'?"

"Don't tell me you haven't noticed." Elizabeth emerged from the stall blotting her eyes with toilet paper. Mascara ran down her cheeks, making her look like a sad clown. "Lucinda's a genius at setting people against each other. If we went back there right now,

I can guarantee you we'd see everyone arguing, some defending me, others defending her, while she just sits there and gloats."

"She must lead a miserable life."

"Don't kid yourself. She gets her jollies by feeding off other people's misery. Look at Judy, for instance. Still single, still living at home with Mommy. Every time she tries to leave, Lucinda finds a way to squelch the poor girl's plans." She leaned over the sink and began to wash her ravaged face.

"Judy owns a yoga studio, doesn't she? She could leave any time she wanted."

Elizabeth's face looked better, but not by much. Now that she'd washed off her makeup, she looked older, and for a woman pushing sixty, that wasn't good. "Judy has never summoned the strength to cut the apron strings. Besides, the studio's in her mother's name. She's the one who fronted the money."

"Lucinda practices yoga?"

"With that mean-mouthed hostility? Of course she doesn't practice yoga! She financed the studio simply to have a financial hold over her darling daughter."

"But Judy didn't have to let that happen."

"You're wrong there. The girl's never been strong. She was a sickly child, in and out of the hospital, and wound up being dependent on her mother for everything. I doubt that will ever change."

"Where's the father?"

"He split a long time ago. Either that, or Lucinda murdered him and buried the body." Elizabeth vented a bitter laugh, then winced as she caught sight of her reflection in the mirror. "Don't ever get old, Teddy. Marry that cute boyfriend of yours right away."

At first I was taken aback by her comment. How did Elizabeth know Joe was cute? When I thought about it, the answer was obvious. She was a writer, and if there's anything a writer knows how to do, it's research. But it gave me the willies to know someone had been researching *me*.

"Joe and I haven't fixed a date yet. Look, Elizabeth, now that you've pulled yourself together, why don't we rejoin the others?

You'll feel better when you get some food inside you, and that salad of yours looked delicious."

She forced a smile. "Good idea. Why should I give Lucinda the satisfaction of thinking she's ruined my entire day?"

When we got back to the table, we found the birders sitting in strained silence. Even Bryndis looked fraught. The only person who acted unconcerned was Ragnar, who was speaking Icelandic to someone over his iPhone.

After killing the call, he said to Bryndis, "I must return to the set. The cinematographer insists the battle scene be reshot right away. Something about the lighting being more ominous now."

"We will go with you," Bryndis said. It was obvious she wanted to get away from the birders, and I couldn't blame her.

I wondered what other nastiness had gone down while I'd been in the ladies' room with Elizabeth. Lucinda wore a faint smile, but the others looked like they'd just witnessed a head-on collision. Considering the woman's all-around obnoxiousness, I, like Elizabeth, questioned Simon Parr's good sense in inviting her along on the trip. But Judy might have refused to come without her mother, and from everything I'd heard, he liked Judy. More than liked.

"That Lucinda, what an awful woman," Bryndis muttered, when we arrived at the *Berserker!* parking lot a few minutes later. Neither she nor Ragnar had said anything since we left the hotel.

"No argument there." I wasn't feeling especially chatty, either.

"Lucinda is not awful, just frightened," Ragnar piped up from the backseat, surprising us both.

"Really! What's she scared of?"

"That Judy will find love and leave her alone forever." With that, he exited the car and headed toward the wardrobe trailer.

Out of the mouths of babes. Or berserkers.

The silent drive from the hotel had given me time to think, enough so that the suspicion that had been bubbling under the surface for the last few days had grown into a certainty.

Why hadn't I seen it earlier? Well, the answer was easy—too many suspects, too many victims, too many reasons to kill. Smoke and fog and misdirection. Last night, while reading the notes I'd typed in at Gullfoss, I'd come up with a theory, but it wasn't until I'd gone over a few more pages that it stopped being a mere theory. I knew who had killed Simon Parr. And Dawn, too.

"Bryndis, when we get back to Reykjavik, I want you to drop me off at the police station. I need to talk to Inspector Haraldsson. I can walk back to the apartment when I'm finished. It's only a few blocks."

"Ah, so you have finally realized how good-looking he is!"

"Not exactly."

"And he is crazy about you."

"I'm crazy about someone else."

"Then why do you wish to see him? Thor is a very busy man, but I know he would make time for love."

I sighed. Bryndis might like to act the rough, tough Valkyrie, but at heart she was a soppy romantic. Same with Ragnar. Those two belonged together.

"I'll tell you why when I'm finished talking to Inspector Haraldsson. For now, let's watch the filming. Maybe we'll get lucky and see another battle." Where the blood won't be real.

As we walked along the beach toward the film set, I noticed the sky had darkened with fat black clouds, and the North Atlantic surf crashed onto the sand rather than rolled. The cinematographer had been right: the lighting couldn't be better for a battle to the death.

Within minutes, Ragnar emerged from the wardrobe trailer, in his berserker loincloth. With a merry wave, he strode toward the set carrying his shield and sword. As we watched, he made it halfway across the marsh, then fell down. No death cries, no twitches, no convulsion, just the same face-plant that seemed to be inflicting other cast members.

Then a camera and a light rig toppled to the ground.

Then Bryndis.

Then me.

The air itself roared louder than the cries of a hundred dying men, but over the roar I could hear shouts and laughter from falling berserkers.

"Earthquake!" someone shouted.

A native Californian, I knew an earthquake when I felt it, so I didn't try to get up, just lay there as the ground rocked and rolled beneath me. After the first startling seconds, I'd relaxed. There was nothing to fear. Earthquakes could be scary, but experiencing one on a level beach felt much less frightening than enduring one in a crowded city. At Vik there were no skyscrapers or freeways to collapse, just a harmless series of bumps to ride out. Heck, I felt right at home.

"Thor strikes the ground with his mighty hammer!" Bryndis called, grinning.

There was no fear in her voice. As she'd once told me, Iceland averaged several earthquakes per week, and its inhabitants accepted them as a fixture of life. The quakes seldom caused any damage. Most were mere tremors, so minor they were hardly noticed. But this one felt like a California-sized whopper.

The roar in the air grew louder, then more specific. Curious, I shifted around to face the direction of the increased noise and saw something that made my sense of invulnerability vanish. Beyond the green hills of Vik, a thick column of smoke rose from glacier-capped Katla.

The volcano was erupting.

Chapter Twenty-three

At that moment, the loudest siren I'd ever heard shrieked an alarm.

"It's Katla!" Bryndis yelled.

Her words were echoed throughout the film set. "Katla! Katla is erupting!"

Almost as one, berserkers, Visigoths, Huns, and ninjas leapt to their feet. Most headed inland, away from the ocean, toward the towering hills and toward Katla itself. A smaller group ran past us, splashing through the marsh.

I scrambled to my feet, but as I stood there, trying to make sense of what was happening, Bryndis grabbed me by the arm. "To the car!"

Her urgency spurred me into a run. We followed the berserkers, emerging with them from the marsh to the beach, then sprinted along the black sand, around the basalt cliff face—which still stood firm despite the earthquake—and through the now-deserted set of *Death on Orion 12.* The astronauts had already vanished, and probably not into their space ship.

By the time we reached the Volvo, I was panting so hard I could barely talk. As she turned the key in the ignition, I asked, "Why…" pant, "…are the others…" pant, "…running *toward* Katla?" Pant. "Are they…" pant, "…nuts?"

She appeared as out of breath as me, so she didn't answer

right away, just sped out of the parking lot behind several that were driving like crazy toward the Ring Road.

When we caught our breaths, Bryndis finally answered, "Most of them are taking shelter at the hotel. Like the church, it is a designated safe house."

"They're not worried about lava?"

"The bigger problem is the glacial flow. The eruption will melt the ice cap, so we want to get out of the lowlands before the runoff reaches the village. Or the Ring Road."

I looked behind, at the hotel high on the hill, at the beckoning church just below it "But what if we don't make it?"

Despite our sprint down the beach, Bryndis sounded calm. "Then we had all that fine exercise for nothing. If the glacial flow has already cut us off—and I hope we ran fast enough—we will turn around and drive back up to the hotel. Do not worry, Teddy, we will be fine. No one got hurt when Eyjafjallajökull blew its top, and no one will get hurt now. The bar at the hotel will do good business and so will the minister at the church, who will be attempting to save the souls of terrified tourists as I speak. We are only hurrying like this because I do not want to get stuck in Vik and miss work. Magnus would be so sad."

She swerved to avoid clipping a brown van with lettering on the side that said, TUMI'S FILM CATERING. She and the van's driver, a bearded man, traded waves. He shouted something to her in Icelandic. Whatever it was, it made her laugh.

Me, I didn't feel so jolly. As we sped along the Ring Road, Katla's plume of smoke grew taller and wider. The smoke was white as the heat from the caldera melted the ice cap, but I foresaw a big problem once it turned dark. Ash. Rocks. The detritus of a billion years. Try as I might, I couldn't help envisioning the thousands of people smothered by ash or flash-burned to death at Pompeii, their bodies entombed by the ferocity of Vesuvius. And as dismissive as Bryndis had been about the threat of lava, you couldn't go anywhere in Iceland without seeing vast stretches of moss-covered lava. Underneath all that solidified magma, I knew, lay the remains of numerous farms and the people and animals that once populated them.

Depressing thoughts, almost as depressing as the one I'd had after leaving the hotel. It was a mistake to wait until we got back to Reykjavik to give my information to Inspector Haraldsson. It would be wiser to call him right now, I decided, reaching into my jacket pocket for my cell phone.

It wasn't there. Mystified, I thought back to the last couple of hours. I had used the camera at the puffin rookery, and at the hotel, where I'd shown my pictures to the Geronimos. And I remembered putting it back into my jacket pocket before we left. Then I remembered falling to the ground when the earthquake struck, my run along the beach…

"Bryndis, can I borrow…?"

"Oh, rats!" Bryndis' voice cut me off. "We are too late!"

I'd been so busy worrying about my phone that I hadn't noticed the Volvo slowing down. Now, as I looked ahead past the cars and vans in front of us, I saw a line of brake lights, and ahead of them, a glistening river where none previously existed. Not your ordinary river, either. This one, as it swept across the highway, carried great chunks of ice, some larger than Tumi's catering van. The river was widening by the second.

Chasing after the glacial river was a thick blanket of white-gray mist. If we got caught up in that, we'd have no visibility at all, and might even drive off in the wrong direction.

Right into the path of that floe-filled river.

Icelanders may be courageous, but they're not fools. To keep their countrymen from being swept away by the runoff, two Visigoths stood in the middle of the road, waving their battle axes to direct traffic away from the river. One by one the column of cars made their U-turns and headed back toward Vik. A Ford Bronco filled with berserkers drove past us, then a Chevy filled with ninjas and Huns. Hard on the Chevy's heels, a Fiat stuffed with astronauts.

Finally, us.

As we sped by the cars still awaiting their own turnaround, Bryndis said, "Looks like it's the Hótel Brattholt for us, Teddy. Katla, that witch, must be feeling pretty pleased with herself."

When we made it back to the hotel, we found a bacchanal in progress.

In the crowded dining hall, the American director of *Berserker!* stood atop a banquet table, leading a pack of berserkers, Visigoths, Huns, ninjas, and tourists in a rousing rendition of "Ninety-Nine Bottles of Beer on the Wall." The more timid evacuees huddled together at a table near the picture window, where they added to the noise level by screaming every time Katla upchucked a piece of ice.

The place smelled like a distillery. Ulfur, in a berserker costume—I hadn't recognized him earlier on the set—displayed his canniness as a hotelier by inventing a drink he called Katla's Kiss, a vodka-Brennivín-crème de menthe concoction every bit as evil as the old witch herself. Served in a heavy pewter tankard, it tasted terrible (I know because Ragnar shared his with Bryndis and me) but it packed an alcoholic wallop. Most of the tourists took one sip, then passed along their drink to a friendly berserker. The Icelanders guzzled the foul concoction so rapidly that Ulfur ran out of tankards midway through the second round and switched to water goblets brandished with the slogan, "Welcome to Iceland, land of fire and ice."

Calling Inspector Haraldsson amidst such clamor was pointless, but there was no way I would walk down that long, dark hall to the relative quiet of the ladies' room. Too dangerous, what with a double murderer hanging around. It was safer to stay here in the brightly lit dining area and hope for a lull in the racket.

"Here, Teddy," Ragnar chortled, thrusting the pewter tankard at me again. "Katlas' Kiss will grow hair on your chest!"

I gave him a pained smile. "That's the last place I want hair."

Tougher than I, Bryndis not only took another sip but ordered a Katla's Kiss of her own. When it arrived, she matched Ragnar drink for drink.

You'd think Ulfur would have been thrilled to have his hotel so crowded with paying customers, but he wasn't. He was still despondent over the theft of his rifle, a.k.a. the supposed murder weapon. From what I was able to overhear from the table next to where we were standing, the loss of the firearm had left his henhouse open to raids by neighborhood foxes, and Ulfur was now chickenless. Which meant eggless.

"No omelets," he grumbled to the American couple sitting next to us, who ordered the *sveppir eggjakaka*, an omelet. "The foxes have killed all my chickens. May I suggest some nice cod, fresh from the sea this morning, served with beurre blanc and duchess potatoes? Or if you're feeling daring, how about some *hákarl*, guaranteed to make you strong as a Viking."

The couple passed on the *hákarl*—smart of them, since it was rotted shark—and opted for the cod.

When we had first arrived, I'd noticed the Geronimos still sitting at the same long table as before. Their lunch finished, they'd moved on to drinks. Most appeared to have tried at least one Katla's Kiss, but Lucinda had three pewter mugs in front of her. Her mouth was rough enough when she was sober, and I hated to think what it would be like now. Yet her hair, released from its tight bun, fell to her shoulders in a silky wave. The change lent a surprising softness to her thin face, reminding me that she was younger than she sometimes acted, possibly still in her forties. Maybe the reason she had let her hair down was the presence of Oddi. She did seem to be sitting rather close to the burly tour guide.

Lucinda's daughter Judy sat across from her, with Tab Cooper's arm around her shoulders. He was on his second Katla's Kiss, but Judy was still sipping at her first. Same with Elizabeth, Adele Cobb and the Walshes, slow drinkers all.

Considering what I now knew, I didn't like the idea of joining the Geronimos, so I tried to hide behind Ragnar, but it was too late. Elizabeth had seen me.

She waved. "Teddy! Come join us!"

Thus caught, I wandered over and tried to act casual. "What a surprise, seeing you folks again. I thought you'd be back in Reykjavik by now."

"Stupid volcano screwed that," grumped Lucinda. Despite her softer look, her tongue remained sharp, if slurred.

As I stood there, the thick mist that had chased Bryndis and me along the Ring Road crept up from the valley below to encircle the hotel. There was a moment of silence from the beer-on-the-wall singers as we watched the curtain of grayish-white mist float by the picture window, but a few seconds later, the chorus struck back up.

"Mind if I sit down?" I asked the Geronimos.

Lucinda scowled. "As a matter of fact, I do, and if you…"

Elizabeth waved her into silence. "What Lucinda means to say is that we'd be delighted." The pewter tankard in front of her had hardly been touched, but the strain of the past week had given her complexion an unhealthy pallor. Her raven locks had dulled, and the crow's feet threading the corner of her eyes cut deeper. But considering the fact that her husband and a friend had died within two days of each other, I guess you could say she was doing as well as could be expected.

Ignoring Lucinda's baleful stare, I sat down. "Long time no see, Oddi," I cracked, shrugging off my jacket. "Sure is hot in here."

"I do not consider an hour to be a 'long time.'"

"Here in Iceland it seems to be. The sun hardly sets before it rises again."

He grinned. "You are correct, of course. We view time differently here. But I see you do not enjoy the Katla's Kiss drink." As befitting someone shuttling around a van full of tourists, he had hardly touched his own. Not that he would be driving anywhere until Katla calmed down and ice floes no longer slid across the Ring Road.

"I'm leaving Katla's Kisses to my betters," I answered. "I'll order a Coke when Ulfur gets to us, which judging by how busy he and the waitress are, may be a long time. By the way, why aren't you acting in one of those movies?" I teased. "Half of Iceland seems to be in one or the other."

"Until they are given permission to catch a flight back home, I will be driving for them. But my father, who normally runs the gift shop down in the village, picks up work on films whenever he can. He and my mother are at the center table, singing with the other actors. Does not my mother have a pretty voice?"

The revelers had reached seventy-eight bottles of beer on the wall, and the purest voice among them emanated from a tiny gray-haired woman dressed as some sort of pagan priestess. She had her arm around a man who, despite his age, looked just like Oddi, except that he wore the bearskin cloak of a Visigoth.

"My father tried to kill my mother this morning," Oddi bragged. "But she killed him with a curse instead."

"He looks no worse for wear."

"Like Ragnar, he knows how to die safely."

"You know Ragnar?"

"He is my cousin."

I blinked. "I guess that's no surprise since I was given to understand that everyone in Iceland is pretty much related to everyone else."

"True, but Ragnar's mother is my mother's sister. We are quite close."

I looked back at Ragnar, who had his arm around Bryndis. Both had joined in singing the "Ninety-Nine Bottles" anthem, which was now down to seventy-six bottles. From behind, Ragnar looked just like Oddi. Come to think of it, the hotelier at Stykkishólmur had strongly resembled Bryndis.

What must it be like to live in a country where you knew you were related to the stranger you just met? Perhaps familial connections accounted for Iceland's almost nonexistent murder rate. For instance, if you were robbing a bank, you wouldn't want to shoot the security guard because he might be your cousin. Then again, being related to everyone did pose problems of the dating variety. I remembered Bryndis' demonstration of the Accidental Incest App. It…

"Good heavens, Teddy, what are you thinking about?" Elizabeth's voice had a smile in it.

"That Iceland is very, very different than the U.S."

"It certainly is. We don't have volcanoes. Not active ones, anyway."

"You're forgetting Mount St. Helens. And there's a super volcano under Yellowstone."

She pulled a face. "Silly me. I even mentioned Mount St. Helens four books back in *Italian Passion*, where Jade L'Amour worked on a dig near Pompeii. She compared life below an Italian volcano to life below an American one, and deduced that the Italians were much more relaxed about it than we are. Just like these Icelanders. Katla blows its top, and what do they do? They have a party! Simon would so have enjoyed this. Still, I'm sorry he ever dreamed up this trip, but he was like that, generous to a fault."

Lucinda couldn't let that go without making another snarky remark. "He was certainly generous enough with his sexual favors."

Elizabeth, her face almost as red as my I BREAK FOR RED-HEADS tee-shirt, shot Lucinda an angry look. "You should know." Then she stood up. "Ulfur will never make it over here, and I need another Coke. How about you, Teddy? Or maybe wine? The chardonnay isn't bad. My treat."

"Nothing for me, thanks."

"You sure?"

At my nod, Elizabeth looked puzzled for a moment, then shrugged and wove her way through the singing crowd to the bar.

Oddi spoke up, but his voice was gentle. "As much as I admire fire in a woman, Lucinda, your words are unkind."

She sniffed. "Elizabeth can handle it. Everyone seems to forget that Arizona is a community-property state, so she got her fifty percent cut as soon as the state released the money. More than three hundred million dollars! But did Ms. Famous Author offer to treat us? No, Simon did that, out of his share. Say what you will about the man, he didn't have a miserly bone in his body."

Maybe not, but unless I was wrong, Elizabeth's comment to Lucinda—*You should know*—inferred that Simon had slept with Lucinda at least once. After Simon's affair with Adele, then Dawn, and now Lucinda, and God knows who else, that wasn't generous, it was promiscuous.

A few minutes later Elizabeth returned with her Coke. "*Skál*," she said, before chugging down half the glass in one gulp. "*Skál* and '*takk*' are the limits of my Icelandic."

"Maybe you'll learn more next time you visit."

"The country's magnificent and the people are wonderful, but there are just too many bad memories here."

Purely to change the subject, I said, "You must be on the road a lot to write the kind of books you do. Where are you sending Jade next time? The Gobi Desert seems like a perfect place for one of her adventures."

Her face stiffened. "I'm not taking that girl anywhere ever again. In fact, I have a new series in mind, a historical set in… Come to think of it, I'd better not tell you or you might beat me to the punch."

"Fat chance of that. I can hardly bring myself to write a letter these days, let alone an entire book." Then what she said sunk in. "Wait a minute. Did you just tell me you're dropping the Jade L'Amour series?"

She nodded.

"But why? They're always best-sellers! And won't Jade's fans be crushed if you leave them in the lurch like that?"

"Nineteen books about her are more than enough." Her tone, almost as harsh as Lucinda's usual grate, ended the discussion.

While reading *Tahiti Passion* I had grown fond of the I-can-do-it-all heroine. What other series had a female archaeologist who could surf a tsunami, escape hands-bound from a deep well, disarm a knife-wielding attacker, and prove that the Vikings had settled Tahiti—all while wearing designer duds? But writers write what they have to, I guess; they were weird that way. Still, I couldn't help wishing that when all this was over, Elizabeth would change her mind.

I wasn't the only person at our table who felt like that.

"Elizabeth, you can't dump Jade!" Judy piped up, shrugging off Tab's arm. "Reading about a can-do woman like her changed me and I'll bet it changed millions of other women, too."

"Millions, my foot," her mother snarled, slanting narrowed eyes toward her daughter. "Her last book didn't even make the best-seller list."

"Okay, that is it," Oddi said, taking away Lucinda's Katla's Kiss. "You have had enough." He set the drink down the table, where Ben Talley snatched it up.

Since I expected an explosion, I was shocked to see Lucinda's smile. "Oh, you!" she said, snuggling up against Oddi's chest. The fact that he wrapped his arms around her and gave her a hug shocked me further.

Judy gazed at them in amazement, then shifted her attention back to Elizabeth. "The Jade books made me realize I didn't have to rely on someone else to make me feel whole. What will girls like me do without her?"

Elizabeth didn't reply.

Enid Walsh broke the silence. "Judy, you always knew how to do things by yourself. You just didn't realize it. When we get back to Arizona, I think you should…"

Her husband cut her off. "You know, I think I'll switch to a Coke. Anybody else? Ulfur's right over there." Perry made a big show of waving his arms to flag down the hotelier, who was just then delivering a batch of Katla's Kisses to a table near ours.

"On second thought, I'll have a Coke, too," I said. "With lots of ice. It's pretty hot in here."

Elizabeth gave me an odd look. "And here I was thinking it was a bit too chilly."

"Just Cokes?" Ulfur said when he reached us. "No more Katla's Kisses?"

"We're drunk enough. Say, what's this I hear about a fox getting at your chickens?"

Once again Ulfur related the sad story of his stolen rifle and the subsequent decimation of his chicken coop. While he bemoaned the loss of his egg producers, I wondered what

Enid's advice to Judy would have been if Perry hadn't cut her off: that she should run away from home and join the Witness Protection Program?

Not that I'd been bypassed by the Interfering Mommy Department. My own mother was just as bad in that way as Judy's, although I'd always known that Caro did it out of love, whereas Lucinda...

Shrugging off Oddi's embrace, Lucinda reverted to type. "You've been working with Inspector Haraldsson, haven't you, Teddy? Always nosing around, always asking questions. You're doing his dirty work for him!"

The table fell silent as the other Geronimos gaped at her, then at me. Ulfur, fearing a looming cat fight, stopped moaning about his deceased fowl and headed back to the bar, his berserker loincloth flapping as he fled.

I tried to look innocent. "Of course I'm not 'working' with Inspector Haraldsson. I'm just a zookeeper, here to pick up a polar bear cub. And a fox and a couple of puffins."

"Oh, really? Well, I just happened to Google you on my iPhone and discovered that this isn't the first time you've stuck your nose in other people's business." She paused to vent a Katla-like burp, then continued. "Funny how you always seem to turn up wherever we go, and don't give me that old story about you and Dawn being childhood friends. You never even went to school with her. Your rich mother sent you to one of those prissy private schools in Virginia."

That's the problem with the Internet. Anyone can find out anything. Before she started in on my felonious father, I snapped, "Look, Lucinda, if you..."

I never finished the sentence because one of the tourists huddled by the window suddenly shouted, "Hey, I think it's over!"

The song-fest ended at sixty-three bottles of beer on the wall when we all rushed to the window. The mist had cleared and old witch Katla had calmed down. The thick plume of smoke which had caused the earlier panic now only emitted a series of weak puffs.

Confident of their safety, people filed outside to survey the damage.

"We should be able to see the Ring Road from the next hill over," Bryndis said. "Ragnar and I are going outside to find out if it's clear yet. Maybe we can make it back to Reykjavik this afternoon."

Eager to remove myself from Lucina's accusation, however accurate, I followed them out the door, leaving my jacket on the chair.

I found myself surrounded by a crowd of movie extras and tourists as we tromped down one hill and up the next. The hike wasn't far, little more than a mile of a fairly easy incline, and after the boozy dining room, the outside air felt refreshing. But when we reached the summit overlooking the Ring Road, we were disappointed. Katla may have quieted, but a cold, thick mist still snaked along the valley floor, obscuring not only the village of Vik but the highway back to Reykjavik as well.

And as for the "hill" we were on, it looked more like a cliff. Good thing I didn't suffer from vertigo, because erosion had sheared away the entire western slope, leaving a straight drop of at least two hundred feet down to the flooded Ring Road. The ground beneath our feet being slippery with ice, I backed away from the ledge.

Bryndis misread my worried expression. "Those are mainly ice particles, mixed with a little ash. As eruptions go, this one is a mere baby."

"Or an old witch blowin' off some steam," someone cracked, in a thick southern accent.

I turned to see the director of *Berserker!* behind me, a Katla's Kiss tankard in his hand. The ground was no longer moving, but he had trouble standing up straight, which probably had less to do with the volcano than with the four empty tankards he'd left behind at the hotel. Given his condition I doubted any more battle scenes would be filmed today. Not all was lost, however, Next to him hunched a cinematographer, and the camera balanced on his shoulder was whirring away, tracking the mist below.

"Think we can rent a room for the night?" I asked Bryndis, as we turned away from the summit and started back to the hotel behind a band of Visigoths.

"Doubtful," she answered. "But since the hotel is a designated safe place, there will be plenty of pillows and blankets. Ulfur is a good guy and he will do all he can to make us comfortable."

Ragnar winked at me. "You can bunk with us, Teddy. Three does not have to be a crowd, if you understand what I am telling you."

Bryndis jabbed him in the ribs with her elbow. "Idiot." But she giggled.

We were almost halfway back to the hotel when something that sounded like a sonic boom pierced the air. The ground began to shake again, and over a series of following booms, I could hear people screaming. When something—ice chunk? rock?—whizzed by my ear, I dropped to the ground and shielded my head with my hands.

Katla. The old witch was erupting again.

It took only seconds to realize that this blast was much stronger than the first. As I lay there cowering, Ragnar tugged at my arm. "Up! Up! We must return to the hotel!"

Despite the flying ice chunks, I scrambled to my feet. Together the three of us began running down the hill with the rest of the crowd. The ground being uneven and strewn with chunks of lava from older eruptions, we zig-zagged around them, which slowed our progress, and somewhere in all that zagging I lost sight of my friends. I finally spotted them several yards away running next to an astronaut and a couple of screaming tourists, but before I could rejoin them, the forefront of Katla's wrath reached us, enveloping us in a thick, freezing mist.

Visibility zero.

I wasn't worried about getting lost. There was no ash yet, only suspended ice particles, and I had a good sense of direction. Besides, all I needed to do was follow the screams and I would make it to the hotel safely. Then Katla could spew all the fire and ice she wanted.

I made good time and continued to keep up with the screaming, when I tripped over an outcropping of ancient lava and fell flat on my face.

"Ow!" I yelped.

Before I could get my feet under me, a dark figure rushed out of the mist. Something metallic glittered in its hand.

"You're not going anywhere, Teddy," the killer said.

Chapter Twenty-four

"Sorry about this," Elizabeth St. John said, as she stood above me. "It's nothing personal. I really quite like you, Teddy, because you remind me of my Jade."

Slowly, very slowly, I turned over to face her. If I remained on my stomach, she could stab me in the back and I would have no defense, but facing her...

"Thanks for the compliment, Liz, but unlike Jade I don't know how to hotwire a van. That's what you did the night you drove from your hotel at Reykjavik to Stykkishólmur to murder poor Dawn, isn't it? Hotwired someone else's car to keep the extra miles from showing up on your rental's GPS system? That's why you were so adamant that Inspector Haraldsson check it, right?"

Keep her talking, keep her talking.

Keep her talking and maybe that old witch Katla will blow again and bean her on the head with a block of ice. In case that miracle didn't happen, I wound my fingers around an uncomfortable chunk of lava poking into the back of my thigh. It reminded me of that old saying, "Never bring a knife to a gunfight," except I'd be bringing a rock to a knife fight.

Elizabeth gave me a congenial smile which, considering the circumstances, appeared terrifying. "You're as smart as Jade, too. Yes, I was going to hotwire a car, even if I had to crack a steering column to do it." She gave me a sly look. "Damn critics call my books 'escapist reading.' They don't realize how much research goes into them. For *Tahiti Passion* I actually bought an old junker to practice hotwiring on so I could write one measly little scene. I was all set to do the same thing in Reykjavik when I remembered seeing the night concierge tuck the keys to her Suzuki underneath the sun visor. They're pretty casual about locking things up here in Iceland. Low crime rate, and all." She actually laughed.

If I lived through this, I was going to have a talk with that concierge.

"But why, Elizabeth? Why kill your husband in the first place? And then Dawn?" I already knew the reasons, of course, but if I had to act dumb to keep her talking, I would play the village idiot.

"You've never been married, have you, Teddy?" She shifted that long steak knife, making the blade horizontal. Somewhere along the line, she'd researched knife thrusts.

Keep her talking. Keep her talking.

"Actually, I have been married, but my husband left me for another woman. Same thing Simon was going to do to you, too, right? Leave you for Dawn?" I knew better, but hoped she'd feel the need to set me straight. Murderers hated being misunderstood.

"Don't be silly. Simon would never have left me for Dawn. Just like he never would have left me for Adele or any of the others. We had an understanding, remember?"

"Then it was all about the Powerball money?" I knew better than that, too.

Her disconcerting smile faded. "Arizona's a community-property state, just like California. I got half the haul. All of it now, not that I care. But I'm surprised at you, Teddy. I thought you were smarter than that. Then again, you kind of gave yourself away back at the hotel when you wouldn't let me get you a Coke. Afraid I'd poison you, right?"

It's hard to shrug while you're lying on your back on top of a centuries-old slab of lava but I did my best. "Something like that. But if it wasn't all about the Powerball money, why'd you kill your husband?" I knew very well why she had, of course, but I was stalling.

She made an exasperated sound. "You *are* dense. Oh, well. To be blunt, since that's what you seem to require, I killed him out of a sense of honor."

Exactly.

It would be next to impossible to spring straight up from my prone position, but the second she made a move, a roll to the side would momentarily put me out of harm's way. That would give me time to shift to my knees, raise the rock and do what I could. Whatever happened, I wasn't going down without a fight.

Still playing dumb, still playing for time, I said, "Honor? I don't understand."

That exasperated sound again. "I really, really overestimated your intelligence! Apparently I have to spell it out for you, so here it is, then, in language you can understand. Winning the Powerball changed everything. Before, I was the breadwinner and I did it in style. Simon was satisfied with that, or at least I thought so. But then, a couple of years ago, my book sales began to fall off, and it made him edgy. As a CPA, he knew better than anyone that fewer book sales meant smaller royalties. Did you see how few people showed up for my Reykjavik signing? That was a nothing crowd compared to what I used to draw."

Were those tears of grief in her eyes? Or were they a reaction to the dense ice-and-ash cloud floating by as Katla burbled and burped?

"Then my publisher dropped me, and we had to take out a second mortgage. We had to sell…We had to sell…."

She coughed as an even thicker cloud swirled by. Unfortunately, her discomfort didn't make her lower the knife.

"Do you have any idea what it's like to be famous, Teddy? To see your books on the *New York Times* best-seller list? To have people stop you on the street and say how much they love your work and ask for your autograph? Then, almost overnight have your books drop out of sight, the accolades stop, your sales plummet, and suddenly you're a nobody? It's humiliating!"

Getting ready. Getting ready.

"When Simon won that damned Powerball I thought we'd revert back to normal, that everything would be all right. And that's how it was at first, but then he started drinking and grew those awful sideburns and conducted his affairs right out in the open instead of with his usual discretion, and then…and then…"

A slight tilt of the knife. Almost time.

"And then, right after we arrived in Iceland, he told me he was sick of being my go-fer and living in my shadow and that because of the Powerball he didn't have to do that anymore. Now he had the chance to go out and do his own thing. *Do his own thing!* He actually used that old canard! He said he was going to divorce me as soon as we got back to Arizona." Her eyes hardened. "You understand, don't you, Teddy? I couldn't allow anyone—especially the man I had supported for so many years—to humiliate me like that. Where was his sense of honor?"

"Yes, Elizabeth, I understand now. But what about Dawn? Why kill her?" I'd already figured that out, too, but I needed more time.

"She was blackmailing me, that's why! For some reason she'd gotten out of bed early that morning, just in time to see me take Ulfur's rifle off the back porch, where he'd left it after taking pot shots at some fox. I didn't know about that until the rest of them went to Stykkishólmur, and she called me and said she wanted a million dollars or she'd tell that horrible inspector what she saw. A million dollars! Can you believe it? Well, I know enough about blackmail—there was a blackmailer in *Nairobi Passion*—to know that it never ends. I told her okay, that although I didn't have that kind of money on me now, of course, I could give her a down payment, then pay her the rest when we got back to the States. We agreed to meet on the causeway at midnight. We met, all right. I had the Suzuki's tire iron, and…Well, it's obvious what I did."

Eyes wild, she stopped for breath, then continued. "But here's the weird thing. I miss Dawn almost as much as I miss Simon! Isn't that strange? Despite everything, I loved that girl. She was the daughter I never had." She raised her knife hand to brush away a particularly annoying tear on her cheek…

Now!

I rolled off the lava onto a pocket of grass and lurched to my knees as she came at me.

Felt the knife slash along my shoulder.

Raised the rock…

And bashed the bitch in the head.

Chapter Twenty-five

While I had been lying on my bed of lava, Katla kept spewing, and the ash in the air was thickening to a dangerous level. Even though Elizabeth had tried to kill me, I didn't want the unconscious woman to die, so I turned her onto her stomach, then took off my I BRAKE FOR REDHEADS tee-shirt. I placed it loosely around her head to keep off the worst of the ash. The downside was that I was freezing, but the upside was that I'd worn my best bra, a lacy pink Guia La Bruna knock-off held together by a safety pin.

Then I left Elizabeth to the temporary mercies of Katla and plunged along the hillside toward the hotel for help. At least, I think that's the direction I was traveling in. Due to the fallout, I couldn't see five feet in front of me. The siren at Vik, which had fallen silent while Katla was getting her second wind, shrilled again, but in the fog it blended with the roar of the volcano to create one huge wall of sound. For all I knew, I was running straight for the cliff above the Atlantic. Or just as dangerous, I could be closing in on the sheer drop-off above the Ring Road.

But I kept running, because there was nothing else I could do.

Blood loss or not, I had to keep moving, otherwise both of us might die—Elizabeth from slow asphyxiation, me from bleeding out.

The ground seemed to be levelling off, which meant that I had reached the deep valley between the two hills. Or maybe

I'd run cross-wise, and was in the valley at the bottom of Katla's slope, a terrifying thought. I stopped, trying once again to get a sense of direction. It didn't help that my brain felt as sludgy as the ground beneath my feet.

I turned right.

Suddenly a flash of white and black rose up in front of me. It came so close I could see a yellow, red, and blue-black beak, feel the brush of a dusky underwing. A puffin! The bird flew out of my sight for a moment, then veered back through the fog toward me. It appeared to be having trouble navigating though the dense fog, too.

But, no.

The puffin circled back and dove at me, uttering the same low growl I'd heard once before—on the cliff at Vik, when I'd wandered too close to her burrow. Still growling, she flew toward my face, getting closer and closer until I could make out the white stripe on her head.

"Good Mama," I whispered. "Protect your baby!"

I reversed direction, turning away from Mama Puffin and the too-close cliff ledge at Vik. Within a few yards, the ground began to climb.

You lose track of time and space when you're running blind, and at first I thought I was imagining things when over Katla's grumbling and rumbling I heard someone call my name. Several someones, actually.

"Teddy!" Ragnar.

"Where are you, Teddy?" Bryndis.

"Yell so we can find you!" The lead singer of "Ninety-Nine Bottles of Beer on the Wall."

"Here!" I yelled back, almost tripping again in my excitement.

Oblong shapes bobbed toward me through the fog, some of them steadier than others, which might have had something to do with the liberal ingestion of Katla's Kisses. I ran toward them, waving with one arm, because for some reason I couldn't use the other.

"Hurry! Elizabeth's been hurt and needs help!"

One by one they emerged from the mist, looking like dirty snowmen. Ragnar, Bryndis, Olli, Ulfur, and a host of barbarians and astronauts.

"We realized you were not following us," Bryndis said, as she reached me. "So we came back. We could not let...Wait. What is wrong with your arm, Teddy? There is blood all over you! And where is your shirt?"

"That is a pretty bra," Ragnar said. He couldn't take his eyes off my chest.

Bryndis made a noise almost like the growling puffin's. "Look the other way, Ragnar." To me, she repeated, "Teddy, your arm. What happened?"

I stared down at my arm. No wonder it wouldn't work. I had lost so much blood I couldn't see much skin, just long streaks of red. "Oh. That. I'm fine, not all mine, some of it's Elizabeth's, but we have to...uh, we have to..."

Why couldn't I think straight?

I turned around and began walking back up the hill toward Elizabeth, taking it for granted the others would follow. "I'll take you to her, but be careful, because she's...uh, dangerous. I took her knife away and threw it down the...uh, the hill, because she killed her husband, and then she killed Dawn because...uh, I'll tell you later, then she tried to kill me, a couple of times, but I...uh, I got away, and then..."

I began to cough.

I was cold. So cold.

But what could you expect with so much ice and ash in the air? Nasty old witch Katla! She wouldn't get me, though. I was walking, still walking.

Someone wrapped something around my shoulders. Bryndis.

"Oh, you're ruining your pretty...uh, your pretty blue jacket!"

Still cold.

"Hafta tell you about puffin," I croaked. "Such a good mama. Uh, she..."

A flash of red to my right.

"Tee-shirt! Joe gave me tee-shirt! Birthday…uh, birthday present."

A few steps more and there lay Elizabeth, my I BRAKE FOR REDHEADS tee-shirt still protecting her.

"See? Geez, what a mess. Head wounds bleed…uh, a lot. Musta read that somewhere, in her book, maybe. Anyway, she needs medical…uh, medical atten…"

Katla must have blown again because the air around me became so dark I could hardly see her even though I stood right over her, but maybe because I was just so tired…

"I'm gonna get me some rest now, so…"

I lay down next to Elizabeth. Funny how soft moss-covered lava can feel.

"Oh, no, you don't," Ragnar said, hauling me to my feet.

"Rude!" I protested.

While he held me upright, Bryndis took off her own tee-shirt and wrapped it around my arm, securing it in place with her belt. Not as tight as a tourniquet, but snug enough to stanch the blood flow.

"Thanks," I told her. Caro had raised me to always be polite, even when I didn't mean it. "But wanna nap."

"I want a Range Rover, too, but that doesn't mean I'll get one," she replied, cinching the belt one notch tighter.

"Mean!"

Before I could complain again, scrambling sounds made me turn my head. Two berserkers and an astronaut had picked up Elizabeth and were hauling her back down the hillside. Like me, she was bleeding, but still alive.

"Oh, good. Not dead. Didn't wanna kill her. Bad.. uh, bad karma."

Ragnar gave me a sharp look, then slung me over his shoulder. I took a little nap.

Two hours later I felt a lot better. Elizabeth, not so much. I could hear her shrieking from the kitchen while I reclined regally in a cushioned booth, drinking orange juice and eating oatmeal cookies. When my head cleared, Bryndis told me the writer had regained consciousness, and Ulfur—after trussing her up like a Christmas turkey—had attended to her head wound. She was now locked in the kitchen larder.

"That's what she gets, stealing my rifle, letting damned fox eat my chickens," he muttered darkly, filling up my glass again, telling me I needed to keep my sugar level up. He also fed me another cookie.

"Oatmeal. Good for you!"

I chomped through the cookie, then chased away its dryness with more orange juice. But I did it left-handed. My arm, wrapped in bandages from the hotel's first aid kit, throbbed from the nasty, four-inch slash Elizabeth had given me. One of the berserkers had volunteered to stitch it up for me but I'd told him thanks but no thanks, I'd wait for a doctor.

"I'd wash my face if I were you," I told the ash and blood-spattered Bryndis when she joined me in the booth.

"Pot calling the kettle black," she said. "Looked in the mirror lately?"

Although more muted than earlier, the party had resumed. So had the choruses of "Ninety-Nine Bottles of Beer on the Wall," which—by the time Inspector Haraldsson and company arrived via helicopter from Reykjavik—was down to a measly three bottles.

When Haraldsson entered the hotel lobby he didn't look happy, but then he never did. Led by Ulfur, he and one of his underlings headed for the kitchen, while two medics hurried to my side. While they were cleaning my wound and arranging a saline drip, Elizabeth's shrieking stopped. What I wouldn't give to be a fly on the wall in that larder.

Whatever was going on in there didn't take long.

"I thought I told you to mind your own business," Haraldsson barked at me, when he finally emerged from the larder. "But no, you just had to keep poking around." He frowned at my arm, my ash-covered face. "Now look at you."

"I'm avoiding mirrors these days."

"How is she doing?" he asked one of the techs.

The tech—the name on his nametag said LARUS—answered in Icelandic.

Haraldsson's frown deepened. "He says you need professional attention, so we will fly you back to Reykjavik. To receive about, say," another peek at my arm, "sixteen stitches." He delivered this in an almost kindly voice.

"Maybe I can get a shower?"

"That, too, can be arranged."

We sat in comfortable silence for the next few moments until I saw two of Haraldsson's men escorting a sobbing Elizabeth outside. The ropes Ulfur had bound her with had been replaced by handcuffs. Although she'd killed two people, then tried to kill me, I couldn't help feeling sorry for her.

"She confessed everything," I told Haraldsson." How her husband was dumping all the women in his life, including her, how Dawn saw her take Ulfur's rifle and was trying to blackmail her, all of it. Will you need me to testify?"

"Probably not, since my trip to the larder confirms your claim that the lady is in a confessional mood. But don't tell anyone I told you."

"Mum's the word, Inspector."

When he smiled, he looked almost handsome. "Call me Thor, Teddy."

Epilogue

Gunn Landing, California: One month later

MEET MAGNUS THE GREAT
AT THE GRAND OPENING OF THE GUNN ZOO'S
NORTHERN CLIMES EXHIBIT

I'd tried to tell Aster Edwina that since "magnus" already meant "great," the sign in front of the little bear's enclosure said "Meet Great the Great," but my boss never listens to me.

The crowd gathered under the bright California sunshine to see the Gunn Zoo's new polar bear cheered as Magnus dove off an artificial ice floe and into his big pond in pursuit of his favorite toy, a bear-proof red Boomer Ball. When he reached it, he grabbed the ball with his little paws, then flipped over on his back and back-pedaled across the pool like a big albino otter.

The crowd cheered again.

So did Joe, who was taking an hour off work to attend the grand opening. Thanks to him, crime in San Sebastian County had slowed recently. He looked sexy in his sheriff's uniform, and as soon as Aster Edwina turned her back, I snuggled up to him.

"Fraternizing with the police in public, Teddy?" he murmured into my ear. "Tsk-tsk. Aster Edwina will have your hide. On second thought, who cares what she thinks?" He nuzzled my ear again.

Another cheer from the crowd.

I looked over at the "glacial" pond, as Aster Edwina insisted on calling the pool, and saw Magnus hoist his Boomer Ball out of the water. He began batting it back and forth across the artificial ice floe.

"He's playing soccer!" piped one small child. "Mommy, can I have one?"

The boy's mother vented a tired sigh. "You already have two baseballs, a soccer ball, a basketball, a foot—"

"Bear! I want a bear!"

"There's your next generation of zookeepers," Joe whispered.

A lot had happened since I left Iceland.

Bryndis, who had returned home after helping Magnus settle in, emailed me an invitation to her and Ragnar's October wedding. I responded with a resounding "Yes!" As soon as she received my reply, she let me know that Inspector Haraldsson-call-me-Thor would be in attendance, too. I didn't know how to feel about that.

The Geronimos' lives had also changed in interesting ways. Lucinda Greaves, she of the intemperate temper and multiple marriages, had moved in with Oddi, the tour director. He was now helping guide her through the long process of getting the Icelandic equivalent of a green card. Good luck there, I thought, but Oddi might be the only man on earth who could handle the harridan. Lucinda's daughter, Judy, snagged a spot in Tab Cooper's upcoming reality TV show, *Wrangler Wives*, and was looking forward to her brand new acting career. Perry and Enid Walsh have returned to their old lives as jewelry floggers, albeit under a new DBA: Icelandic Diamonds.

And the heartbroken Adele Cobb? She was the biggest surprise of all. An article printed in *Publishers Weekly* reported that Doubleday paid her a six-figure advance for her upcoming "true" crime book, *Iceland: Land of Passion and Death*. In the book, Adele describes her torrid love affair with Simon Parr, his and Dawn Talley's murders, and reveals how she used her "expert detection skills" to track down the killer. The article also hinted that a movie deal was in the offing, starring Angelina Jolie as Adele. In a red wig.

Which brings me to Elizabeth St. John.

Under Icelandic law, Elizabeth's confession was not to be enough to send her directly to prison. Inspector Haraldsson and the other detectives assigned to the case had to provide material evidence that she'd carried out the murder of two people with malice aforethought. No problem, though, since she led them to the volcanic flume in which she'd hidden Ulfur's rifle. (Poor Ulfur still doesn't have it back and to this day, remains chickenless.) The tire iron from the night concierge's "borrowed" Suzuki with which Elizabeth killed Dawn was dredged from the harbor at Stykkishólmur, Elizabeth's fingerprints still on it. And on Ulfur's rifle. And on the steak knife she'd slashed me with.

Elizabeth was now doing a fourteen-year-to-life sentence at the new prison near Reykjavik, but Bryndis advised me that hardly anyone ever served more than fourteen years, no matter how many people they'd killed. The prison sounded rather nice, since—like all things Icelandic—it had been designed to hold wayward relatives. Elizabeth enjoyed a private room with a toilet and shower, as well as access to a common kitchen and dining room, a gym, and a living room where she either could watch TV or read books from the well-stocked prison library. The private visiting room available for her guests was being put to good use, too.

When the story of her crimes hit the newspapers, her book sales went through the roof. She was visited by her agent and her former publisher, who, during a long, kiss-and-make-up session, offered her an eight-figure advance for her new Jade L'Amour novel, *Icelandic Passion*. She was already halfway through.

Well, more power to her. Elizabeth may have tried to kill me, but I still had a sneaking liking for the woman. I, too, took honor seriously.

Not that I'd ever kill for it.

"You have the strangest expression on your face, Teddy." Joe's voice startled me.

"Oh, just thinking about this and that. Like, how happy I am that Magnus is happy."

The polar bear cub had cleared quarantine with flying colors. Thanks to the excellent care he had received at the Reykjavik Zoo from Bryndis and the other keepers, he wasn't infested with worms or other parasites. His radiographs were clean, with no signs of broken bones or diseased organs. In short, Magnus was as fit as any polar bear cub could be.

So were my own pets, DJ Bonz and Miss Priss. They appeared overjoyed when I picked them up at Mother's house, but Toby, my half-Siamese cat, was more tepid. On my first night back he refused to return to the *Merilee*, preferring to remain on Cathie Kindler's houseboat, *S'Moose Sailing*. But early the next morning the little devil finally padded home to snuggle with his doggie foster-father DJ Bonz. Still, Toby is Toby, and considering his roving eye, I think he's already on the lookout for another boat to mooch around on.

Not so the Icelandic foxes or puffins. They love their new homes. Speaking of which...

"Follow me to the new puffin rookery," I told Joe, taking him by the hand. "I have something to show you."

I led him to the southern end of the Northern Climes exhibit, where Sigurd and Jodisi had their own pool, almost the size of Magnus'. The two puffins lived in a human-made rookery built to resemble the clifftop at Vik. Bright green moss covered a cement-and-stone surface, but several spots had been hollowed out so they could choose and furnish their own burrow. As a result, they now dwelt in a snug little nest lined with twigs and grasses scavenged from the "litter" I had placed at the corner of the exhibit.

"Look carefully and tell me what you see," I said to Joe.

"Two fat black and white parrots walking around. The smaller parrot has a white stripe across its head."

I gave him a playful slap on the arm. "Try again."

"Okay, not parrots. Puffins. What you've been calling a 'breeding pair.'"

"Old news. Keep looking."

"Boy and girl puffin?"

Another playful slap. "Look just to their right, and do it quick, because Jodisi's about to climb into the burrow."

He squinted his eyes. "Something...something..." He squinted harder. "Why, it's an egg!"

I would have clapped my hands, but I didn't want to startle the birds. "She laid it last night, and in around forty days, we'll have a brand new puffin chick at the Gunn Zoo. Forty-five days after that, it'll be strong enough to live on its own."

"Then Mama and Papa Puffin go their separate ways?"

"Puffins mate for life, so no one's leaving anyone."

Joe smiled. "Like penguins, then."

"And swans. And wolves."

He nuzzled my cheek. "And turtle doves."

I nuzzled back. "And gibbons, and prairie voles, and bald eagles, and..."

He shut me up with a kiss. When he was finished, he whispered, "And us."

"Yes," I gasped, once I caught my breath. "And us."

To receive a free catalog of Poisoned Pen Press titles, please provide your name and address in one of the following ways:

Phone: 1-800-421-3976
Facsimile: 1-480-949-1707
Email: info@poisonedpenpress.com
Website: www.poisonedpenpress.com

Poisoned Pen Press
6962 E. First Ave. Ste 103
Scottsdale, AZ 85251